FAMILY
Jewels

Dix Dodd Mysteries

The Case of the Flashing Fashion Queen
Family Jewels
Death by Cuddle Club
Covering Her Assets (coming Fall 2013)

FAMILY Jewels

A Dix Dodd Mystery

N.L. WILSON
(the writing team of Norah Wilson and Heather Doherty)

PUBLISHED BY:

SOMETHING SHINY
P R E S S
Norah Wilson / Something Shiny Press
P.O. Box 30046, Fredericton, NB, E3B 0H8

Cover by The Killion Group, Inc.
Book Design by Hale Author Services

Note re Bonus Material

Please note that bonus material in the form of an excerpt from *Death by Cuddle Club: A Dix Dodd Mystery*, appears at the end of this book. That bonus material will make this book appear several pages longer than it actually is. Bear that in mind as you approach the end and are anxiously trying to judge how much story is left!

Chapter 1

THINGS WERE LOOKING up.

Since solving the case of the Flashing Fashion Queen, business had been booming for this PI. Though I'm not one to rest on my laurels, no matter how enticing laurel-resting may seem, every once in a while I just had to put my feet up on my desk, link my hands behind my head and lean back in my chair to savor the feeling. And I only fell over the first time. Damn chair.

The publicity generated from that infamous case had drawn so much business our way, Dylan Foreman (PI apprentice extraordinaire and hot as hell to boot) and I were extremely busy. Crazy busy. Stagette-with-a-host-bar busy.

True, most of our work still involved digging up dirt on cheating spouses, but we'd been handed some other work in the last few months. We'd found missing relatives and missing poodles. Deadbeat dads and surprised beneficiaries. We'd been hired a few times to do background checks on potential employees for big corporations. Oh, and I got one call from a B-list celebrity client who had us chasing all over Southern Ontario looking for his 19-year-old son who'd gone AWOL with his dad's credit cards. Naturally, the client had wanted the kid found yesterday, but he wanted it done on the QT. Dear old Dad hadn't wanted to involve the police, nor his estranged wife, or her new hubby, or the kid's current girlfriend or last girlfriend, and holy hell, not the last girlfriend's older brother, and especially not the media. So we had to track the son of celebrity down the old fashioned way — knocking on doors, asking the right, carefully-put questions of the right people. And, of course, by tapping into my trusty intuition. (Okay, granted, when chasing a 19-year-old male, maybe hitting the strip clubs didn't exactly take a lot of intuition, but we still had to pick the *right* clubs.)

Also, Dylan and I had done a fair amount of business locating lost loves for those who still pined away for them. Apparently, in some cases, absence *does* make the heart grow fonder. Or stupider. Lost loves are lost for a reason, in my humble opinion.

"You're too cynical, Dix," Dylan would tell me whenever one of those lost sweetheart cases came our way and I voiced this sentiment.

Maybe he was right. Maybe I do have a little bit of a chip on my shoulder when it comes to men. Or a big bit of a chip. Or a great big chunk of firewood. But, once burned ...

Suffice it to say that while Dylan still had a streak of the hopeless romantic in him, I did not. Nada. And at the agency, I was still the bearer of bad news to the clients on the way in the door, and Dylan was still the sympathetic ear and shoulder to cry on on their way out. But that was one of the things that made us so perfect together.

I mean, so perfect *working* together.

And the best part of our growing business since the case of the Flashing Fashion Queen — we moved the Dix Dodd PI Agency! Nothing fancy, nothing too pricey — just a step up from the bottom-of-the-barrel rental we had before. Fewer broken bottles in the parking lot. And a few blocks closer to my mother's condo where I lived while she was in Florida. (I still didn't have a condo of my own; things weren't booming quite that well yet.) We were still in Marport City, of course, with no plans to relocate to a bigger center. There was enough under-the-covers action for undercover work in this burg. We were just doing it from a better address now.

We'd bought ourselves some new equipment and furniture. Cozier seats in the waiting room, and my personal favorite, a high-tech honey of a coffee machine. That puppy not only ground the coffee beans and delivered the coffee into an insulated carafe that kept it fresh and hot for hours, but — oh, bliss! — it also delivered frothed milk in 10 seconds flat.

Dylan's indulgence? A voice changer. We spent the better part of an afternoon working the kinks out of that machine — calling people up and saying "Luke, this is your father" in our best Darth Vader voices. But who knows? A voice changer might come in handy some day for more than just freaking out the guy at the comic shop (especially with the caller ID we spoofed!).

We also got newer phones and computer telephone-call recording software, which we run on our newly upgraded computers. And I had to place a whole new order for business cards. The ones that read

Dix Dodd, Private Investigator.
There's power in the truth. Let Dix Dodd empower you.

The business card had been Dylan's design. Dylan's words. I still get a little choked up when I think of it. His pursuit of the perfect motto for the agency had, by turns, driven me crazy and kept me sane during the Flashing Fashion Queen case when it looked like my future might involve stamping out license plates in a federal correctional facility for women. But enough of that.

We also bought a fancy copier/printer/fax machine that sounded like a tweety-bird when a fax came in, replacing a slow-as-death desktop printer, a perpetually moody copier, and an ancient fax machine that squealed like a cat in its death throes. I hated that old fax machine, and no matter where I was in the former office (hell, if I was in the bathroom down the hall) that squealing sound would make me cringe. I'm talking nails-on-a-chalkboard cringe. This new machine was top-of-the-line! It had all the bells and whistles — and a gigantic paper tray I wouldn't have to fill again for six months. Not to mention virtually unlimited fax capability. No more 50-page memory limit.

Not that I'd ever gotten a fax that long. But if such a monster did come in — hell, if ten of them came in — I was now ready for it.

So it was a bit of a thrill when the fax tweeted these days and started punching out the pages faster than the speed of … well, the speed of my old fax machine.

Usually I got that little thrill. But not always.

And definitely not the day I got the fax from Sheriff's Deputy Noel Almond of the Pinellas County Sheriff's Office. I groaned. "What is it this time, Mother? Skinny-dipping in the seniors' pool again? Prank calls to the local radio station saying you're the original Bat Girl?" Probably not the latter; Mom had already done that twice. For Pete's sake, she was seventy-one! Couldn't she knit something? And would it kill her to sit in a rocking chair once in a freakin' while?

I leaned back in my chair, blowing out an exasperated sigh. But as I looked over the pages, I sucked that sigh right back in on a gasp.

My mother, Katt Dodd, was under suspicion in the matter of the theft of stolen jewels. Lots of them. Tens of thousands of dollars' worth. That was bad. But it wasn't the worst of it. That first paragraph was just the opening jab. The second paragraph of Deputy Noel Almond's letter delivered the punch: mother was a person of interest in a man's disappearance.

That was the second time I fell over in my chair.

Which is exactly where I was when Dylan walked into the office — flat on my back, shoes up in the air, eyes pointed toward the ceiling, head sunk to the ears in the plush carpeting.

"Trying a new yoga position, Dix?"

My gaze shifted from the ceiling to Dylan's grinning face.

"No," I said. "I'm trying to figure out just what we should pack for Florida."

I accepted a hand up from Dylan, righted my chair, and handed him the faxed pages I still clutched. And watched his laughing eyes go serious.

Thus began the first time I'd ever pressed my PI skills into service for family. And not just any relative. My mother. My MOTHER!

Of course, I dubbed it the Case of the Family Jewels.

"What's a seven-letter word for *fire-rising bird*?" Mrs. Presley asked from the back seat.

"Phoenix, Mrs. P." Dylan answered, not missing a beat.

But I could have gotten that one. Not that it was a competition between Dylan and me. Much. Not that we were keeping score. Out loud.

"OE or EO for phoenix?" asked Mrs. Presley.

"OE," I shouted. That should count for something.

Dylan gave me a grinning sideways glance.

I bit down on a grin of my own.

A few months ago when we worked the Weatherby case, we'd fallen into bed together, literally. Not that we'd had sex. Well, not *sex* sex. Still, there'd been a little tension between us for a while after that. We were getting back to normal now, though. Well, as normal as it got when your male apprentice-slash-assistant is smart, sexy, tall and handsome, incredibly good-smelling and funny. Oh, and young. Did I mention young? All of 29.

"And a six-letter word for *highest point*? Fourth letter's an M."

"*Climax*," I shouted, half turning in the seat and oh-so-proud of myself.

"No," she said. "No, starts with an S ..."

"No fair. You didn't say —"

"*Summit!*" Dylan didn't turn in the seat. Which was good considering he was driving at the moment. He did, however, cast me a wicked grin.

"But I like your word, too."

"Try this one." The seat squeaked as Mrs. P shifted her position.

I heard the tapping of the pencil on the seat behind us. This time, I'd be ready. Dylan tightened his hands on the steering wheel beside me.

"Eight letters. *Close and often passionate relationship …*"

"*Cybersex!*"

Dylan snorted a laugh. "Could it be *intimate*, Mrs. P?" he said.

She looked down at the paper. "Why, yes … yes it could be *intimate*. Thanks, kids. I think I'm good for now."

"Anytime, Mrs. P."

For the record, I liked my answer better.

I sank back in my seat. The moment silence prevailed again, my mind drifted right back to that fateful fax from Deputy Almond that started this odyssey.

The fax had come in late yesterday afternoon, and we'd left early this morning, grabbing a drive-thru breakfast and supersizing our coffees. We'd swung by the office and picked up all the fancy new PI equipment we might need. Then we'd picked up Mrs. Jane Presley.

Of course, driving wasn't my first choice. I'd wanted to jump on the first flight. But Dylan, in that damnable voice of reason of his, had persuaded me we'd be better off driving. Mother wasn't in custody, so we didn't have to be in a hair-on-fire hurry. Plus it would give me the chance to return my mother's BMW, or Bimmer, as she called it. And as I, too, quickly learned to call it. She refused to let me drive the thing until I stopped calling it a *Beemer*, which apparently is reserved for BMW motorcycles.

Not that I was aching for a chance to lose the luxury ride, which had fallen into my possession the last time mother had been to Marport City. She'd hooked up with Frankie Morrell and decided to return to Florida with him, leaving me the use of the car.

At this point I should say I never liked Frankie. And I liked him even less now. Because Frankie was the one who'd gone missing — the one the police suspected Mother of … um … disappearing. (The letter hadn't said murder, but I could read between the lines.)

Anyway, Dylan had pointed out that: a) we needed our equipment, which would be easier to transport by car; b) we'd need wheels in Florida anyway; and c) we needed the think time.

He'd been right, of course.

So how'd we gather up Mrs. P? All too easily.

I'd swung by the Underhill Motel to ask if Cal or Craig — Mrs. Presley's hulking sons who helped her run the motel — could stop by the condo while I was away, just to check on things. Not that there was a cat to feed or plants to water. Cats didn't like me and only the hardiest of plants could survive my inattention. Hardy being plastic. Preferably self-dusting. But there had been a couple break-ins lately in my neighborhood. Mrs. P was all too happy to offer up her sons to watch the place. Plus I knew that Cal was still seeing Elizabeth Bee, now that she'd broken up with Craig, and I thought maybe they could use some alone time.

"Gee, I've never been to Florida, Dix," Mrs. P had said. "And I haven't had a vacation in years." She pulled a pen from her shirt pocket and a small notepad from the pocket of her skirt, and began making a list.

Leave meat pies for the boys.

Tell Cal none of that spicy pepperoni till I get back.

Pack the sunscreen.

"Well, it's going to be pretty hectic, Mrs. P and —"

She kept writing.

Get new underwear.

Pack the summer pajamas — not the footies.

"I've always wanted to go, but never got the chance. But you know, I might get there someday. Someday someone might do me a favor. You know, like I do favors for other folks. Especially friends in trouble. Not that I'd ever expect anything in return, no matter how much jeopardy I'd put myself in for their sakes."

"Okay, okay," I said. "You had me at 'jeopardy'. Would you like to come to Florida, Mrs. P?"

"Why how nice of you to ask!"

"See you at seven a.m.," I'd said, backing out of the Underhill, pushing the door open with my ass as I did.

"Make it six, Dix. I'm a morning person, you know. I'll be ready."

"Six it is, Mrs. P."

"Oh, and Dix ..."

I stopped with one butt cheek out the door. "Yeah?"

"I had you at 'Gee'."

When Dylan and I had pulled in the next morning at *quarter* to six, Mrs. Presley was standing outside the motel, her long-faced sons at her side, red suitcase at her feet, and tasseled sombrero in hand. She had four big pillows with her, and a blanket — not a bad idea really. Mrs. P liked her comforts. She wore sunglasses that covered half her face, the very same Roberto Cavallis she'd loaned me once for a disguise. Bermuda shorts floated below her knees, and the wildest Hawaiian shirt I'd ever seen covered her top half. And in the front pocket of that shirt, tucked in a pocket protector — pencil-pen-pencil. She always wore that at the front desk of the hotel.

"Thinking of doing some work, Mrs. P?" I'd asked, nodding to the shirt pocket.

She pulled a rolled-up magazine from her armpit and waved it at me. "I love crossword puzzles, Dix. Don't you?"

Actually, I hated crossword puzzles.

Craig looked like he was going to cry as he opened the door for his mother. Cal wasn't far from snuffing back a few wet ones himself. I looked at him.

"Allergies," he said. "Damn lilacs."

"It's October, Craig." I said. "Lilacs are long gone."

"Goddamn *super* lilacs then ... they're the worst."

The boys were 28, but still very much their mother's sons. They were a close-knit family, and in its own way, I thought that was pretty cool.

"Now, you call as soon as you get there," Craig said.

"Yeah, collect," Cal added. "And it doesn't matter how late you get in. You know we'll be waiting up for you."

She kissed them both goodbye, and we loaded up the car.

"Now if either of you two need me to navigate," she offered. "Just say so. I never sleep in a car."

"You know I'm on business, eh, Mrs. Presley?" I'd said as we started on the highway. "Dylan and I are going to be pretty busy with my mother's ... er ... trouble."

"Ah, Dix, we all got troubles," she said. "But don't worry, you won't even know you've brought me along."

That had been a few hundred miles and a few dozen crossword clues back.

It turned quiet in the back seat, and when I looked back, sombrero over face, head on pillow and blanket pulled up to her chin, Mrs. Presley was sound asleep.

Good. I needed some time to talk this over with Dylan.

It was still Dylan's turn at the wheel, so I put the faxed pages before me to look things over one more time. Not that I needed to look them over again. Pretty hard *not* to commit the words 'a person of interest in the disappearance of one Francis Morell' to memory, and the whole stealing jewels things didn't exactly escape my mind either.

But no way. No way in hell would my mother do any such thing. Okay, she wasn't a model citizen. But any trouble she'd gotten into had been 'fun trouble' and usually dealt with by a not-so-stiff warning from some cop trying to hide a smile. No one could be all that stern with Mrs. Katt Dodd, 71-year-old resident of the Wildoh Retirement Village, Complex B.

Dylan glanced over at me. "So what do you think?"

"Well, for starters, what I *know* is that my mother is innocent of all charges."

"And you know this because …?"

"Because she's my mother!" I snapped.

"Good. That's out of the way." Dylan nodded to affirm. "Now, you know she's innocent because …?"

With anyone else, I might have been offended. But with Dylan, not a chance. I knew his legally trained mind was doing just what it should be. Helping me build my case, helping me order my facts.

I sighed. "Well, let's look at this piece by piece, starting with the thefts. Mother's not what you'd call rich, but she's comfortable enough. The condo in Marport City, the Bimmer, the condo in Florida — she owns it all outright."

"Right, and all in use. Would she sell if she had to?"

I thought so. Didn't I? Mother owned the condo I lived in. She insisted on keeping it, wanted me to live there, and wouldn't take a cent of rent. Would she tell me if she needed me to move out so she could sell it? *Dammit, Mother.*

I dug my fingernails into my palm. "If she was having money trouble, she would come to me or Peaches Marie."

"You sure?"

Was I? My sister, Peaches Marie, was currently vacationing in Europe with her college professor girlfriend. She was certainly closer to Mom. They lived closer to each other and they were more alike. Peaches was just as carefree as Mother, just as irresponsible. I was the steady one. The serious one. Peaches was well-educated, with that coveted PhD in Philosophy, but I was the one doing better in business. I was the take-charge older sister. Surely if Mom was having financial problems, she'd tell me. We weren't close, but were we really so far away?

I must have drifted too long into my thoughts for when Dylan spoke again, he startled me from them.

"What did your mother do, Dix? For a living?"

I shrugged. "She was our mother. Things were different in my day." Yes, as soon as I said the words I caught myself. *My day.* As if he needed a reminder of the age difference between us. As if *I* did. I pressed on, before he could dwell on that too much. "When my mother was in her mid-twenties, she married my father, Peter Dodd. He was a musician and toured North America. So she quit her own job and followed him. Until I came along, that is. And Peaches two years later. Then we all followed him on tours when we were very young. I can remember some of it — the lights, the instruments, the other musicians. Me and Peaches running around the tables and playing under them while the band set up in empty clubs, preparing to play gigs that we would never see. But that didn't last. Dad took sick. All those smoky nightclubs finally got to him, and he had to quit touring. But music was all he knew."

"Bummer. How'd your family survive?"

"Dad knew music, and ... well, music knew him. Peter Dodd was famous in the club scene in Ontario and parts of Quebec. So if he didn't have the lungs to sing the songs, he still had the mind to write them. Eventually, his work got some attention. I can remember the first time one of his songs played on the radio. Then the first time that one topped the R&B charts. And I remember the first thing Dad did was call the jewelers and order my mother a honking big diamond ring. God, she loved that diamond. Not the most practical expenditure, but Dad always said it was worth it. He was in a wheelchair then, but looked ten feet tall as he put that rock on Mother's hand. Mom saw that too. She dubbed it our lucky diamond. She said that nothing bad would ever happen to us because of that rock. She said it was magic. Things got better then. More secure. More songs on the radio. Big-name stars calling the house. It was pretty wild. Before Dad died, he'd tucked a bit away I know. Probably thinking it would last our mother a lifetime."

"But times changed," Dylan said. "Age isn't what it used to be. Lifetime isn't what it once was."

"No, but I'm sure Mother is doing fine. But even if she were having difficulties, Katt Dodd would not steal." I bit my lip. Of course she wouldn't steal. Not in a million years.

"Dix?"

"Yeah?"

"What did your mother do before she married your dad?"

I looked half hopefully at the approaching sign indicating food, gas and lodging available at the next exit. A fresh coffee sure would be nice. Of course, if we stopped, Mrs. P would wake up and restart our crossword contest. It was a long drive to Florida. Abandoning the idea of coffee, I shifted in my seat. "Mom was an entertainer, too."

"A singer?"

"Ahhh, no. But she did spend a lot of time on stage."

"Oh, you mean she was a dancer. I guess that's where you got those great get-away sticks, huh? Dancer's legs."

Okay, that shut me up. Since when had Dylan Foreman been checking out my legs? And how? I wasn't exactly a high-heels-and-miniskirt kind of girl, although there had been a few times undercover ...

I cleared my throat. "No, not quite that kind of an entertainer, either. Mom was more of a ... well ... more of a show girl, if you know what I mean." When Dylan still looked in the dark, I continued. "She went on stage ... skimpy costumes ... feather boas ... applauding gentlemen ..."

I could practically see the wheels spinning in Dylan's mind. Just about there ...

"Holy shit!" His eyes saucered wide. "She was a peeler!"

"Dylan!" I clapped a shocked hand to my chest. "That's my *mother* you're talking about."

"Oh, shit. I'm sorry. But you said —" He relaxed when he saw my 'gotcha' smile. "Okay, you got me. So, what was she?"

"Magician's assistant," I supplied. "And from what I've heard, a damn good one. She worked mainly with this Lazlo Von Hootzeberger fellow. I gather more than a few other magicians tried to lure her away, but she stuck it out with Lazlo. She toured with him all over Europe and North America before she met and married my father."

"Did she ever teach you and your sister any magic tricks?"

I shifted back in my seat. That was a tricky question. And I wanted to answer slowly and get this right. And I really didn't want to try to explain it again. "You have to understand my mother. She doesn't do tricks. She does magic. That's what she always told us."

"Like the Harry Potter stuff?"

"Not quite. But somewhere along the line, she convinced herself that she really had the ability to do magic and not just sleight of hand. Don't get me wrong: she's perfectly sane. But she's ..."

"Fun?"

I had to smile. If I ever had the privilege of picking out business cards for Dylan Foreman, they'd read *Dylan Foreman — Diplomat*.

"That's a nice way to put it," I said dryly. "Mother always told us she despised tricks. But she loved the *real* magic in the world. We believed her as kids. And you know, I think she believed it too." I shook my head.

In the back seat, Mrs. P snorted in her sleep. (Well, it was loud and ripping so we'll go with 'snort'. I rolled down the window.)

I looked at Dylan, and unfastened my seatbelt. "Now's my chance."

"Dix, what the —"

I turned, leaned over the back of the seat and gently took the magazine from Mrs. Presley's sleep-loosened grip. I plunked myself back down in the seat beside Dylan. "Let's copy all the answers from the back for the next few puzzles." I began flipping through the pages. "That way, when she asks for a clue we can — wait a minute!"

"What?" Dylan flicked a glance at the book on my lap, then back to the road.

"These aren't crosswords." I snapped it closed. "It's a circle-a-word book. Mrs. Presley was just trying to get us to talk dirty."

From the back seat I thought I heard another sound. I turned around quickly to see a sweetly-sleeping, angelic Mrs. Presley.

Chapter 2

MY ASS DIED on the highway. About six hours after the A/C did. Somewhere on Interstate 75 between Atlanta and Macon, Georgia, my hindquarters officially called it quits. That's what 23-odd hours in a car will do to you. Between all that sitting, the lack of sleep, lack of a good meal, and my all-consuming desire (spelled N-E-E-D) for a long, hot shower, I was glad to see this road trip nearing its end.

Mrs. Presley had stretched herself out quite comfortably in the back of my mother's car for most of the trip. True, Mom's Bimmer wasn't that big, but neither was Mrs. Presley. Shoes off, of course. She wore moisturizing patches on her eyes and a dark sleep mask over that. When she wasn't sleeping, she did her 'crosswords'. She sang along with the radio and pulled out a small hand-held battery-operated fan. Cal and Craig had packed her a picnic basket for the trip, and she chomped most of the way there.

She was in prime shape by the time we hit the Sunshine State. Fresh as a daisy.

Dylan on the other hand wore a scruff of beard. And, damn him, it looked good. Sexy. Manly. I wanted to run my hands over it to feel the roughness against my palm. Not that I would, of course. It had been awkward enough the few times we'd bumped each other in the closeness of the BMW.

No, there'd be none of that. Not while we worked together. And shit, not with that decade between us. Still, there was a spark there.

Man, he even *smelled* good, which should have been an impossibility. Granted, we'd freshened up in rest stop bathrooms along the way — a splash of the face and a quick swipe of the pits. But whereas I was beginning to smell like old socks left in a gym bag too long, Dylan had an earthy, musky man-smell thing going on. And it worked for him.

Well, okay, it worked for me.

(I said my ass was dead — other parts of me were very much alive. Compensating even.)

That was Dylan Foreman, though — sexy without trying. And if *his* ass had died somewhere along the highway about the time mine had checked in with the coroner, well someone forgot to tell the jeans that packaged it.

Frankly, I was anxious for Mother to get a look at Dylan. Yeah, juvenile, I know. Especially given the seriousness of Mother's situation. But Katt Dodd was certainly one to appreciate the finer things in life. She loved men. Handsome young ones, distinguished older ones. She appreciated class. She appreciated looks. She liked when a man refilled her wine glass and opened doors for her. And Lord knew she certainly appreciated the young men at the strip clubs. (According to Peaches, she was on a first name basis with more than a few of them.)

Which is why it had surprised me when she cut short her visit with me in Marport City and took off back to Florida with that Frankie Morell. Frankie was not much of a looker.

I'd had misgivings about Frankie from the start. He was a little too smooth to be glass, a little too clean to be squeaky. Yet his leather-soled shoes squeaked with every step he took. I should have run a criminal records check, had my sources in Florida ask around about him, check out his credit history, INTERPOL background check, fax his mug to America's Most Wanted to see if anything cropped up. You know, normal daughter stuff.

But I'd been busy. I'd put my misgivings about Frankie Morell on the shelf. And now my mother was apparently paying the price.

Coincidence?

I feared not.

Missing Frankie — missing jewels. There had to be a connection. I'd have to find it. True, my intuition wasn't 'calling' yet, not pointing me in any particular direction. But give it time …

While Dylan, Mrs. P and I landed in Pinellas County as a trio, it was only Mrs. P and me who were going to the Wildoh Retirement Home (Motto: We supply the *wild*; you bring the *oh!*). Dylan would follow later, but not as my assistant and not as a guest. To investigate fully, he'd need to find a way to come in undercover. Before we'd even hit the Florida state line, we'd formulated a plan, made some calls and put it into action.

Dylan would be staying at the Goosebump Inn, about a mile from the Wildoh Retirement Village. Just a quick jog down the road for the fit Mr. Foreman. We checked him in to Room 46, along with all the fancy electronic equipment we'd brought with us. As command central for our operation, the room was on the small side, but on the plus side of the ledger, it was around the back of the motel and away from traffic.

Did I mention it was small? Barely-turn-around-in small, with a three-quarter sized bed and a chair that looked downright menacing, huddled there all lumpy and mean. Dylan gave it one look, then began piling it high with equipment. There was a small TV in the corner perched precariously on a too-small, too-wobbly chrome stand. In the bathroom, the showerhead was mounted so low, Dylan would have to crouch down to catch any spray.

"And the pool is open for the season," the receptionist had gushed. All of 16 by my guesstimate, with a nametag that read *Rosie Sinatra*, she'd eyed Dylan very thoroughly as she showed him to the room.

Dylan thanked her, but pool play was the last thing on our minds.

We'd checked on the Internet, made a few phone calls — that's what had led us to the Goosebump. I wanted Dylan close, but discreet. Not that I had any illusions that he'd blend in. With that six-foot-four frame and lean good looks, that wasn't going to happen. But I wanted him separate, seemingly moving in another world. He'd get himself into the Wildoh one way or another.

I felt a twinge of guilt hiding Dylan's part in the plan from Mom, but it was for her own good. (Jesus, I felt old just thinking that.)

Mrs. Presley had so not been down with the plan as we'd formulated it en route. She hadn't liked the idea of keeping mother in the dark, even to a small degree. "Family doesn't do that, Dix. Family sticks together. Trusts each other. Counts on each other, through thick and thin. You hear me, Dix?" she'd said from the back seat. "*Thick and thin.*"

My dead butt had slunk down further in the seat with every word of admonishment.

But finally we'd convinced Mrs. P to play along. Well, okay, we'd bribed her. One night of bingo before we left Florida, and …

"Okay, you two," she'd said. "Here's the deal. If you answer my cross-word question in 30 seconds, I won't breathe a word to Katt about Dylan. Ready? Give me a six-letter word for 'style,' starts with D … and *go!*"

Drape? No that's five letters.

Dashing? I counted on my fingers. Crap!

Style, style …

"*Doggie!*" I'd shouted at the top of my lungs, pumping my arm in the air. "I got it! It's doggie-style!"

"I think the word's *design*," Dylan had said dryly.

Mrs. P had sat back, tsking. "Gracious, Dix, what is it with you?"

But we'd gotten her on side, and that was the important thing.

It was late afternoon before we got Dylan settled and made our way over to the Wildoh.

As I stood outside Mother's little apartment waiting for her to open the door, I squinted my eyes to the slanting sunlight, all Clint Eastwood like. Hands on hips, feet spread wide apart, shoulders back, I braced myself. Steadied myself. Steadied my nerves. Steadied my mind and body before the inevitable.

Katt Dodd opened the door, took in the sight of me, then threw her arms around me and hugged me tight.

Must. Breathe. Now.

I love my mother. I'm just not the touchy, feely type.

"Why, Dix," she said, finally releasing the death grip. "What a surprise! What are you doing in Florida?"

That was Mother. Not oblivious to the gravity of her situation, but totally making light of it. Not just keeping the stiff upper lip, but keeping it in a smile. Yet there was something more there. I'd seen it when my father had died — those last few weeks when mom had stayed with him night and day. There was worry behind those sparkling blue eyes.

Her apartment — Suite 101 of Complex B — was on the ground floor. I'd not been pleased with a ground floor suite when Mother had told me she'd bought the place, but she was determined this was the one for her. This was the one with the best 'vibes', she'd said. And I knew there was no changing her mind after that. The complex itself was nice, and complete with everything — laundry service, bus service into town for those who didn't like to drive, a recreation room (and I hear a pretty competitive cribbage gang gathers there) and a tennis court. There was even a driving range set over a man-made lake, complete with little floating islands for distance markers. Mother didn't play golf, but from her frequent emails, I know that the range was a pretty popular place.

"Surprised to see me, Mom? Well, I bet you're not nearly as surprised as I was when I got the fax from Deputy —"

"And you can be no one other than Mrs. Presley," Mother said, turning to Mrs. P and effectively shutting me up. "Dix has told me so much about you."

"Call me Jane. I like your lipstick."

"Do you?" Mother smacked her lips. "Why thank you. It's Pinch-Me Pink."

I rolled my eyes. If there was one opening line that could seal a friendship between the two, that was it. They'd bond like schoolgirls now.

"What am I thinking, keeping you on the doorstep?" Mother stepped back. "Come on in."

We followed her into the foyer of her tiny apartment.

"What a great place you have here." Mrs. P left her bags by the door (don't worry, Mrs. P I'll get those later), and strolled into my mother's living room.

"Thank you, Jane! I like it too. Please make yourself at home."

She would.

Mrs. P sat on the sofa, kicked off her shoes and put her feet up. "You get the wrestling here, Katt? I just love those wrestling boys. All slicked up and broad-chested and stuff."

I cleared my throat. "You know it's staged, eh, Mrs. P?"

Mrs. P and my mother looked at each other then looked at me as if I were an alien. "And that matters because …?"

Great, two hormonally elevated little old ladies to contend with over the next few days. I felt like the mother of two teenagers. Except I couldn't ground these two.

Mother glanced at her watch. It was a new one, I noticed — delicate and thin gold band, dainty safety chain, and I swear those were real diamonds glittering around the outside. And by 'swear' I mean I said, "Holy shit! Mother where'd you get the watch?"

She looked at the watch as if just noticing it for the first time. A little shocked at seeing it, perhaps. She pulled her sleeve down and covered it quickly. The Pinch-Me Pink disappeared for a moment as she sucked in her breath. "The watch was … it was a present from Frankie. Before he … before I …"

Mother recovered. She straightened, and said. "Try channel 137, Jane. I think wrestling is on in ten minutes."

Mrs. Presley began flicking.

"Let me get you a drink," she said to Mrs. P. "You must be parched after such a long trip."

"Well, yes, it was tiring."

I stifled a snort. Mrs. P was tired?

"Mother, I really think we should talk about —"

"Not now, Dix, we have company." She turned back to Mrs. P. This was getting frustrating as hell. "Can I get you a beer? Iced tea?"

"Do you have something with an umbrella in it?"

"Let me see," Mom answered. "I think we have some left over from Maudine's stagette party."

"Stagette party? Mother don't you think you're a little too old to be hosting stagette parties?"

If looks could kill, I'd have it from both ladies.

Mother sighed. "Dix, when are you going to get that stick extracted from your butt?"

"Never, thank you very much."

I was beginning to be even gladder that Dylan hadn't come along.

"Oh, I almost forgot, Jane. Two very pleasant young men have been calling — Cal and Craig — they seem anxious to know you've arrived."

"That'd be my boys." She shook her head. "Those two just can't get along without their mama. I'd better call them."

"Aren't children wonderful though!"

I followed Mom into the kitchen — and made myself at home. Not that I was familiar with her kitchen, but she was my mother so it was by default that her refrigerator was mine to snoop through and I had automatic dibs on any cookies I found. (I said a prayer for chocolate chunk.) I plunked down on a cushion-covered kitchen stool that deflated with my weight. Having found no cookies, I grabbed a bag of Doritos from the counter and, ignoring the 'you'll-ruin-your supper' raised eyebrow glance from my mother (on which *she* had automatic dibs, being my mother), opened them and munched one.

"Dix, will you see if there are any ice cubes, please?"

I jumped up and checked the freezer compartment of her tiny refrigerator — moved around the frosted bags of tiny peas (no one ever eats the tiny peas, so why bother with them?), Pizza Pops and what looked like a vodka/fruit slush concoction.

"No ice cubes, Mom."

"You sure about that?"

"Sure."

"Very sure?"

"Yes, very sure."

Mother stepped up then down from the little step stool — bag of multi-colored drink umbrellas in hand. But she didn't rush around the kitchen in usual company mode. She dallied, and Katt Dodd rarely dallied in this life. I took that as my cue.

"What's going on, Mom? Why did I get a fax from the local Sheriff's Department telling me you're in legal trouble?"

"Well, Dix, because I told them to fax you. How else do you think they'd have gotten your fax number?"

That wasn't what I meant, and she knew it.

"How much do you know?" she asked.

"The Sheriff's Deputy faxed me that —"

"Oh, Noel Almond? You'll like him. So handsome! Beth Mary MacKenzie called 'dibs' as soon as she saw him drive into the yard and step out of his cruiser. But she didn't have her teeth in so we all pretended not to hear her. And Mona Roberts — she's in Suite 222 — just about fainted. Which didn't go over well with Big Eddie Baskin, let me tell you. I think he's sweet on her. I'd never seen the woman looking so pale! And Tish McQueen — she's staying with Mona for a while — out and out flirted with him."

"Big Eddie?" I said sarcastically. "Let me guess, Big Eddie is the guy who wears leather, slicks back his hair and does the wheelies on his motorized cart? Oh, and I bet he wears at least a half dozen gold chains dangling down in his wide open shirt collar."

"Don't be a smartass, Dix. You have no right to mock my friends."

Okay, she was right. That was uncalled for. It was just so damn frustrating trying to get Mother to focus. And truthfully, I was worried. But it was always like that. Well, since Dad died, anyway. Mother had always been fun loving, but had so much responsibility taking care of Dad in his later years. And stress. And though she never let on to Peaches or me, I knew there was more worry behind her smiling face. Peaches might be the one with the academic smarts, but I was the one who could read people. And I could read the strain on her face no matter how well she hid it behind the Pinch-Me Pink.

"Sorry, Mom," I said. "I'm an idiot."

I waited for her to correct me on that.

And waited . . .

"Er, did I get something right?"

"Okay, young lady. But those chains and charms are very fashionable these days."

I couldn't wait to meet Eddie.

And mom couldn't wait to tell me more about Noel Almond.

"Deputy Almond is tall and so good looking. Deepest blue eyes. Honey-blond hair and he does this adorable comb through thing with his fingers. And that body!" She scrunched her shoulders up and down as if hugging herself. "Broad shoulders, long legs. And Dix, if I'm any judge of these things — *and I am* — Deputy Noel is so goddamn wonderfully hung —"

"Mother! I don't want to discuss how well hung the Deputy is!"

She feigned shock. Poorly. With a dramatic hand to chest gesture. She swung open the door to the living room and called out to Mrs. P, "Jane, does Dix always talk so filthy?"

"She does." Mrs. P paused in her channel surfing. "Gotta watch that one of yours, Katt. The words that come out of her would make a sailor blush. You should have heard her in the car on the way here. I didn't even know some of them words, to tell you the truth."

She let the door swing shut again. "Why, Dix Dodd!" Mother said. "I was going to say the Deputy is so *hung up* on finding out the truth about the strange happenings around here."

"No you weren't"

She grinned. "No, I wasn't."

"Mother, do you really think it's a good time for shlong jokes?

"Is there ever a bad time for them?"

She had me there. Despite myself, I finally smiled. "Good to see you, Mother."

"Dix," she said. "I'm so glad you're here."

I let out an exasperated sigh. And by the eye roll I got from my mother, she knew my fakes as well as I knew hers. But this was serious. And I had to get her to realize that. "Mom, no matter how good looking Deputy No Nuts is, or how grandly he's hung ..." (oh I wanted to go places with this one myself) "... *up* on finding the truth, that's not really important right now."

She looked at me strangely, a minute. Then snorted a laugh. "Oh I get it — *Noel Almond*, No Nuts! That's good, Dix."

I guess my penchant for naming male police officers wasn't restricted to Detective Richard Head, (aka Dickhead) of Marport City. But come on, his name was Noel Almond. That was a *kick me* sign waiting to happen.

I pulled off a strip of paper towel to dust my Dorito-orange fingertips on. I thought it would be easier to start with the thefts. Hit less close to home. "So, tell me about the missing jewels."

She hauled out the small cutting board and began chopping. Her back to me, she began talking. "They started about two months ago. Vanessa Trueman's ruby earrings went missing. She's a dear, but a little on the forgetful side, so we all just sort of thought they'd surely turn up somewhere. But then Quinn Foster's diamond ring went missing, the next day Annamarie Tildman checked her jewelry box and all the diamonds out of her antique broach were missing. Plucked right out! The alarm went up, Dix. This wasn't just a matter of a few things going missing. This was a shitload."

I hated to ask. But I had to. "The diamond ring, the one Daddy got you, Mom ... our lucky diamond ... is it ...?"

"It's safe. I don't keep it in my jewelry box. I keep it in the wall safe, behind that picture of you and Peaches Marie that I love so well."

I knew the picture. Peaches and I had been 5 and 7 respectively. Playing at the beach. Building a sandcastle while the waves played in the background. And over the two sun-drenched smiling Dodd girls, our mother's shadow ... holding the camera in one hand, waving with the other. And you could feel the delight of her doing so.

I also knew the safe. Well, not *it* specifically, but a zillion just like it. The Wildoh condos were fairly new, but cookie-cutter similar in construction. Just like the eat-in kitchen and the convection oven, the mini wall safe was no doubt standard in all the condos, though each would have its own combination.

"I didn't steal the jewels, Dix," Mom said.

"I never said you did. Never thought it for a minute."

"No, but I wanted you to hear it from me. We have to be upfront about everything with each other. That's what families do."

I swallowed down my guilt at hiding Dylan away. *For her own good*, I reminded myself.

"There's a lot of ... a lot of suspicion around here. And a lot of it is aimed at me."

"Why?"

She shook her head. "I don't know. Well, I didn't know at first. But ... but with Frankie's ... hopping off like he did. People just naturally turned their suspicions on me. They stayed stuck on me."

I wasn't suspicious of my mother, but was starting to have suspicions about Frankie. I kept them to myself for the moment. "And what about Tish, Beth Mary and Mona? Do they suspect you?"

"Don't underestimate the power of female friendships, Dix. Mona wouldn't ever say a word against me. And by default therefore, neither would Tish. And there are others here who are so very friendly. You'll meet them all tomorrow."

And I couldn't wait. Inserting myself into the flow of life at the Wildoh would be a piece of cake. Unless … "You didn't tell them I was a private investigator, did you?"

"Of course not!"

I relaxed. "Excellent, better to have them off guard."

"I told them you ran a bordello."

"Mother!"

"Kidding, Dix. Lighten up! I told them you wrote erotica. And that you were here doing research for a book. Told them you'd have some questions for them."

I waited for the sly grin, the 'ha-ha, got you again'.

And waited …

Ah hell.

"What about Beth Mary and Big Eddie."

She rolled her eyes. "Beth Mary is as jealous as the day is long. She's been after my Frankie since the day I introduced them."

Jesus, I hated to ask: "This is only a one-bedroom suite. Does Frankie … live here too?"

She laughed. "Of course not. He rents a little bachelor place in Complex A. Moved in just after we met."

My shoulders lowered and I sighed with relief. There are some things a daughter just doesn't want to picture about her mother.

"But often he'll sleep over after sex, especially if we've gone around two or three times."

Shoulders of steel! Back ramrod straight. Mind cringing.

She turned. Somehow in the midst of our talking she'd made a tray of sandwiches, cubed up some cheese and put some fancy little pickles on a plate. There were three different kinds of crackers and some kind of pâté thing. None of her domestic skills had rubbed off on me. She was fine china and haute cuisine. I was chili in a Styrofoam bowl.

"Bring the drinks, Dix."

They clinked in the glass as I grabbed them. "Ice? Weren't you … weren't you out of ice?"

She smiled. "Did you forget? I'm magic."

She started toward the swinging door again to join Mrs. Presley. But I had one more question.

"Mom." I approached this carefully. Diplomatically. "Where do you think Frankie disappeared to?"

"Oh, he didn't disappear."

"Huh?"

"He changed. I changed him."

Did she really think she could change that man? Apparently, she did.

Mother continued. "I told him I didn't like his flirting with all the women. I wasn't about to put up with it! So I told him it had to stop — or else."

"What did he say?"

"He croaked."

Croaked! Oh, sweet Jesus, she'd killed him! I could picture poor Frankie Morell now — his smarmy smile, his bushy sideburns and inch-high eyebrows, stuffed in the freezer. Ice hanging from his fingertips. Frost stuck to his nose hairs. Where the hell had these ice cubes come from?

"Mother you ... you ...?"

"I changed him into a frog." She plucked an olive off the tray and popped it into her mouth. She was serious. Three chews later: "That'll teach him to flirt with other women."

Oh shit! She really thought she'd changed him into a frog!

Mother rolled her eyes. "You've always known I have the magic, Dix. I just used it."

She backed into the door to push it open with her butt, her hands occupied holding the tray. "Close your mouth, honey. You'll catch a fly. Frankie's gonna need those."

I closed my mouth.

Chapter 3

You'd think after such a long drive, I'd have slept like a log once I'd finally showered, put my PJs on (baggy t-shirt and boxers) and finally crashed on my mother's pullout sofa in the living room. And, well, you'd be right. Holy shit, did I sleep!

Despite all the drama and tension, once I closed my eyes, I was out. I know that I snored. I know this because at least once during the night, Mrs. P came out and rolled me onto my side to get me to stop. The pullout wasn't the most comfortable bed in the world, but I'm a PI. I can sleep practically anywhere. Besides, the beautiful Florida night more than compensated for any shortcomings the bed might have had. I'd left the French doors open right up until bed time, and the breeze had blown right in through the screen. It was closed and locked now (both Mother and Mrs. P double-checked it, thank you), but I could still faintly hear the palm trees in the yard swaying and rocking me to sleep. And it was blessedly quiet compared to Marport City.

Mrs. P bunked in with Mom. She had a large double bed in her room, which she insisted Mrs. P take. And she herself slept on a small, foldout bed that we brought up from her storage locker in the basement. I know the two stayed up late talking. Before I turned out the lights, I could hear the giggling through the thin walls. Mother and Mrs. P were so very different, yet alike in many ways. Both widows who'd done a lot of the childrearing on their own. And both looking for fun in life now. Despite everything going on, Mom was determined to make Mrs. P's visit to Florida enjoyable. As much as she frustrated me by times, I had to hand it to her. She did have this way of connecting with people, making everyone feel like they belonged.

Even me.

I did of course spend my pre-sleep hours going over (and over) everything mom had told me. The conversation hadn't ended in the kitchen of course. One thing for sure, she was really smitten with Frankie Morell. Mom's one tough lady, strong as they come, but she obviously had a soft spot for Frankie. She felt awful about him 'hopping' away in a huff. But she had to teach him a lesson. And she hadn't expected him to hop off before she turned him back.

Yes, Mom really believed she'd turned him into a frog.

Now there was a vision for you — a geriatric frog waiting for a kiss to turn back into a prince. Good luck with that one, Frankie.

Why was mother doing this, though? Was she going senile?

True, she always attested to being 'magic' and with a conviction that made Peaches Marie and me believe it when we were younger. She could pull rabbits from hats and sneeze out flowers. She could make white milk into chocolate! And she always, *always* knew when we were lying. Or holding something back from her. Guess that's where I got my own intuition. Of course, as we got older, we (or at least I) realized that kind of magic just didn't exist in the world.

So, yeah, I was worried about Mom. If she didn't tell us what really happened to Frankie, she'd be in deep shit. But would her pride let her? She might have to admit he'd left her, or worse, left her holding the bag. If he'd stolen the jewels, taken off and left her to take the blame, this didn't bode well for Mother. I had to find Frankie. I had to find the jewels. Thus I had tossed and turned with these thoughts in my sleep, waking on the floor half under the pullout and half out (and not the sunny half), my pillow bunched tightly in the crook of an arm. Damn that REM sleep behavior disorder.

But when I did awake, it was to the smell of bacon, eggs and toast. Mrs. Presley was in her element whipping up breakfast. Mom was just getting in from her early-morning power walk, looking like a million bucks in her white tracksuit, hot pink sneakers, and flawless make up. And best of all — carrying a tray of coffees.

I had a funny feeling I'd be needing that caffeine today.

And, was I ever correct on that.

You see, yesterday had been golf lesson day. Big Eddie had taken the ladies out to help them improve their game. They'd shot balls into the lake. That meant today was lake-cleaning day. And mother assured me I wouldn't want to miss that.

Personally, I had my doubts. I mean, come on! How boring could life be here?

"So tell me, Ms. Dodd ..."

"Please, Mona dear, call her Dix. Just because she's a rich and famous author doesn't make her pretentious. Why, she's very down to earth."

I flashed my mother an I'm-right-here look that she chose to ignore.

We were sitting in the front room — the recreation room. And it was beautiful. The sun shone in through the floor-to-ceiling windows. Outside flowers bloomed and trees hung lush and green. There were a few people strolling on the walkways over the lawns, and each one turned and waved. And the man-made lake was well within sight — less than forty or fifty yards from the rec room. Close enough that I could see the water's surface was dotted at intervals with floating markers, distance indicators on a watery driving range. According to Mother, this was quite the popular spot, though she didn't golf herself. At least I didn't think she did. *(Yes, yes, another stab of guilt.)* There were lawn chairs out front, so that anyone could watch Big Eddie and his golf instructions. My first visual had been of swimmers getting whacked on the head with golf balls, but Mom had assured me that no one swam in the lake during driving practice. There were swim times (though everyone used the heated indoor pool instead), there were driving-range times, and there was the time when Lance, the pool-boy-slash-diver guy *(We call him Lance-a-lot ... get it Dix? / Yes mother. Ha, ha. I get it. / No, I don't think you do.)* cleaned out the golf balls from the previous day's session.

Mom sat there, practically purring as she introduced me, her erotica-writing daughter, to her Wildoh friends. I smiled through the introductions. Smiled so hard my jaw ached. I'd gone undercover in some pretty strange situations before, but I had to admit this was one of the weirdest.

When I first went into the PI business, I asked mom to keep things hush-hush about my career. True to her word, she had over the years evaded any and all questions as to her eldest daughter's profession. So granted, when faced with the task of inventing a career for me, she'd probably had to think fast. But *erotica writer*?

Why couldn't she have given me a normal career, like a doctor? God no, not a doctor! I'd be screwed if someone needed anything beyond a hangnail fixed.

Seamstress? Nah. Someone was bound to notice I fix my hems

with staples.

Maybe mother could have told them I was Marport City's finest orthodontist (finally realizing the dream of my buck-toothed high school guidance counselor, who wistfully urged everyone he ever counseled to become an orthodontist). That would have been perfect. I mean, how many seniors citizens have braces on their teeth? (Yikes, wouldn't that look scary in that jar over night?)

At least Mother's imagination had made me popular with the crowd at the Wildoh. Sought after, even.

"All right then, Dix," Mona continued. "I know you do a lot of research for your books —"

"How do you know that?" *Smile. Keep smiling.*

"Why, that's what your mother told me."

Mother smiled at me adoringly. Molars crunched molars as I smiled back. Then I turned to address Mona again. Okay, game on: "Well, you're quite right. I do a great deal of research." I crossed my legs and dangled/bobbed my left foot in the air. Don't ask me why I dangled/bobbed. It just felt right for Dix Dodd, sex goddess writer woman. "Hours and hours of research."

"Why don't you tell us all about it?" Mrs. Presley said. "Every little detail."

Collectively, everyone at the table leaned forward. I looked around at the eager and anxious faces. It was looking like Christmas Dinner at the Wildoh and I was in charge of the stuffing.

"Please do," Tish McQueen invited, but her voice rang with a clear challenge. "I'm sure you could enlighten us all."

That was just after she'd given another one of her looks toward my mother.

Yes, another one. I'd caught that transaction between these two women early. Tish was a stunningly beautiful woman, and though my mother is a pretty hot ticket herself, Tish had a hell of a figure for an old gal. Hell, she had a great figure for any gal. When she'd swooped into the common room, she'd looked like she was dolled up for dancing. High heels that would have killed me, tight Capri pants that would have killed themselves had they found their home on my ass, and a diaphanous blouse. She had earrings that dropped to her shoulders, bracelets that jangled every time she moved an arm. Tish's makeup was a little heavy for the bright lights of the common room, and by the yawns she tried to stifle, I wasn't so sure she hadn't been out dancing all night. She wore her silver blond hair up, and she lifted a hand to touch it every so often. More than touch it ... she readjusted pins and tucked in strands that had no business being out at this early hour of the day.

Tish might be rooming temporarily with Mom's friend Mona, but I believed dear Mother was wrong on the automatic extension of loyalties there.

"Well ... Tish, is it?" I flipped my hand with an I'm-too-important-to-care condescending wave to go along with the dig. I knew her name. That was snide of me, but what the hell. And too, I wanted to appear a bit on the flaky side. That's more of a smart blond trick than a private investigator trick. Let them underestimate you, when it suits your purpose (ideally, just before you nab them).

Tish McQueen didn't miss a beat. "That's right, it's Tish. But don't worry, dear. Lots of people start forgetting names when they get to be our age." She raised her arms to re-stick a piece of hair — dipping her cleavage as she did. Holy shit! I know she did that on purpose to give me a gander, but ... holy shit. I was never that well-endowed (and I had the fake boobs at the office to prove it). But more to the point, you'd think gravity would be more on my side than hers! Surgery? Pretty expensive endeavor ...

"Please, Dix, do tell us about all the *research*," Tish repeated.

She was one up on me. Maybe even on to me. Or potentially on to me. I'd better make this good. I searched my memory banks for all my personal expertise. Well, that was a quick little withdrawal. Then my mind flipped to Dylan. And I sat up a little straighter. True, we'd only been close-close that one time. And it hadn't gone all that far. But the memories of lips on mine, his hands in my hair, his eyes on me, looking me over with a hunger that matched my own ...

"Dix? Dix!" Mother's voice snapped my attention.

"Oh! Sorry!" For some strange reason I caught myself waving a fanning hand to cool me off. "You ladies keep it warm in here."

"Oh, that's just you kicking into sexy writer mode," Mona said. She laughed, but sincerely. With me, not at me. I did like Mona, and could see why she and Mom were such good friends. Mona seemed more down to earth than the rest of the Wildoh residents. Her clothes looked thrift store and her makeup was nonexistent. Her shoes caught my attention. More than a little on the scuffed-up side.

Yet Mona was a genuinely happy lady. That was obvious. At least, most of the time. But even I could feel the tension when Tish walked in the room. Friendship? Sure. Civility? Absolutely. But caution. There was just a tightening to Mona when Tish came along. Words came out a little too quickly, and gestures were made a little too hesitantly. Others might not notice that, but I was, after all, Dix Dodd, world famous erotica-writer ... I mean, PI.

Beth Mary MacKenzie adjusted her teeth. (meaning she took them out, looked at them and put them back in again). Then she smiled her thousand dollar smile. "Do you watch videos, Dix? Those sexy ones? Do you interview lots of men? Good-looking ones I bet." She was talking a mile a minute.

Beth Mary was an odd duck (and being the self-proclaimed queen of the odd duck brace, I know my odd ducks). Instantly, I liked her. She wore her gray hair long and braided down her back. She wore jeans and a plain white shirt that was two sizes too big, and I envied the comfort.

The other two people at the table were Harriet and Wiggie Appleton. In my entire life, I'd never seen anyone sit straighter than Harriet Appleton. And that line of her back was only rivaled by the perfect pleats in her skirt and the creases in her blouse. Man, this was no laundry-out-of-the-dryer chick. But it wasn't just her appearance, Harriet gave new meaning to the phrase, stiff-upper-lip. It was one straight line across — thin and barely there.

Wiggie, her husband of 40-odd (and, oh, I can believe they were very odd) years, sat beside her. Not so stiffly. Wiggie slouched in his seat, and I would wager the mismatched tracksuit he wore had never seen an iron.

"I'm not so sure I want to hear about ... any kind of research a *pornography* writer would be conducting." Harriet sniffed the air in a I-know-who-farted manner.

"No one's forcing you to stay, Harriet," Mona said, pleasantly. "But this might be fun."

She sniffed. "If you ask me, people are having a little too much *fun* around here."

"Amen on that one!"

Good one, Mother.

Harriet didn't think it was such a good one. "Humph!"

"I'd like to ask Frankie Morell just how much fun you've been having, Katt Dodd. Oh that's right, he's gone *missing*. How convenient."

"Not convenient for me, Harriet," Mother said. It unsettled her. I know that it did.

"Oh? And why is that now, Katt? Because you're a suspect in

his disappearance?"

It was official: I did *not* like Harriet Appleton.

Mother waved a dismissive hand, "No not that. It's because I'm horny as hell and this kitty wants to purrrrr."

Beth Mary's teeth clacked just before her jaw dropped. Mona snorted a laugh. Tish nodded appreciatively. Mrs. Presley of course, laughed out loud. I was never so proud of my mother.

Harriet Appleton shook her head in disgust.

Out of the corner of his mouth, Wiggie smiled at me. Weakly and slyly, but his eyes sparkled as Mother put Harriet in her place.

It was all I could do not to reach over the table and give Mother a high five.

On that note, I was bound and determined to give the gals and Wiggie an earful of my best research. I just had to figure out what the hell that was.

"Well," I said. "Research? Ah yes, research." I tapped a finger to my temple as if thinking. Then I tapped it again. Once more for good luck ...

Did I mention I was pathetic at stalling for time?

"Yes," I finally said. "Of course I do a lot of research. A great deal of reading of the classics in erotic literature." I tried to sound authoritative.

"What classics would that be?" Tish asked. She twirled a silver blond lock in her fingers. "I'm quite widely read. Actually, I used to work at a bookstore. Maybe I've heard of them."

Damn, damn, damn. It wasn't that I didn't have a good book or two tucked under my mattress. But there was a reason certain pages were dog-eared. Those were the juicy parts. If I tried to elaborate on plot, I'd be screwed.

And not in the good way.

I'd have to make up some new titles.

"Oh you may not have heard of the modern classics."

"Such as?"

"Yeah." Mrs. P smiled. "Such as what?"

I couldn't give her the kind of glare I wanted while staying in character, but I'm sure she interpreted my fierce smile appropriately.

"Well, what firstly comes to mind is the Syvanna Sly series. She's a wonderful new author. Writes from a women's point of view. Pure lust. Pure sex. They are hot!" I had to think fast, talk fast, and boy, was I winging it. "The series revolves around the sexual escapades of this middle-aged woman."

"What's her name?" Mom asked.

Not helping! Not helping!

"Daphne. Daphne Delicious."

Okay, now I was just not helping myself.

I continued. "And she's you know, middle-aged."

"Got that. Go on." Tish prodded.

Fine. I would. "So Daphne Delicious is busy in the world finding herself. In every way. She has a new career. Well, not really new. More ... more like she finds more independence in her career these days. But she's also finding a newfound sexuality. But here's the kicker ... she likes men, but she doesn't exactly trust them. Not anymore. She was burned, burned badly before and be damned if that would happen again. Then into her life comes this young man. Tall. Handsome. Smart and sexy in a smart and sexy kind of way."

"What's his name?"

"It's Dyl ... Dilson, Mrs. P. His name is Dilson."

"Why, that's an odd name."

"Yes, it is." *Keep grinning.*

"Is he handsome?"

"Yes, Tish, he's drop dead gorgeous."

"Does he work for you, Dix?" Mrs. P says. "Oh sorry, I mean does he work for Daphne Delicious?"

I gritted my teeth. "As a matter of fact, he does."

"Yum. Does she do him?"

Mona swatted my mother. Playfully of course.

But I had to wonder myself ...

"Well, she better!" A male voice boomed into the room. "Can't tease a fellow like that forever, can you, now, ladies?"

Collectively, everyone turned.

Harriet drew herself even straighter and Wiggie gave a friendly wave. Mom smiled. Tish twirled her hair and Beth Mary stuck her fingers in her mouth to readjust her teeth.

"Hey ya, Big Eddie," Mona called out.

"Hey ya, Mona."

He came over and kissed her on the cheek. "There's your birthday kiss!"

"Ah, Eddie," she gushed. "You know my birthday's not for three more days. You've been laying a kiss on me every day for the last two weeks."

He winked. "Just practicing up for the real thing."

He turned his attention to Beth Mary. "All set for our golf lesson, BM?"

"Oh, I don't know, Eddie," Beth Mary said. "I don't seem to be making much progress. I'm just about ready to give up on those balls."

"I've got just the thing then. We'll use the lucky balls."

Beth Mary smiled. "The orange ones?"

"The very same. I got a lucky orange one here, I'm warming up for you." He rolled his hand around a golf ball in his deep pocket (God, I hoped he was rolling his hand around a golf ball deep in his pocket).

They had to be doctored or course. Weighted or some such thing to send them farther. And painted orange to distinguish them from the non-weighted balls. What the hell, wouldn't hurt. And if Beth Mary thought they brought her luck, then maybe they did.

When he stood upright again, I got a full view of Big Eddie. All five-foot-two of him — in platform shoes. Wearing heavy socks. I half squinted my eyes as he moved closer. The sun reflecting off the several layers of chains around his neck was almost blinding. Okay, maybe not *blinding*, but the guy definitely had a thing for bling. The chains he wore were gold — well, gold in color. And he had more trinkets hanging from them as if he was wearing a charm bracelet around his neck. Four leaf clovers, medallions, the obligatory diamond-studded horseshoe. Or, I suspected, diamond-ish. One thing for certain, whoever was pinching the jewels at the Wildoh would not be hitting Big Eddie's place any time soon.

Mother had told me Big Eddie lived in the staff quarters. Had his own tiny bachelor apartment in exchange for bi-weekly golf lessons and generally taking care of a few things around the Wildoh. Not all the employees had apartments on the premises, but Big Eddie was more than a golf instructor. He was kind of a social director at the Wildoh, from what I'd heard. This was Florida, and most staff were young and transient. But Big Eddie had been with the Wildoh for a while now.

"Who's the little lady?"

I waited for someone to answer.

Oh *me*.

I extended my hand. *Please just shake it. Please just shake it.*

He wiped his hands on his pants, depositing the bit of white powder there that had to be from a sugar donut, held my dangling fingers a little too long in his damp grip, then pulled my hand forward and kissed it loudly.

"Dix Dodd," I said, pulling my hand back and fighting like hell to keep from wiping it on my jeans. It wasn't an Eddie thing. It was a slobber thing. "Pleased to meet you, Edward."

"Please call me Big Eddie. Heavy on the *big*."

Men in polyester pants shouldn't say those things.

"Are you moving in to the Wildoh?" he asked. "I know they've been renovating the C Complex. Fixing up some cute little places there. Are you looking at one of those apartments?"

Okay, that's it—I wiped my hand on my pants. He didn't notice. Crap. I hardly thought I looked old enough for a retirement home. After all, wasn't forty the new thirty?

Mrs. Presley laughed out loud. "Well, there you go, Dix. Nice little retirement home all ready for you."

"This is my daughter, Big Eddie. She and Jane," Mother nodded towards Mrs. P, "are staying with me for a few days."

"Well, that's just lovely. But are you sure she's not your sister, Katt?"

"I'm sure Big Eddie."

Mother wouldn't blush in a million years, but she grinned a Cheshire cat grin. I had to admit, Big Eddie was a charmer with the ladies. With the *older* ladies.

"Good Heavens," Harriet hmphed again. "Edward, you're full of yourself again this morning, I see."

He chuckled, but a little too deeply with just a tad too much time between the ha-ha's. There was no love lost in either direction.

"Harriet, dear, you're looking well this morning."

She rolled her eyes. "Why it is that you think you have to flirt with every woman who comes into the Wildoh is beyond me." She glared at my mother. "And especially those of . . . the criminal persuasion."

What the f —

"Now, just wait a minute," I said. "My mother is not a criminal. She'd not guilty of anything. From what I hear, there's nothing but circumstantial evidence and unfounded rumors floating around. That's hardly a conviction in my books."

Mother put a cautioning hand on my arm. Or maybe it was an appreciating one.

"Oh, I'm surely not interested in *your books*, Ms. Dodd."

It took me a minute to realize she was referring to my erotica. Or my supposed erotica.

"Well, maybe if you'd get the broom handle extracted from you backside, you would be."

Well, *that* shut her up. In fact, that shut *everyone* up. Except for Tish, that is. She snorted a laugh.

Wiggie squirmed in his seat.

"Now, ladies, please," Big Eddie said. "Let's not have any more craziness around here. We're all just under a bit of pressure with the ... things going missing and such." His eyes more than slid to my mother before quickly sliding away. Why the hell was everyone thinking my mother guilty? There had been no trial! There was no evidence against her! It was that damned Frankie Morell. This was all his fault, with that disappearing act he'd pulled.

"Big Eddie's right," Mona said. "We're all just tense and —"

"Some of us more so than others." I glared at Harriet as I said this.

"Why don't we all just cool down?" Mona jumped from her seat. "I know! I'll grab the crib board. Nothing like a good old-fashioned crib game to ease the tension. You know fifteen-two, fifteen-four —"

Her crib talk was interrupted — loudly and strangely musically — by a car horn. One of those musical ones like the General Lee from the Dukes of Hazard. But this one didn't play those few notes from *Dixieland*. The driver of this vehicle played a few unmistakable sounds from a Rod Stewart tune. And if the leaping and squealing of the ladies at the table was anything to judge by, yes, they did want his body and thought him sexy.

"It's him!" Beth Mary shouted. She tipped her chair over and left it on the floor as she raced to the picture window, thumbing her teeth back in as she went.

"Who?" Mrs. Presley asked, but she herself was already on her way across the room. "Him who?"

Tish grabbed under her boobs, adjusted them left-right-center in one deft motion. "Lance-a-Lot. Golf lessons were yesterday; ball retrieval today."

"Oh."

Mona grabbed Mrs. P by the hand, "Come on, you got to get a look at our Lance."

Even Big Eddie sauntered his way over to the window.

"It's time for us to go, Wiggie." Harriet grabbed her husband by the shoulder (and I couldn't help but wonder what she grabbed him by when they were home).

For all that, Harriet was taking her sweet time leaving. And with each step, she craned and rotated her neck around just a little more until I thought she might snap it clear around (and if there was one demon-possessed woman in that room, my money was on her).

"Leaving so soon, Harriet?" Mother asked sweetly.

Harriet stopped short. "I am not going to lower myself to your level of entertainment, Katt." She spat my mother's name out as if it spoiled in her mouth. She waved a flustered hand to the window. "And this ... this ... spectesticle I do not need to see."

She practically pushed poor Wiggie through the door and it swung firmly shut behind her.

I leaned in to Mom, "Did she say spec*testicle*? Now there's a slip of the tongue."

Mom looked up at me, trying to give me a genuine smile, and it broke my heart that she didn't quite pull it off.

As if on cue, the doors swung open again. A dozen other women came rushing into the room. Some said hello to Mom, others — very obviously — did not. Chairs began to fill up as the women, and yes, Big Eddie too, took their seats in front of the window. Seven or so more ladies strolled to the front of the building and claimed the lawn chairs there.

"Got a chair right here for you, Katt. Right beside me," Mona yelled, and I felt the relief flowing off my mother.

Mona Roberts was definitely going on my Christmas card list. Which brought that list to a grand total of ... one.

Mom led me along by the arm. "You've got to see this, Dix!"

She took her seat beside Mona, and I stood beside my mother's chair. All eyes were forward focused, looking out the window waiting for this Lance guy to clean the lake. I scanned the crowd of anxious faces.

Okay, like how boring *was* this place? There they sat, a group of senior woman and Big Eddie looking out the window as if Frank Sinatra himself were going to jump out of that truck. They leaned forward, they grinned widely. Why, you'd never catch me acting like that. No chance in hell. Not in a million years. Not in a —

"Oh my God!" There was a high-pitched squeal.

That was from me.

Lance-a-Lot got out of the truck. He was average height I supposed — just under six feet tall. His black hair looked almost blue with the sunlight on it. He was tanned, muscular, and wearing nothing but the happiest pair of Speedos on the planet. Yes, Speedos. *Bursting* with happiness, if you get the picture. Overwhelmed with joy — if you know what I mean.

Okay, enough of the euphemisms. The guy was hung. And at full attention.

"Mercy!" Mrs. P shouted. "What's that freak of nature?"

"Gotta love mother nature," Tish commented appreciatively.

With my sharp investigative mind, I watched the diver closely. I was a PI after all, I had to catch every little detail. And every big one, too.

Lance Devinny obviously knew he had an appreciative audience. He strolled a few feet from the truck, stopped suddenly and gave a quarter turn to wave at the ladies and beamed a full smile. Big Eddie grumbled, "Now, what's that boy got that I ain't got?" He ran a hand through his own dark hair — thinning as it was. The hair, not the hand.

Out of politeness, no one answered.

Did I mention Big Eddie wore polyester pants?

The group continued to watch as Lance turned back around, flexed his butt cheeks — left, right, left again — and made his way to the water. He walked out to his waist, then quick as anything dove into the shallow lake.

With a collective sigh, the group leaned back. And there was an appreciative moment of silence. And by moment, I mean, literally, moment. But tranquility shattered pronto.

"Help! Somebody help!"

Everyone jumped. Even the ladies who'd taken chairs outside came in to see what was going on.

The voice was coming from the hallway. So was the sound of low-heeled shoes thumping down the hallway along the tiled floor. The door to the rec room swung open, and Harriet Appleton stood there, one hand on her chest, one hand on Wiggie's. Poor Wiggie looked more out of breath than she did.

"What's wrong?" I asked, immediately taking charge of the situation.

"My mother's wedding ring!" Harriet shouted. "It's gone. Stolen! It was one of a kind, precious and priceless. It was an antique! It was my grandmother's," she wailed. She glared at my mother. "You did this, Katt Dodd! I know dang right well you did!"

"You're wrong," I said. "And you'd better stop making accusations you can't back up." I gave her my best glare.

She didn't miss a beat. "I had the ring out late last night. I was giving it to my great niece for her own wedding ceremony. I put it back in my jewelry box — Mr. Appleton saw me do it." Wiggie nodded on cue. "And now the ring's gone."

"I had nothing to do with this!" Mom said.

Harriet huffed. "A likely story. I'm calling Deputy Almond. You're a thief, Katt Dodd. And most likely a murderer, too." She turned to me. "And we'll see whether or not there are accusations that can't be backed up!"

"Harriet, I'm innocent!" Mother pleaded to her. I couldn't help but notice everyone else moving away from my mother. Everyone but Mona, of course. And Mrs. P. "I would never take your ring." She looked around the faces of the crowd gathered there. "I'd never steal anything."

Even Big Eddie turned away.

Chapter 4

So you'd think things would be a little crazy by this time. Well, you'd be thinking correctly.

All hell broke loose. Accusations were flying, rumors were flying. Teeth were flying (Beth Mary sneezed). Evil looks were being pinged around the room from every direction, and unfortunately only heading in one direction — my mother's.

The questions started. Yes, Mom had been out for her pre-dawn walk. So what? She always walked in the coolness of those hours. And of course there was the fact that Mom had been a magician's assistant, something she'd told all her peers at the Wildoh. Why not? It was a past she was proud of. She never told them how the magic was done, of course. She'd been sworn to secrecy all those years ago, and still felt bound by her oath. And Mom had told them about the things she'd escaped from, and places she'd popped herself into. Also, she'd mentioned the fact that she'd never met a lock she couldn't pick (a skill I seemed to have inherited).

That, combined with the fact that Mom was famous for her early morning walks, sealed the deal for most of the residents. And oh yeah, half the residents had already spun a dozen wild yarns about how she had disposed of poor Frankie Morell. Hefty bag in the swamp. Hair in the hamburger. Some old fellow in Complex D thought he found a toenail in his almond pecan ice cream. (Had to be Frankie's, of course.)

And now that Harriet Appleton had reported her ring missing, suspicious minds were overheating. Mother had means. She had motivation (there certainly was no love lost between Harriet and Mom). She had opportunity.

Crap.

But frankly, I was getting suspicious of Harriet Appleton.

What if she were lying?

Maybe Harriet and Wiggie were trying to cash in on the recent thefts? File a false insurance claim and collect some money for nothing, while laying the blame for the 'loss' at my mother's feet? Or maybe they were responsible for all the thefts! What if that uptight, proper facade of Harriet's was just a cover? What if they were really criminal masterminds? What if the crown jewels were tucked under their bed? The Hope diamond hidden away in the sock drawer underneath the support hose?

Oh, oh … what if Harriet was a Harry? Or Wiggie a Wanda? (Okay, that was pretty far out there, not to mention irrelevant, but it *could* happen. Hell, it *had* happened with my last case.

But would Harriet, or Harriet and Wiggie, go so far as to off Frankie Morell and blame my mother? I'd seen worse in my line of work. There had to be a connection between the thefts and the missing Frankie. Logic dictated it.

I was bound and determined to find out the truth.

And so was the soon-to-arrive Sheriff's Deputy Noel Almond.

It was Big Eddie who appointed himself taker-charger in the situation. Yes, that was his terminology. At least he didn't dub himself the 'decider'. He flipped open his cell phone and punched in a single number. Number two on his phone, by my reckoning of the bend of thumb. Efficient man. Now that was a taker-charger for you, with the local sheriff's office on speed dial. Less than two minutes later, Deputy Noel Almond's white Dodge Charger sped into the yard. No sirens blared and no bar lights flashed, but he arrived at a pretty good clip.

Deputy Noel Almond was everything Mother had described him. Tall and handsome and, God, yes, *hot*. He was everything my Marport City nemesis Detective Richard Head was not. Besides a man, I mean. Deputy Noel Almond was no Deputy No Nuts.

My immediate, utterly instinctive reaction was to go over and begin giving the good Deputy my professional take on the situation. With one leg twined around one of those muscular, khaki-clad legs.

The sheer outrageousness of the impulse shocked me a little. I mean, I like men. I enjoy men. But at 40-something, my hormones had been around the block often enough to have adopted a more laid back approach. Even they knew that men are trouble, and that a guy needs to demonstrate they're worth the aggravation. And here they were zipping and zinging around my body like teenager hormones.

Funny, as … gifted … as Lance-a-Lot had been as he'd made his way to the lake to retrieve the golf balls in those happy Speedos of his, the good deputy in his Florida Sheriff's green police pants and close-fitting short-sleeved shirt turned me on the more.

But what was I to do? Nothing! Certainly not straddle him then and there. I had to remain in character, remain part of the scenery to get more information to clear my mother. I had to sit back and watch and listen. He of course, knew that I was a private investigator; he had sent the fax to my office, after all. I just hoped Deputy Almond had the good sense not to expose me in front of everyone.

I'd much rather be exposed later when we were alone.

Oh boy.

Big Eddie and Deputy Almond huddled themselves away from the crowd to converse. Glancing over to the rest of us, mumbling and jerking a thumb or nodding a head toward our group every so often. The Deputy caught my attention more than once, and I saw the hesitation there.

"You're becoming quite the frequent visitor, Deputy." Tish purred the words as she sashayed up to Almond. She settled a hand on his bare, tanned, muscular forearm and let it slide down.

God, her timing was inappropriate. But her taste was bang on.

"Good morning, Ms. McQueen," Deputy Almond drawled. "You're looking just pretty as a picture again this morning. Fresh as a daisy. Cute as a button."

Oh, God, one more cliché and I'd puke.

Like Big Eddie, Deputy Almond seemed to know how to work the older ladies. Notice I said *older* ladies. Handsome as he was, I was immune to his charms.

"That's a lovely outfit," he said to Tish.

"This old thing?" Tish batted her eyelashes. "Why, thank you, Deputy."

Yeah right, *this old thing* had the price tag still attached to the back, a fact I happened to notice when Tish did another of her dip/squeeze/show-hooters things.

Tish beamed at the Deputy, and he beamed right back at her. Smart man. He knew that a little flirting goes a long way. Well, for those folks who are susceptible to such tactics.

When Tish sashayed herself away, Deputy Almond addressed the crowd.

"Now, Big Eddie tells me we've had another robbery."

We?

Mother must have caught the disconcerted raising of my eyebrows. She leaned in and whispered, "He's been here often, and it's a small community. Everyone knows everyone, including Deputy Almond."

Okay, so the local cop was one of the gang. I got it. But I didn't know if I liked that. Would that make him likelier to believe the gossip about my mother?

"This wasn't just any old robbery!" Harriet jumped from her chair. "My grandmother's antique ring was stolen!" She glanced at me before she continued. "And I know it was Katt Dodd. Most likely with the assistance of her thieving, smut-talking daughter, Dix Dodd."

Excuse me?

I was about to step out of Dix Dodd erotica-writer mode and into Dix Dodd geriatric-ass-kicker mode, but it was the Deputy who opened his mouth first.

"Now, Mrs. Appleton ... Harriet." There was no sweetness here, no flirting and flattering. "If you've got any proof of your accusations, then I want to hear all about it. In fact, I'll want to talk to all of you." He scanned the room. "But first, I have to check out the crime scene."

Of course he'd want to talk to everyone.

Harriet stood. Wiggie stood up right after her, as if pulled by a string. Together with the Deputy and Big Eddie in full taker-charger mode, they headed out of the rec room.

"There goes Lance-a-Lot," Mona called. But few heads turned toward the window to see.

I ventured a glance though the window at the wonder wood coming out of the water. He walked with all the bravado of a professional stripper. He dropped the bag of golf balls on the green, their wet whiteness shining in the sun. He raked his hands through his hair, arched his tanned body in a stretch, and smiled toward the rec room. Oh this guy was a showman. Pity no one was watching the show.

I glanced at Mom. Her gaze appeared to follow Lance-a-Lot as he shook himself and got into his car, but I knew she wasn't really seeing him. Though she smiled and projected a damned good 'haven't-a-care-in-the-world' attitude that probably fooled some of the residents; it didn't fool me. I knew she was faking it. But I admired her *fuck you* face. She refused to let them see her sweat, and I was so proud of her.

It turned out to be a long afternoon. I'm sure every resident of the Wildoh strolled into the rec room at least once over the course of it. Of course, that had something to do with the fact that Deputy Almond had made the polite 'request' that all residents come in and answer a few questions. Who could refuse? Everyone wanted these thefts cleared up and the thief caught. Refusal meant suspicion. Suspicion meant rumors breaking out. In a small community like the Wildoh — a rumor would travel like the wind once it was broken.

Nobody wanted to break wind.

Slowly but surely Deputy Almond made his way through the interviews. After his inspection of the Appleton suite (yes, the lock appeared to have been picked, yes he dusted for prints, no he didn't find any, and yes, double dammit, he did see a picture of Harriet's antique ring and the insurance papers). It had been a doozie.

Deputy Almond set himself up in a little room off the side of the rec room. Sort of a kitchen-type thing. (Okay, I guess those in the know might actually call it a kitchenette, but when your domestic skills are as non-existent as mind are, it's a kitchen-type thing). It held a little two-burner stove, a fridge that might hold two cases of beer, tops, the world's smallest table, and two God-awful plastic orange chairs. The room was glassed-in, which allowed me to watch the interviewing process. Of course, it also allowed Deputy Almond to scan the crowd of those who waited to see who was nervous and who wasn't, who talked to whom. Who tried to stroll toward the door, who watched the door. Smart man.

Smart, good looking, totally ripped man.

Time and time again, as the Deputy finished an interview and escorted the person out, he would pause to meet briefly with Big Eddie. The two of them would confer, then scan the rest of us in the room. The Deputy would nod, then Big Eddie would step forward and call a name. Jesus, it was like a junior high school dance, without the testosterone. Hell, without the estrogen in most cases. But breaths caught and tension rose when the Wildoh residents waited to see who was next.

I kept my gaze averted from Big Eddie. Kept it ducked every time so as to not get the 'you're next' with a nod and authoritative jerk of the taker-charger thumb. Not because I was intimidated or scared. Not at all. But because the longer I was here, the longer I could watch the residents react to the police presence. One at a time.

Oh, and it gave me plenty of time to get my ass whooped at crib.

Mona hauled out the cribbage board when it was evident we'd be there for a spell. She called out, "Who's up for a game while we wait?"

Surprisingly, some of us were.

Not that I like crib. Nor that I'm any good at it. But as I watched Mona head toward the small card table at the back of the room, crib was just an excellent idea.

I took one of the chairs (more of the plastic orange variety) and sat with my back toward to the wall so I'd get the best view of the interview room. Mom sat across from me; she had no desire to know what was going on behind her in that small room. This wasn't easy for her. A tall redheaded gentleman, Roger Cassidy — who did a slight little bow thing that was really kind of charming — sat on my right. Mona sat on my left. She squeezed mom's hand once, shuffled the cards with a flash and flair that would shame a Vegas dealer and started passing out the cards. We played cut-throat, every man for himself. The stakes, at Mona's suggestion, were two bucks a game, double for skunk. Of course, she won repeatedly. She played with a ferociousness that hockey coaches would love to bottle, pegging the bejesus out of me. Of course, it didn't help that I was distracted.

I was in full PI mode as I watched Deputy Almond work the residents. Every fidget, I caught and registered. Every careful mutter, I witnessed.

Most of them knew nothing or little, which was easy to tell by their reactions. But this was told in different ways: some people were overly animated in their defense, some were under animated. Most maintained eye contact, while a few looked away nervously, but not with the guilty type of nervousness. Of course, my intuition was on full alert as I waited for the feeling to crawl up my spine as the right Wildoh resident went in for the interview.

Didn't happen.

Every time Big Eddie called someone else forward, I'd get a little niggle of anticipation and I'd think, *this is it. This is the one.* But as soon as the interviewee sat down and started talking … nothing. The feeling went away.

"I'll go next," Mrs. Presley said, impatiently after the first half dozen people filed in and then out of the little interview room. "I'm here on vacation. And besides, this shouldn't take long." She was right of course. Short and sweet it was. I watched, amused, really. It was obvious right from the get-go that Mrs. P (who has lots of police-interviews under her belt being the proprietor of the Underhill Motel) wasn't a bit scared of Deputy Almond. If anything, she was enjoying the interview. Hell, she seemed to be *conducting* the interview. When she finally rose to leave, about five minutes after Almond had prompted her with a polite right hand on the door and his left hand adjusted in a right-this-way directive, Mrs. P was well in command of the conversation.

The door opened.

"So, it's five letters, and starts with a 'w'. Any idea, Deputy?"

Oh, no. She wouldn't.

Almond's eyebrows knit in a pensive expression. "I'm thinking, Jane."

"I don't know why I can't get it." Mrs. Presley shook her head. "Five letters, starts with W ... Dammit, what was that clue? Oh, now I remember!"

Oh, she couldn't!

"It was ... a laughing cartoon bird."

"Woody!" Deputy Almond shouted.

Mrs. P (who by the way had excellent hearing) turned and cocked her ear toward him, "What did you say?"

"A happy cartoon bird ... it's gotta be Woody."

"Gotta be *what*?" She cupped her hand around her ear.

"Woody!" he shouted. "You're looking for Woody!"

"Yes, of course!" She snapped her fingers. "Woody! That's it!" She paused, looked thoughtful then nodded her head. "Those dang crosswords. Thanks for helping a little old lady out, Deputy." She winked at me on the way out.

One by one, the crowd dwindled down.

Roger, having lost himself six dollars to Mona, didn't seem too displeased when Big Eddie called him to go talk to the Deputy. He did the nod-bow thing again and pushed his chair all the way in to the table before going to join Almond.

I didn't watch that interview very closely. If Roger had something to hide, I would have sensed it at the table.

I was watching Mom by this time. Now, Mom is a pretty amazing card player. She used to kick my ass at crazy eights when I was a kid, not to mention the days of go-fish card parties we used to have. But her mind hadn't been on the game today. She'd miscounted her hand more than a few times. Whenever Mona pointed out the missed points, Katt just shrugged and insisted Mona mug the points. "That's the rule. I missed it. You take it." Obviously, she was nervous about the impending interview with the Deputy.

When Mother's turn finally came, I watched her approach the small glassed-in interview room. I watched Big Eddie take her elbow to shepherd her inside. And that's when it hit me. That feeling I'd been waiting for, that tingle …

No. No way. Jesus H. Chris, she was my mother! She could *not* be guilty.

But what would I be thinking if she were someone else? Someone unrelated?

I'd damn well think she was guilty, that's what …

Almond straightened when Mom walked into the room. Any trace of friendliness left his face. He assumed a profile of complete authority. No good cop here — just the bad. It was clear he suspected Mom of something, too. He was, after all, still investigating the disappearance of Frankie Morell, and she was still a person of interest in that investigation. How long would his patience last with the crazy lady who turned her boyfriend into a frog?

Frankie Morell. Frankie Morell who was conveniently missing now.

What if he wasn't missing? What if he was hiding out somewhere nearby? Maybe still on the premises? Still stealing jewels. What if he hadn't just hopped on a bus out of town? What if he was still around somewhere, framing my mother?

Grrrrrrrrr.

"Was that your stomach growling, Dix?" Mona asked.

"No." I smiled at her through gritted teeth. "Just me."

Deputy Almond didn't look at my Mother much. I quickly decided that was a deliberate tactic on his part, depriving her of eye contact. He spoke, wrote, spoke, wrote. Mother sat there, growing more nervous by the moment. Which was weird for my mother. Katt Dodd didn't do nervous. But to my discerning eye, and possibly to Mona's, she was clearly restless as she sat with Almond. She touched her hand to her cheek a few times. She crossed her legs then uncrossed them twice. And she kept pulling at her left shirt sleeve, pulling it down over her wrist.

And despite keeping his gaze down, I have no doubt Almond noticed.

The interview was long. As was Mona Roberts' interview. Both women headed out of the room quickly when Almond dismissed them. That left just me in the room when Big Eddie came out to give the nod and the thumb jerk.

"That's all right, Eddie," Deputy Almond said, coming out of the interview room. "Everyone else is gone, I'll interview Ms. Dodd out here."

Big Eddie straddled the chair. Jesus, that was one more thing a man in polyester pants shouldn't do. He sat in the chair Roger the crib player had vacated not too long before. Almond sat where Mona had been — to my left.

His knee touched mine as he pulled his chair in. Yes, I felt the jolt — and not in my knee. Which annoyed me. This man had just made my mother very uncomfortable. I was going to have to have a talk with those hormones of mine about loyalty.

Oh well. Knee should move any second now. Contact happens. No big deal. Tall man/small table accidents occur all the time — probably account for at least five percent of all hospital visits. Amazing more people didn't do the knee bump thing. These damn tables should come with a warning sign. Yep. Waiting for knee to move back. Any second now.

It didn't.

Oh.

Okay.

"Eddie, I think I can take it from here."

Big Eddie looked like a broken-hearted puppy. "You sure, Deputy?"

"I'm sure, Eddie. I can handle Ms. Dodd."

Oh, man! What had happened to the air-conditioning?

Big Eddie Baskin glanced at his watch. "Well, I'd better get going anyway. You call me if you find anything out, okay?"

Almond gave him a firm nod. "Will do."

Big Eddie smoothed a hand over the back of his neck as if he'd just worked a double shift at the factory and his muscles were sore. His necklace — chains and charms and all — jingled against his skin.

Deputy Almond watched him go and didn't say a word until the door had swung completely shut behind Big Eddie's retreating form. Then he turned to me, "Okay, Dix Dodd. Where's the missing ring?"

Okay, I moved *my* knee away.

"Whoa, Deputy, I just got in town, remember? You think *I* stole that ring? Is that the way law and order works down here? Can't solve a simple crime so you lay it on the first newcomer to wander in? What are you going to try to pin on me next? The Kennedy assassination? Maybe I'm the one who killed the Black Dahlia? Mind you, I'm a little too young to have committed those crimes, but what the hell. Are you so damned incompetent that —"

He smiled.

Crap.

"No, I don't think you stole Harriet Appleton's ring. Never thought it for a moment. What I think is that you've watched everyone in this room for the last few hours, just as I did. Maybe *better* than I did. You're a trained PI, and from what I hear from my Ontario contacts, a pretty good one."

Ontario contacts? I wanted names, numbers and a great big pack of thank you notes.

"Why the hell do you think I left you out here so long?"

"Whoops. My bad."

Leaning back easily in his chair, he ran a hand along his lightly whiskered chin.

I bit down on the half grin (mine, not his, more's the pity) that threatened to break through. Hell, if Deputy Noel Almond got any more relaxed, he'd be undoing his belt buckle.

I bit down harder. God, Dix, get a grip. This is the same unsmiling man who just finished grilling your mother. The man who thinks she had something to do with the disappearing jewels, if not the disappearing Frankie.

"How much did you lose to Mona Roberts in crib?"

"Six bucks."

"She let you off easy."

"You know her?"

"I know everyone here. And maybe that's part of the problem. Why I've not solved these thefts or the matter of the missing Frankie Morell. I'm too close maybe, and that's why I need your take on things."

Damn, it felt good to be appreciated. As did the idea that he might be keeping somewhat of an open mind about whodunnit. "Well, here's what I think —"

He stood. "Nope, not now. I have to get some paperwork done, head back to the Appleton apartment one last time, stop by to see Big Eddie, then get to my office to type up these notes." He waved a handful of sheets of yellow legal paper in my direction as if proving the point. "We'll talk tomorrow — give you time to mull things over, sort out your own thoughts."

That was weird. "You want me to come by your office?"

"No, I'll stop by here. Say about seven. In the evening. And it would be best if we didn't talk here. Wouldn't want to make the residents suspicious. Wouldn't want to blow your cover. I'll pick you up and we'll go out to dinner somewhere."

Okay, if this was a date, it was setting up to be the strangest date I'd ever been on. But *was* it a date? Or was it an interrogation? Shit!

"Okay, then," I said. "I'll be ready at seven."

"Great, it's a date." He stood.

Did he mean *date* date? Or did he mean business date? Did I want it to be a *date* date?

Of course, if it were, if the attraction was mutual, surely I could use that to my advantage, or rather to Mother's advantage.

"Looking forward to tomorrow night," he said.

I smiled. I'd be cool, but not coy. Smart, but not sassy smart. Confident. Poised. "I'm looking forward to it to, Deputy Allman. *Almond.* Deputy Almond."

Jesus Christ! I'm an idiot.

My face burned, and Almond grinned from ear to ear.

"Just call me Noel," he offered, setting a warm hand on my shoulder. "That's probably easiest."

Noel. That I could handle.

With a grin, he turned and walked away. I watched him — every rippling muscle in his wonderful physique.

Yep, that I could handle.

Chapter 5

MOTHER TRIED. SHE really did. And I knew it was for my sake as well as Mrs. Presley's that she kept the smile on her face. Chin up; shoulders back. That was Katt Dodd. I'd seen that smile when Dad was so sick all those years ago.

That wasn't the smile I wanted on my mother's face.

But when Mrs. P suggested we all go out for dinner, an invitation that under normal circumstances Mother would never decline, she put on her bravest face . . . and declined.

"Don't put yourself out cooking, Katt," Mrs. P had said. "Let's get supper out on the town. Dix's treat."

"Oh, Jane, please let me cook something special. I just love to cook. We'll go out tomorrow night."

"Okay, but how about we head out to bingo afterward, Katt? Dix would love to drive us."

"You know, Jane, I love bingo . . . but just not tonight."

As she nudged my mother with one fun-filled suggestion after another, I could see what she was trying to do. Could see how she was trying to cheer my mother up. She didn't really give a rat's ass about going out this evening. Yes, she loved bingo (and she'd brought along a six-pack of dabbers and three multi-colored-hair bingo trolls to prove it). And yes, she did remind me of my promise — a.k.a. bribe — to take her to bingo before we left Florida. But a night out wasn't foremost on her mind this evening. Mrs. P was simply trying to get Katt Dodd's mind away from all her troubles.

I admired these women, and got a lump in my throat just watching the kindness between the two of them. They both tried for the other. That easily, they'd become friends. And that thoroughly and that loyally.

But that was women for you.

Speaking of loyalty, Mona Roberts called Mother repeatedly. Not to play crib this time. She first asked if we all wanted to go for a walk later on. Mother declined. She called a second time and offered to cancel her golf lesson with Big Eddie, scheduled for the early evening, to come over and visit. Mother insisted she not cancel.

"Hit that orange ball right across the lake, Mona!" Mother told her.

Mona called a third time, and asked Mother to put her on speakerphone.

She asked, "How many Harriet Appletons does it take to change a light bulb?"

None of us knew.

"Can't be done. Even light bulbs run like hell when she says she wants to screw them."

Yes, it was lame. It was awful. But we laughed like hell.

Mother invited Mona over for supper then. Mona accepted.

The meal was great (Mom's cooking rivals the talents of a Cordon Bleu chef, whereas my cooking rivals Chef Boyardee). I couldn't help but notice, though, that Mother scrimped on the olive oil and the cut of steaks was not the finest that she usually bought. The wine, which she'd sent me out to fetch, was passable (hey, it had a cork; that had to count for something), and as the evening went on, the conversation was lighter. Kind of fun.

On my wine run, I'd called Dylan. I needed him to check up on a few things for me. He had the equipment to do it at the Goosebump Inn, of course. He had the time. And not surprisingly, he'd already made some local connections to cash in on.

Wrestling.

When I clicked on the remote the first channel I came to was wrestling. There was a guy bent over in a head-lock with his red-shorted butt to the camera. I don't care what Mother and Mrs. P thought, this just was not sexy! Faster than the speed of light, I hit the mute button. Unfortunately, my speed of light apparently wasn't quick enough for Mrs. Presley's sharp hearing.

"Was that wrestling, Dix?" she called from the bedroom.

She and mother had retired about a half hour earlier. And I had thought after the big meal, the bottles of wine and the fairly uneventful and restful evening, the two would be sound asleep by this time.

"I'd get up for wrestling you know, Dix."

I didn't want to lie to Mrs. P, but I needed some time alone to relax and think. Quickly — so I wouldn't technically be lying — I flipped the channel. "Wrestling is not on the television, Mrs. P."

"You sure?"

"Positive." Not on this TV right now.

Remote still in hand, ear cocked toward the bedroom, I waited for more questions. Nothing. Apparently, sans wrestling motivation, Mrs. Presley had resettled for the night.

And I settled a little easier back into the pull-out again.

What *was* on?

I flicked through the channels. Not that I was in much of a mood to concentrate. And not that I was much for TV at the best of times, unless there was a kick-ass CSI on (and they're all kick-ass). But tonight, I clicked right past all of them — Dallas, Vegas, and especially Miami.

Horatio and the gang would have a field day if Frankie the Froggie came into the morgue.

Parking it on CNN, I stretched on the sofa bed best I could (which surprisingly was pretty well). I wore my pajamas, which consisted of gray t-shirt and sleep shorts fresh from the dryer, but I wasn't cozy-cozy yet. I reached around, and undid my bra in the back, did a few contortions, then pulled it out through an arm hole. There. *Now* I was cozy-cozy.

Mother had set out two blankets for me, but being used to cooler climes, I was fine with just the thin sheet. I set the blankets on the decorative white rocker beside the bed. Definitely decorative. It cradled three teddy bears and the runners on the bottom hadn't so much as one crack in the paint from wear.

As Piers Morgan droned on in the background, I went over and over again in my mind the details of the day. When my thoughts started circling back on themselves like a snake eating its own tail, I gave up in disgust. The Case of the Family Jewels wasn't going to be solved tonight.

Okay, TV it was. I picked up the remote again and started flipping. Mindlessly.

Nope, I wasn't even thinking at all as I surfed up the numbers. Looking for nothing in particular as I clicked up higher and higher. Yep, just flicking away …

"Holy kamoly!"

I sat crossed-legged on the bed and leaned back against the head of it and watched the tangled trio — *okay, outie, innie, outie … yep that was a trio* — for a moment.

Now where did that remote go? Oh, yes, somehow I'd managed to toss it across the bed. I reached for it, of course. Eventually grabbed it, and yes my hand was edging in on those numbers.

Research!

My hand stilled.

Yes, definitely research. After all, I had to keep up the Dix Dodd erotica-writer persona. No doubt Tish would be at me again tomorrow looking for more details on my literary career. I'd be prepared. I'd be damned prepared. Why, if I had to watch this channel into the wee, wee hours of the morning, I would. All for the sake of getting off. I mean, all for the sake of getting my mother off and clearing her good name.

I turned up the volume just enough — just barely enough — now I *really* didn't want Mrs. P and Mother coming out here to catch me doing my research.

Yes, volume certainly added to the plot. Not that I'd have been lost without it. Oh, and I got to hear that really cool music you just couldn't find anywhere else.

There was a tall, handsome blond guy in the flick, moving to the *waw-waw-wawwww* music pretty well. That is, pretty well, for someone with such a massive distraction. I half waited for him to stand up and trip over it. And of course tall blond guy got me thinking about the good deputy and our 'date'. I still hadn't decided if technically it was a date. I wasn't so naive as to think Deputy Almond was only asking me out to get my take on things as he'd professed. And it was more than a straight he/she date kind of thing. I knew he was playing me, or trying to, rather. Hell, he'd played all the parts perfectly in the rec room earlier in the day. Best bud to Big Eddie Baskin. Charming young man to Tish and Beth Mary. Consoling gentleman to Harriet and Wiggie. (So why had he been so stern with my mother? He'd play me to get information, probably on my own mother. Deputy Almond was a looker, but those blue eyes and good ol' boy charm would only get him so far with me. I'd be playing him right back. I'd let him think I was being charmed while I found out everything he had to know.

Hee hee hee. I swear that giggle had come from the wine glass.

And since no one likes to laugh alone, I poured myself a second glass and snuggled down under the thin sheet, my head nestled down into the soft pillow Mom had provided.

And so there I found myself late that Florida night, cozy in my near-nothing, laying back in the darkened living room, enjoying a nice glass of Shiraz with only the glow of the television washing over me as I watched the happy — couple now — on TV.

I stretched out my legs and wiggled my toes. I played a fingertip around the edge of the wine glass. Slower and slower.

And I damn near threw the fucking glass across the room when I heard someone outside my mother's patio door.

Miraculously, I didn't scream. Fighting back the rush of adrenaline, I set the wine glass down on the small end table with barely a click. Staying out of the light from the television, I tiptoed my way to the patio doors.

The jewel thief? God, wouldn't that be convenient?

Or, hey, Frankie Morrell, maybe?

Whatever the case, someone wasn't using the front door here. Someone was breaking and entering my mother's apartment. My mind went immediately to our family's lucky diamond. The one Dad had given Mother all those years ago. If someone was coming in here with a mind to steal that from my mother, they'd be getting one hell of a big surprise.

I'd be their welcoming committee. Hell, I'd be their worst nightmare.

The doors were locked, of course. Both Mother and Mrs. P had checked them twice, including the patio's French door. But a locked door wasn't much of a deterrent to a determined thief. These condo locks were fairly high quality (I'd checked), but they weren't the high-security jobs with the floating collars that resisted picking and drilling. They wouldn't thwart someone who knew what he — or she — was doing.

I stood by the door and quickly looked around for something I could use as a weapon. Mother had deposited a few personal items on the nearby table. Her pierced earrings? Sure, poke him to death with the stems. Her hair brush? Sure I could brush him to death.

Fuck!

I hadn't brought my gun. Guns and border crossings just do not mix. But I was clever and resourceful, Dix Dodd, private eye.

Shit! Why are there no brass candle sticks lying around when you need them? Why no lead pipes? No wrench? (Clearly I'd been playing too much Clue.) Besides, it was likely a geriatric jewel thief. Old people had thin skulls, didn't they? And brittle bones. Wouldn't want to kill anyone by coshing them.

I heard the click as the cylinder turned and the lock gave. I heard the faint snick as the door opened.

Show time.

Fine, I'd use my hands to take down this intruder, and my feet, of course. (I'd long ago learned to never underestimate the power of a well-placed foot.) Oh shit, I'm a woman ... I'd use my brains.

I leaned forward just enough to catch the edge of the sheet from the pull-out and I pulled it in toward me.

I readied myself in attack mode — crouching down low, ready to spring. I was ready to kick some ass. Gently, if need be. But harder was good, too. The door opened enough so that the culprit could enter. *Oh, please God, let it be Harriet Appleton.*

The intruder poked a leaning head into my mother's apartment, and I jumped into action.

"Gotcha!"

It wasn't a shout, for I really didn't want to alarm Mother and Mrs. Presley until I had the criminal fully apprehended. Yes, showing off, but if there was going to be a fight here on my hands, it wasn't something I wanted either of those two ladies getting in the middle of.

I flung the sheet over the intruder, muffling an exclamation.

Oh, shit! Male! Definitely male. A shot of adrenaline fueling my muscles, I tackled him onto the sofa with a move that would have made an NFL defensive end proud.

"What the hell?"

Okay, that sounded familiar. And so was this physique that I was now straddling on the sofa bed.

"Dylan?" I asked in a harsh whisper, then pulled the sheet off.

"Jesus, Dix." He matched her stage whisper. "Are you trying to give me a freakin' heart attack?"

"Give *you* a heart attack? What did you think you were going to be greeted with when you broke in? A bouquet of flowers?"

I still held him pinned (yeah ... moving must have slipped my mind), but he managed to shrug against the white sheet. "I thought you'd be asleep, and I wanted to practice my technique."

"I appear to have taught you well, Grasshopper."

He grinned. "Apparently. But I'm disappointed in you, Sensei. This is the best weapon you could come up with. A *sheet*?"

"I thought you were Harriet Appleton, or maybe Wiggie Appleton, and I didn't want to kill them. Besides, it worked. You're caught."

"Yes, but what if I was a real intruder, not a willing captive?"

Oh, God. *Willing captive.* The way he said the words — oh, Christmas, it just *did* it for me. I felt a low hum start deep in my belly.

I jumped off him fast and sat on the edge of the bed. It wasn't the sex that made me jump away. It was the closeness. You know how it is. Once burned ... to a crisp like a goddamn marshmallow in the face of a flame-thrower.

"Well, if you were a real intruder, you might not be willing, but you'd still be captive."

Dylan drew himself up on his elbows. He wore a dark turtleneck and a dark tuque (perfect cat-burglar material) though of course with his dark hair, the hat was not really necessary. But he was fully prepared for any situation.

"So Dylan, is that a flashlight in your pocket, or were you just happy to see me?"

He smiled. Under the glow of the television it looked so damn — *Glow of the freakin' television! Ack!*

"What are you watching?" Dylan sat up. Or rather, struggled to sit up. Hard to do with a full-grown forty-year-old woman body slamming you back to the bed again.

"Hmph."

"I'm watching ... I'm watching ..." One arm on Dylan symbolically if not actually holding him down, and one hand frantically searching the pulled-apart bedding, I scrabbled for the remote. Mid *waw-waw-waw-wwwww*, I found it and clicked as quickly as I could. "This is what I was watching."

Oh God. *The Lawrence Welk Show*. How uncool was that! How positively geriatric.

"You *like* this show?"

"Duh. Why else would be I watching it?" Certainly not because I was truly watching porn and just about got caught by my hot, hot assistant.

"Cool." Dylan looked at the screen. "Man, that Sissy and Bobby sure can dance, huh? I wish I were that light on my feet. Hey, remember old Lawrence conducting? A-one-and-a-two-and ..."

I arched an eyebrow.

"My grandparents used to love this show," he explained. "They couldn't wait for Saturday nights to sit down after supper to watch it. Whenever they babysat me, I'd watch it with them. I had a real crush on Sissy. But I was just a kid."

I couldn't help but smile. The mental picture of a young (okay, younger) Dylan Foreman in his jammies with a crush on the dancing Sissy ... well, it was just too cute.

"Hey, remember that theme song? I had it memorized. I used to sing along with it every week."

I could literally feel the dilation of my pupils. And it had nothing to do with adjusting to the light. Dylan was the world's worst singer. He just didn't know it.

"Every week?" I asked.

"Well, every week until my grandmother started turning the television off about two minutes before the show was over. Weird."

"Huh," I said. "Go figure." I muted the television quickly.

Dylan spotted the wine. "Mind?" he asked.

I poured him a glass and refilled my own as I did. We tasted. We sipped. And then it was time to talk shop.

This wasn't just a social call. Dylan Foreman wasn't sneaking about on this fine Florida night to join me in a Lawrence Welk marathon.

"I retrieved the office voice mails," he reported.

"Anything special?"

We did have a few things on the go, but nothing that couldn't wait until we got back. And I'd notified current clients of our absence, so I didn't expect there to be much.

"Not much. But you won a week at a timeshare in the Dominican Republic. You just have to pay the taxes on the prize."

"Gee, what's the catch?"

Dylan chuckled. Even in the low lighting of the room, I knew his eyes were sparkling. And chances were mine were too. What was it about this guy?

"Seriously though, nothing urgent." He took a long swallow of wine that matched mine.

I topped up both our glasses. "So," I said. "Any luck checking on our newfound friends?"

The look on his face changed instantly. When Dylan Foreman went to work, it was all business. The guy was smart, and I loved that intense look he got when we were working on a case. After his apprenticeship was over, he was going to make one hell of a good private investigator.

"Where do you want me to start?" No notes, no hand-held gadget to retrieve the information. It was locked solid in his mind.

"Tish McQueen."

"You mean 'Tish the Dish'?"

Tish the Dish? I sat up straighter.

Apparently, Dylan had already gotten an eyeful of Miss

Above-the-Law-of-Gravity Tish McQueen.

"You've seen her?" I followed the question with a drink.

"Nah. That was her stripper name."

I almost *pffted* out my drink out onto my chin. Yes, just almost. This was wine, not coffee.

"Apparently, our Miss Dish had quite the career in her younger days. Worked from Florida to Toronto. New York to Vancouver."

"And all ports in between?"

"And she not only worked under Tish the Dish. But also Trixie O'Treats. Tish Tush. Oh, and my personal favorite — Tish the Fish."

I blinked.

"Mermaid theme," he elaborated.

"And when was this?"

"Early sixties. I found some posters on the Internet from her stripper days. I tell you, Dix, she was a headliner. Built like a …"

He didn't finish the thought. But my shoulders pressed back even farther as I did.

"Let me guess," I said, a wee bit snarkily. "She made a mint and put it all into an orphanage for impoverished children?"

Dylan waved a dismissive hand. "Nah, that's whores who have hearts of gold, not peelers."

"Fine line," I grumped. "So what did she do with her show-biz money?"

"Invested it. Property in Northern Alberta, just before things really started booming out there. I'm telling you, Tish McQueen is loaded. And from what I've read, she's one shrewd business woman."

"I wonder how she knows Mona. Mona doesn't look like the stripper type."

"Geez, I should hope not. She's 70 now," Dylan said. "Even if she had been a stripper once, she'd hardly look like one now."

"Huh. You haven't seen Tish yet," I muttered. Stomach in, chest out. If it sat up any straighter I'd be leaning backwards. *Oh, the hell with it.* I slouched back into my normal posture. "What did you find out about Mona?"

He got that pensive look — that sexy, thinking-man, pensive look that drove me wild.

Drove me wild? Where the hell did that come from? Suspiciously, I looked into my wine glass.

"Mona Roberts," he began. "Age 70. Widow of ten years. Homemaker.

Married thirty-two years to the late Theodore Roberts of Brunswick, Vermont. He was in insurance sales and did quite well. Left Mona a tidy sum."

"Did they have any kids?"

"Just one. A daughter. She's still in Brunswick. Married with a teen-age daughter."

"So nothing much of interest on Mona, then?"

Dylan twisted his lips. "Not quite. The tidy sum that Theodore Roberts left Mona? It's gone. And it went quickly — in the last two years."

Interesting. "Where's it going?"

Dylan took a sip of his wine. "Hospital bills. Her granddaughter's been in and out of the hospital a dozen times over the last couple years. Cancer treatments."

I felt a stab of sympathy for Mona. When she'd left this evening, Mother had packed her a plate of food for tomorrow. Mona had demurred, of course, but even I could tell it wasn't real. How hard up *was* Mona Roberts? Hard up enough to steal?

Jesus, I hoped not.

"Big Eddie Baskin? No, wait! Let me guess." I held up a hand before Dylan could answer. I was after all, Dix Dodd, people-reader, private eye extraordinaire. I'd impress Dylan with my great observational skills here. I scanned my memory banks on Big Eddie — good with the ladies, liked to be in charge, makes his way taking care of the things at the Wildoh …? "Got it! He ran a bordello."

"Ah, no, Dix."

"Close?"

"Not a bit. Big Eddie Baskin is retired from the US Army."

"No shit?"

"No shit. He was a machinist."

That of course would explain one of the little dangling charms hanging from the chain around his neck — amongst the ones of golf clubs, half a heart, and the obligatory horseshoe, had been one of a mini screwdriver and mini wrench.

"Clean record?" I asked.

"Choir boy," Dylan responded. "Never married. No kids. Likes to bet on the ponies, but nothing too serious."

Dylan proceeded to give me the 411 on the other people I'd asked him to check out.

Beth Mary MacKenzie, the pup of the crowd, was a mere fifty years old, though she looked a hell of a lot older. Of the group, she was the newest Wildoh resident. She'd taught school in Northern Alberta up until a year ago, when she'd retired and bought into the Wildoh.

"Fifty is young to retire," I murmured.

"Not if you win the lottery."

"Did she?"

"I couldn't find any records of a win online, but not all winners get the press. If it wasn't a giant one, who knows? Sometimes they just go for the ... um ... *media friendly* types for their promotions."

I hated that, but Dylan was right. Beth Mary was one ugly woman. Unless she won a shitload of money, it probably wouldn't have been newsworthy. A modest win — just enough for a comfortable future — could easily have gone under the radar.

"Or she might have inherited something. From my cursory search, I'm not seeing anything like that, but give me time. I'll dig deeper."

"Who's next?"

I listened with greatest interest when Dylan brought up Harriet and Wiggie. And with the biggest disappointment also.

"He was a patent lawyer in a small Orlando law firm, and she —"

"— sucked the blood out of the rest of the clients?" I offered.

"She was his secretary for many years."

"Kids?"

"Nope."

"Financial woes?"

"Not that I can find."

Crap.

Make that *crap, crap, crap!*

I'd been hoping for an 'aha' moment. For that one trigger to my intuition that would lead me along. Was I too close to this case? Too much at stake here?

"And what did you find out about Mom?"

He took a sip of his wine. "You didn't ask me to check out your mother."

"No, I didn't. So what did you find?"

While I'd been sitting on the sofa bed, Dylan had maneuvered onto his side — leaning up on one elbow. Suddenly, he had eyes only for the wine in his glass. "Okay, so I did make some inquiries."

"And?"

"She's been doing quite well financially lately. Very well, in fact.

In the last two months, over thirty thousand dollars has gone into her bank account."

Well, that sucked. Mother received a small pension from a plan Dad and she had invested in many years ago. There was insurance money and, of course, royalties from songs still trickled in. I racked my brain trying to think of any way in hell that thirty big ones could suddenly start popping into her account.

And my brain racked back... I didn't like any of the possible answers.

By the look on Dylan's face, I knew there had to be more. "What else?

"Your mother and Frankie Morrell had been fighting the night he disappeared. Loudly. Threats were uttered, on both their parts."

I shook my head. Not good. I *knew* that my mother was not capable of committing a crime. Well, a serious crime. Katt Dodd was a good person. Honest as the day is long. The salt of the earth. She was my *mother*, for Pete's sake! She was not a criminal. Not a thief and certainly not a murderer. No matter where the evidence pointed. But I was far from naive. In the eyes of others, the evidence, circumstantial as it was, did not bode well for Katt Dodd.

"Just want to get all the information on the table," Dylan said. "Best way to protect your mom."

He was right of course. "You know she's innocent, right?"

"Absolutely," he answered.

And bless him, I believed him.

Silence.

I'd pretty much been looking at him while we'd been talking. But now I caught myself staring into my wine. Staring into my thoughts. And somehow, now, drifting into the feeling of being so very close to Dylan Foreman.

When I looked at him again, he was looking back at me. *Seeing* me.

He set his glass on the end table, then reached for mine. Heart pounding, I surrendered it. He placed it beside his, then turned and hauled me down beside him on the bed. Gently. He never would have pulled me hard enough to lie down beside him if I hadn't met him halfway. But I went willingly. And there we were, face to face, body to body.

Come morning, I would probably blame it on the sagging middle of my mother's pull-out couch, but right now I knew it was something entirely different. It was two magnetically charged bodies moving toward each other, following the immutable laws of physics. And sweet gentle Jesus, it felt good! I think I missed this the most about being celibate, the solidity of a male body beside me, the warmth of his breath on my skin, the feel of his heart thudding as hard as mine was.

Then he slipped his hand under the hem of my t-shirt to find a breast.

Correction — *this* was what I missed the most. I reached for him, my fingers bunching the denim at his lean hip, pulling him closer with my hand and with the leg I'd looped over his.

"Dix …"

He found my mouth with his. And unlike that first time all those weeks ago when we'd shared that one kiss, there was nothing tentative about the way this one started. He kissed me like he was sure of his welcome. Maybe that had something to do with the way I was moving against him like I wanted to crawl inside him. Or maybe because of the way I was kissing him right back, with lips and tongue and teeth.

When he lifted his head, I wanted to pull him back down to me, to taste again the wine's soft, ripe tannins on his tongue. Then I felt the air on my skin as he pushed my t-shirt up and decided I liked his plan better. He applied that talented mouth to my breast, and a soft gasp escaped me.

Okay, *this* was what I missed most.

He pressed me down onto my back … and right onto the freakin' remote.

The volume blasted just at the very same time the channel changed to last channel selected. *WAW-WAW-WAWWWWWWWWW.*

"What the —" Mrs. P's distinctive voice cut into the living room.

The light snapped on in my mother's room, as evidenced by the clear bar of light showing under the bedroom door. Mother called out, "Everything all right, Dix?"

"Everything's f-f-fine, Mother."

I pulled my shirt back down and Dylan jumped off the bed. With one hand he adjusted himself in his pants and with the other he frantically began searching for the remote (yes, it was somewhere under my butt).

"Omigod, what a huge dong!" the appreciative red-headed female in the movie cried out.

"What's that, Dix? Did someone say 'dong'?"

"No, Mrs. P." — *where was that fucking remote?* — "It's an old movie. King Kong, I think. Yeah, that's it … a huge King Dong!" *Shittttttt.* "I mean King Kong!"

Through a frantic flap of the sheets, I flipped the remote onto the floor. Dylan grabbed it and clicked the TV off again.

The room was in darkness except for the light from beneath mother's bedroom door. I could hear Dylan's breathing. Oh, I liked his breathing. Then I could hear his giggling. It was pretty much matching my own.

We waited a few minutes, without of course admitting we were waiting a few minutes, but the light stayed on in mother's room. God, I felt like a teenager all over again. Horny as hell. Young and smitten. Falling head over —

That did it for me. I pulled myself back in. Dix Dodd didn't do close. Not anymore.

Dylan sighed, as though he sensed the change in me.

"I'd better get going." He walked to the patio doors. "Gotta hike it back to the Goosebump Inn, and I've got an early day tomorrow."

I followed him to the door, at his insistence. He wanted to be sure that I locked it after him. I wrapped a sheet around me, and walked with him outside onto mother's little patio and wiggled my bare toes on the patio stones.

"Some dark out here, Dylan," I offered. "Better use your flashlight."

He grinned, oh so handsomely under the light of the Florida moon. "I didn't bring a flashlight, Dix."

He walked away after I locked the door.

Probably a good thing, I reminded myself.

Yeah?

… Yeah.

Chapter 6

No, I DID not wake up with a hangover. Not a bit of it. Though I did have a slight headache. And I couldn't really stomach the big breakfast Mrs. Presley offered to fry (yes *fry*) up. I was a tad on the dry side, but well, Florida air must be dryer than Southern Ontario air. And fine, I admit, I really could have used an extra hour or so of sleep. And a Tylenol.

But hungover?

Not a chance.

The first thought/image that crashed into my mind on awakening was that of banging Dylan Foreman. All. Night. Long. Every way imaginable. (And I have a very good imagination.) Feeling those hands that had explored my breasts exploring even further. Feeling that lovely erection of his sprung from those snug jeans.

No, I had not banged Dylan Foreman. Hands had not explored brave new worlds, and Dylan's spring had remained (sigh) unsprung. But I couldn't have stopped those thoughts with a . . . thought stopper thingie.

I hate metaphors.

Suffice to say, I had every confidence that if Tish, Beth Mary or any of the gang down at the Wildoh rec room wanted to discuss my erotica-writing career today, I could match them fantasy for fantasy. Inch for inch. Lusty comment for lusty comment. Tit for . . .

Yet truthfully, had we done it, had we gone there, I knew deep down inside that I would have awoken with more than a non-existent (I'll never admit to it!) hangover. There would have been regrets. Big regrets, and there would be no going back. I knew this. So it was best that we stopped when we did.

Right.

Getting close to Dylan — hell, to any man — would only lead to heartache. One colossal heartbreak in one lifetime was enough to last

... well, a lifetime.

For the record, I am completely over Myles Gauthier. Yep. Over and done with. That time I'd caught him at the Underhill Motel in the arms of the proverbial other woman had done it for me. The first time hadn't, but that second time ...

I know. Pitiful, isn't it? But I'd let the worm off the hook the first time. I'd even accepted some of the blame. Accepted his tearful apology and his pledge that it would never happen again. Then it happened again. I'd sworn off Myles Gauthier that night. Sworn off all men for that matter. And it was working out just fine.

But Dylan Foreman is nothing like Myles Gauthier.

Damn inner voice. And with that, the thoughts of Dylan began creeping back in ... the warm ones. And it took every bit of willpower I could muster to shove them back out. This was one matter on which intuition would be taking a back seat to logic.

Besides, I had other things to worry about. This was going to be a hell of a day. I'd promised to take Mrs. P out sightseeing. I know, I know, I was here to solve a case — a case of great personal importance — but I had my cover to consider. I had to make sure I looked suitably touristy to the occupants of the Wildoh, and I wasn't going to achieve that hanging around the Wildoh all day, every day. Also, my biggest clue-seeking expedition was dinner with Deputy Almond this evening. I could afford to take some time with Mrs. P.

Speaking of the Deputy, I had every confidence he was planning to play me. I was, after all, his prime suspect's daughter. But Deputy Noel Almond had no idea who he was dealing with. I squared my shoulders. I looked in the mirror, narrowed my eyes and gave my best evil laugh/ snicker/snort.

And wiped the spit off my chin.

Mrs. Presley had made a list of the places she wanted to go. I had her list-topper figured for bingo (they have bingo around the clock down here!), but it wasn't. At least not today. Today, the one item on her list was 'Mall'.

"First, thing I need," said Mrs. P, "is a new crossword book."

Oh, joy.

"I want to get some souvenirs for the boys. Cal wants a Panther's hockey sweater and Craig wants a Buccaneers jersey. Oh, and I've got to pick up some underwear for Craig. He's got holes all through his. Damn, I don't know why that boy's so hard on underwear. And Cal's getting low on sport socks. I better pick him up a few pairs. I have to get him the one-hundred-percent cotton ones. His feet sweat so bad." She shook her head. "I don't know what those boys would do without me."

Shudder to think.

Cal and Craig — the 'boys' — were damn near 30 and she still mama'd them. They still loved it.

As Mrs. P took a couple hundred bucks in bills and eight rolls of American quarters from her purse and deposited them in her fanny pack (God help the fool who tried to wrestle it from her), I told her we absolutely had to be back in time for the late-morning gathering at the recreation room.

"Relax, Dix," Mrs. P said as she folded up two one-hundred-dollar bills and put one in each side of her bra. "Have I ever let you down?"

Okay, she had me there. She'd not. And she wouldn't start now. She'd have me back at the Wildoh on time.

And with suspicions running high, it was just where I needed to be. Everyone would have to show up to avoid being suspected. Avoid being talked about and collectively declared guilty by dis-association in this instance. And of course, the gossip itself would keep people coming back.

Mother would be going, too, but not for the gossip. She'd go to the Wildoh rec center to keep suspicions about her from growing even further.

Granted, she hadn't ventured out last night, and she didn't go on her early morning walk today (had not donned her walking suit and shoes at all and was in fact still wearing her housecoat). But I knew Katt Dodd. She'd put on her Pinch-Me Pink lipstick, some dangling earrings and hold her head high as she walked into that rec room, even if it killed her. But it didn't take bucketloads of intuition to know it wouldn't be easy for her. Katt Dodd was one tough cookie. She'd handle what she had to. But still ...

I swallowed down the lump in my throat.

Never had a case been so important to me.

Though the last one had been close, when it was my own ass in the sling.

"Gonna let Mona kick your ass at crib again?" Mrs. P teased when I mentioned our need to be back in time. "How much you going to lose to her today? Eight bucks? Ten?"

Mona was a gambler, that's for sure. Small dollar amounts, but I saw the desperation in her when she played. That was one woman who absolutely craved a win like some people craved a smoke.

"We'll see, Mrs. P."

"Oh, and don't forget that Lance fellow. Eh, Katt?" She elbowed my mother, trying to draw her into the teasing. "Is he coming around today?"

"Let's see," Mother said. "Yes, Big Eddie instructed golf yesterday, so Lance will be around to dive for the balls today."

"There you go then, Dix! Gonna bring your camera?"

I rolled my eyes. Shook my head. Tsk-tsked. Discreetly pocketed my digital camera.

Okay, yes, I knew this was going to be a weird day … I just didn't know how weird.

Mrs. P and I were on our way out the front door, waving goodbye and promising to pick up a few things at the store. It was then that I (sharp PI that I am) noticed something else about my mother this morning.

She was screaming.

Her eyes were saucered wide, and her hand shook as she pointed to the floor by the patio door. The exact same door via which Dylan Foreman had entered the condo last night and made his way into my bed.

"Oh my God! He's been here! Right here in this very room last night!"

Crap! Busted!

Weirdly, this felt like the time in high school when I'd been caught sneaking Cody McNally into the house late one night. (We were just going to watch a movie together, I swear.) Not that I thought I was in for the same lecture now as I'd gotten then. But still … Dylan Foreman's presence at all was something I necessarily had to keep a secret from Mother.

And the other stuff … *that* I definitely wanted to keep under wraps.

"I … I can explain, Mother," I sputtered.

Mother looked at me like I'd lost my last marble. "Why would you explain anything?"

"Guilty conscience, Dix?" Mrs. Presley's grin spread across her entire face. "Something we don't know you'd like to tell us about? Something about last night?" Mrs. Presley gave an exaggerated wink.

Damn, she knew. Her catlike smile confirmed it.

Thankfully, while I was silently instructing Mrs. Presley (okay, pleading with hands clasped together in prayer and mouthing *no, no, no*) not to tell Mom about my visitor, Mom was crouched down staring at the floor. I joined her.

There was a puddle of water on the hardwood floor. A very small puddle. Barely noticeable, in fact. Mother picked something up as I looked at the lock on the patio door.

Goddamn it! I *knew* that door had been locked when I'd gone to bed! But now it was open. And no one had been out yet this morning. The lock itself was unscratched. Very few lock pickers can actually do the job without there being at least one or two tell-tale nicks and scratches (present company excepted, and Dylan, too, it seemed). The unannounced company of last night had either had his or her own key, or been damn good at what they were doing. This was no hack job.

"Did Frankie have a key, Mom?" I asked.

"Of course! How else would he have gotten in?"

Was she finally ready to admit Frankie could be the culprit? Was she finally admitting that the man remained in human form after all? Was she —

"Though it's beyond me how his little green arms could reach all the way up to unlock the door," she said.

Crap.

I crouched and touched the water on the floor. As I suspected, it was cold. I looked at it on my fingertips as I rubbed them together. Nothing out of the ordinary. I smelled the water — odorless.

Okay, in case you're wondering, no way in hell was I going to taste it.

It had not rained last night. Florida weather is unpredictable at best, but a quick check of the weather station this morning confirmed what the tanned, blond, bubbly weatherman had promised last night. No rain in sight.

So where did the water come from?

I looked up at the ceiling. No drips.

Open door, water on floor — there really was only one answer.

Someone else had broken into my mother's home while I'd slept soundly through it. That unsettled me. Big time. They'd have seen me sleeping. They might have *watched* me, and I had not stirred. They might have stood right over me ...

"Mother!" I gulped. "Go check the lucky diamond."

"But Frankie would never —"

"Just humor me, okay?"

She tsk-tsked, but went to the wall safe. Discreetly, with an 'I'd better go pee again', Mrs. Presley headed to the bathroom rather than be there when Mother opened the safe.

Mother laid the picture of me and Peaches Marie flat on the table. I watched over her shoulder as she worked the clicking dial. Not that I was trying to see the combination. I knew it, of course; Peaches and I both did — 2 left, 18 right, 4 left. But what red-blooded offspring wouldn't be at least a bit curious to see what their parent kept in their wall safe. It was like snooping through the bottom dresser drawer when your parents are out. Finding a lost love letter in someone's old coat pocket — you had to read it, it was practically the law, wasn't it?

But it's not like Mother was trying to hide the safe's contents!

My heart beat hard and fast as the safe door swung open. I looked and ...

The ring box was there. Safe in the safe. And the small box was solitary in its occupation of that 12-inch square box.

"See," Mother said. She waved a hand to the opened safe for emphasis. "It's right here."

"Open the box," I urged.

This time there was no protesting tsk-tsk. She snapped open the box with a flick of the wrist. And before she opened her mouth to say the ring was there, I knew that it was. I could tell by the look on her face as she gazed lovingly at the gift that Peter Dodd, her husband/my father, had given her.

"You know, your Dad was so proud on the day he gave me this diamond. I guess I'm so used to having it there. Safely there. It's like a part of Peter's still with me, you know. I always felt ... that nothing bad would truly happen to our little family as long as we had that diamond." She gave half a mocking laugh. "I just don't know what I'd have done if I'd opened that safe and that diamond had been missing."

Nor did I. I sighed my relief.

"I knew it would be here," Mother said. "Frankie would never take my lucky diamond. He's crazy about me and he knows how much it means to me. Besides, Frankie Morrell knows damn well better than to come in here without wiping his feet, I mean his flippers ... I guess."

"Mother," I said. "This insisting that you turned Frankie into a frog really isn't helping."

"Then how do you explain *this*?" She held her palm flat, and in the center of it lay a little heart-shaped piece of green. Not quite grass, not quite a leaf ... It was more like —

"It's a piece of lily pad," Mother asserted. "And it's a gift from Frankie."

Okay, I'd heard of cats bringing dead vermin 'gifts' to their owners as a show of affection. When we were kids, Peaches Marie and I had a great big tabby that left field mice at the foot of our beds. Great fun to tiptoe to the bathroom in the dark at our house. My grandmother supposedly tamed a great big bobcat (she called him Bently) when she was a girl in Northern New Brunswick, and he used to bring her bunnies.

But a lily pad gift? As a show of affection from Frankie the frog? That would be assuming a lot, most particularly that Frankie really had become a frog.

This was just getting too weird.

"Let me see it," I said.

She held her palm out, but didn't hand over the little piece of greenery. It was kind of heart shaped. It could very well have been a lily pad. But one thing for sure — it was a clue.

"Hang on to that, Mother," I said. "Put it ... put it in the fridge to keep it fresh."

She looked at me strangely, a look to which by this time I was immune.

The toilet flushed and a few seconds later, Mrs. Presley emerged from the bathroom.

"I don't know, Katt," Mrs. Presley was said as she tucked her flowered shirt into her Capri pants. "You'd think Frankie would be showing up with something a little more substantial. Like an apology for being an ass. An apology, flowers and dinner for two."

Oh, God, dinner for two from the swamp.

Mother said, "Frankie's not cheap. He is one for flowers and candlelit dinners, Jane. Oh, and did you see that watch he got me? It's beautiful." She pushed up her sleeves and touched her left wrist first before then touching her right. "I must have set it down somewhere. I love that watch," she said worriedly. "I certainly hope I didn't lose it."

"That would be a shame, Katt," Mrs. Presley said. "It's a beautiful watch. I'll help you look for it."

"No!"

My head shot up as my mother raised her voice. It wasn't an angry raising of voice so much as a panicked one.

"Sorry, Jane," she said. "Didn't mean to shout. I just ... I just don't want your visit to Florida to be all about my troubles and woes and looking for misplaced watches." She rubbed her wrist again, as if willing the watch back on her arm. "You and Dix go out and get those things you wanted for the boys. See some sights. Play tourists. That watch will turn up somewhere."

"If you're sure, Katt ..."

"Mother, why don't you come with us?" I really did want her to come along now. If she were traveling along the malls with Mrs. P, I could check in with Dylan and see if he had any more information, maybe even check in again with the Deputy. If I could drop these two at the mall and do a little checking at the local pawn shops, it would save me from having to go back later. But moreover, I was worried about my mother. She looked tired to me. Worn and worried. God, for the first time in ... ever ... Katt Dodd looked old to me.

"Yes! Come with us, Katt. You know how stuffy and boring Dix can be. I'd love some real company."

It wasn't to be.

"Dix," Mrs. Presley said when we were out the door, "you know we don't have to go. I mean, your mom's looking pretty miserable back there."

I sighed. "She'll want the time alone now, Mrs. P. She'll sit for a bit, and think things through, and then, if I know my mother, she'll be up doing the dishes and putting on her dancing shoes."

"And looking for that watch," Mrs. Presley added.

"Yeah."

I was taking Mom's BMW, of course. I'd opened the passenger door for Mrs. Presley, who'd adjusted the seat and belted herself in. I walked around the car and was just about to open my own door when I heard a, "Hey there, Dixie!"

"It's not Dixie ... just Dix."

Big Eddie Baskin grinned from ear to ear. "Oh sorry, Dix. Me and my old brain ... not what they used to be. I'm terrible with names." The multiple charms/chains on his neck jingled as he raised an arm to point to his head (as if I needed a visual on where his brain was located). He was standing by the garden, making a half-assed attempt at horticulture (half-assed being there was a clump of lime at his feet and an overturned lily looking for attention.)

Mrs. P rolled her window down and called, "Hey, Eddie."

"Well, hello, Jane. You're looking lovely this morning."

"As always," she answered.

Big Eddie smiled back at me. "Just wanted to let you know that with all the troubles we've had, we've hired an extra security person. I'm telling all the folks I see out and about this morning. I'll introduce him to everyone officially at the rec room later this morning, but he's right here. Just give me a minute and I'll introduce him.

I fidgeted with my keys. "We're kind of in a hurry this morning."

"Oh, it'll just take a second." He turned to face one of the other Wildoh buildings (Complex A, which from the outside was identical in every way to Mother's Complex B). I looked at my watch and reminded myself I was posing as an erotica writer. Not a PI with a 'tude against people who said 'this will just take a second' when clearly I was in a hurry. Grrrrrrrrr.

"Hey," Big Eddie called. "Hey ... hey, New Guy."

He turned back to me and pointed to his brain again.

"Yeah, I get it. You forget names."

I waited. I stomped my right foot a few times. I — I said "Holy shit!" as Dylan Foreman came jogging around the corner. So this was what he'd meant when he'd said he had an early day tomorrow. But ... holy shit. I mean, I knew Dylan was smooth, but to land a job so fast?

And just wait until the ladies at the Wildoh got a load of him. Six-foot-four and hot as hell. And those jeans ...

Whoops. Guess those early morning fantasies hadn't departed so very far after all.

But nor had the early-morning ... regret.

Dylan beamed a smile when he looked at me, with a little bit of something extra behind it. Those sexy brown eyes were sparkling. And when he shook my hand he squeezed it with suggestion. I pulled away.

Nothing that anyone but the two of us would catch. And of course Mrs. P who had leaned over to look through the driver's side window (she was laughing in there, I know damn well she was).

"The name's Dylan," he introduced himself.

"Got a last name, Dylan?" I asked. I had to play the part. Did not want Big Eddie thinking we knew each other.

"Sure do," said Dylan. He waited. I waited. Big Eddie ... kind of waited too.

"Why don't you tell her what it is," suggested Big Eddie.

"What what is?"

Eddie threw his hands up. "Your last name!"

"Oh, that! It's Hardy. Dylan Hardy. Heavy on the "har". Get it? Har, as in laughing." He put his hands on his flat belly and mimed a head-tossed back, har har har of a laugh.

Oh God, that was *awful*.

I smiled. He'd not used that cover name before. Chances were that by now he even had a fake Florida ID with it. "Well, nice to meet you, Dylan Hardy."

He flashed me one last grin before he looked to Big Eddie again. "Want me to patrol that C place again, Big Eddie?"

"Sure, sure kid," he said. "You go right to it. Oh, and you know, why don't you vacuum around while you're there? Polish the mirrors and shine up all the buttons on the elevator."

"Do security guards do that, Big Eddie?" Dylan asked.

"Oh, yeah, all the time."

With a salute to Eddie and a golly-gee kind of wave to me, Dylan jogged off.

"Heavy on the 'Har'," Eddie echoed watching Dylan head off to Complex C. "Thick as a brick."

But I had to smile as I watched him go. He truly was a genius.

Chapter 7

I AM *NOT* stuffy and boring, contrary to what Mrs. P might claim to my all-too-agreeable mother. I'm a PI, for God's sake. Posing as an *erotica writer*, no less. How is that boring?

Okay, maybe it didn't help my image that the only two things I bought at the mega-mega mall were a turtleneck sweater and some granny panties. But I look great in turtleneck sweaters. And honestly, what woman doesn't really love her granny panties?

Speaking of the mall, I'm here to tell you that no one on the planet can outshop Mrs. Jane Presley. Not outshop as in who can spend the most money the fastest, but as in bargain hunting. Mrs. P could find steals like nobody's business. And she was quick about it, which was good. Both of us wanted to get back to Mother as soon as we could. But not *too* soon. I really think Katt Dodd needed some time alone for a damn good cry. Get it out of her system, and step up to the plate again.

No, Mrs. P was not the dallying type. More like a general with a battle plan. She got in, she got out, and she invariably got what she came for at bargain-basement prices. Which was great with me. My traipsing through the granny-panty aisle notwithstanding, I'm not the shopping type. Though Mrs. Presley did dither once. She spent more than a few minutes pondering a completely tacky Florida Gators bobblehead collection. She kept tapping their little plastic-helmeted gator skulls and setting them ... well, bobbling.

She didn't buy them (thank God!). But she did get great buys on the perfect jerseys for the boys, which had her smiling from ear to ear. And for a moment, Mrs. Jane Presley really did look like a sweet little old lady to me, standing in line to pay for the shirts for her boys. Family. Strange, the warm feeling that gave me.

Which lasted all of two minutes. Right up until Mrs. P led me to the men's underwear section.

The underwear she held up to her waist went around her twice. She nodded her head knowingly. "These'll fit Craig all right. He's lost a little weight. Probably lost more since I've been gone." Apparently Craig was a boxers man (which raised every man a notch in my humble opinion). Mrs. Presley stretched out the waist of the underwear; she pulled at the crotch. She examined the stitching at the hem and she rolled the fabric between her fingers. Okay, this was just a tad much. Truthfully, I was growing a little impatient as she started humming and hawing through the multi-colored packages.

"Well, this is the style and size. But which do you think Craig would like, Dix?" she finally asked. "Think he'd like the white, green or red?"

Well, everyone knows white underwear is the dumbest invention known to humankind. And green always seems well … just too damn grassy. Craig wasn't the Tarzan type. "I think red would be best, Mrs. P," I answered, hoping like hell we'd be moving along now.

"Red it is, then!" She tossed six pair of red men's boxers into her shopping cart. "I'll tell Craig you thought the red underwear would suit him best."

Lovely. Gee, thanks. And thanks, too, for saying it so loudly.

I couldn't see the smart-assed smile on her face as she walked ahead of me pushing that cart (past all the inquisitive underwear-buying gentlemen who were staring at me now), but damn, I knew it was there.

It wasn't too far to the sock aisle. Mrs. Presley pulled onto her hands a few pairs of the display socks (they went up to her armpits). Three pairs later she found the ones she wanted for Cal.

"Cotton, Mrs. P?"

"Cotton, Dix."

With a satisfied nod to the cashier, she pulled the money out of her fanny pack and paid. Then she shoved the parcels at me to carry.

"All set?" I asked.

"Just a quick stop at the magazine store for my crossword books. Were you hoping I'd forget?"

"Of course I wasn't."

Of course I was. Crossword books … yeah right! My three-letter word for derrière.

I had every confidence Mrs. P was buying more circle-a-word books under the ruse of crosswords to have some more fun with Dylan and me on the way home (yeah, like I'd be talking dirty on a fully-packed jumbo jet).

All in all, it was a good morning out. And then we were set for the good morning in. We were back in plenty of time for the mid-morning gathering in the Wildoh Recreation Room.

So was everybody else.

There was still a worried look on my mother's face, but I was glad to see that at least it was behind the Pinch-Me Pink lipstick.

Mother was dressed in a soft brown, long-sleeved caftan blouse, crisp white Capri pants (at least one Dodd woman can iron) and open-toed sandals. She'd painted her toenails to match her fingernails — a pretty pink that perfectly matched her lipstick. Mother wore antiqued gold half-moon earrings, and a matching necklace. Actually it was the set I'd sent to her last Christmas, the one Dylan had helped me pick out. But Mother's wrists were still watchless. And I knew she was conscious of the fact as she kept her arms straight down at the sides, thus the sleeves falling down over her wrists at all times.

But leave it to Katt Dodd to look like a million bucks as she stared down the suspicious gang that would be gathered in the Wildoh Recreation Room. Leave it to her to get the crying over and done with, then throw back the shoulders, and go face them all. She wouldn't be wilting in the corner. No way in hell.

But that was a woman for you.

No matter who was saying what — loudly or in whispers — Katt Dodd would face them all.

And she damn well did.

The hush was absolutely complete when we — Mother, Mrs. P, and I — swung open the doors to the rec room. The silence was short-lived, of course, but damned obvious. As were the quick turn-away snubs and the curt smiles and nods delivered by others. I read people — I read people very well — and these few seconds after entry were more than a little telling of what was on the minds of the Wildoh residents.

Beth Mary gave half a wave to Mother without a full half glance. Yes, she was heading toward the kitchen and moving at a pretty good clip when we came in, but still, there was no warmth whatsoever in that greeting, only caution.

Tish did a little snort-huffy thing and bobbed a hand to her perfect hair. "Hello, Katt," she said, every fucking syllable breaking down and standing out on its own. "Any sign of Frankie Morrell yet?"

Bitch.

"Afraid not, Tish," Mother answered. "But if you're back out trolling the swamp later, let me know if you see him, okay?"

Harriet Appleton apparently had another great big stick up her butt this morning and didn't bother to pivot on it to so much as look in Mother's direction. And Wiggie was looking, well ... Wiggie-ish ... as he slouched in his tracksuit beside her. He glanced up at us, and gave the barest of smiles. All in all, there were more than a few cold shoulders turning toward my mother.

And a couple very warm ones.

"Hey, over here!" called Mona with a great big wave and smile from her crib-playing corner, and we headed in that direction. From the look of woe on Roger's face, he was already set back a bit. Roger, ever the gentleman, stood when we approached the table. His smile to Jane was genuine, but to me and Mother, less so. Not that it changed from one of us to the next, but that it *didn't* as it moved along the row. It was just that plastic ... just that forced. Mother took a seat beside Mona. Mrs. Presley sat opposite her and I sat between them, again so that my back was to the wall.

"That's it for me, Mona," Roger said.

"Are you sure, Roger? I'm up for another game."

I didn't like the desperation in Mona's voice. The flash of it in her eyes.

"Quite sure," Roger answered. "I'm down twenty on the week. Besides, I want to get my hands on Beth Mary's buns before everyone else does."

Ever the gentleman? What kind of place was this? Retirement home for geriatric pervs?

"Close your mouth, Dix," Mother said. "He means her sticky buns."

I blinked. "And that makes it better?"

"The sticky buns that you *bake*, Dix," Mother said dryly. "You know ... that thing people sometimes do with their ovens?"

"Geez, Mother!" I rolled my eyes appropriately. "I figured that."

I hadn't figured that. Sticky buns?

"Beth Mary makes them a couple times a week," Mother said. "She cooks them in the oven down here so we can enjoy them hot. And they are just to die for."

Huh. I couldn't picture denturally-challenged Beth Mary eating sticky buns. (Then I *could* picture it and I shuddered.) But from the group gathered around her in the kitchen now as she was taking two pans out of the oven, and the group just outside the door waiting with napkins in hand, she must be pretty good at making them. There were a few abstainers, notably Tish — wearing stilettos and a pair of pants so tight they were biting back — standing in the corner talking to Big Eddie. No wonder she wouldn't wait in line for a bun. One bite of sticky bun and the seams would rip. But food was probably the last thing on her mind. Currently, she was finger-walking (somehow I always hurt the guy whenever I tried this) her way along Big Eddie's shirt — right from his custom-made state of Florida belt buckle to the start of his he-vage (we're talking maybe a 3-inch trip here). Eddie was so giddy he full-body giggled. I could hear the charms around his neck rattling clear across the room. Like a life-sized bobblehead.

Mona got up. She'd seen what was going on. Hell, everyone had. And she'd been a damn sight more patient with things than I would have been. "Well, guess crib's over for a while. Want me to grab a sweet for you ladies?"

"Grab one for all three of us," Mother instructed.

"Oh not for me thanks," I began. "I'm —"

I'm ... shutting up now thanks to that good kick in the shin!

"Sorry," Mother continued. "Yes, Dix, Jane and I would each love one. Could you grab napkins too while you're up? We'll take ours to go."

"Sure I will ..." Mona walked away, holding her hand to her pocket as she went. She looked to Tish and Eddie flirting in the corner but walked right on by.

I looked at Mother questioningly as I bent down to rub my shin. "What was that all about?"

Mother leaned over to me and spoke just low enough for Mrs. P and I both to hear. "Mona's having a hard time these days. Financially, that is. I always ask her to get me a bun ... or whatever else someone might be having, and then conveniently forget to take it with me. She takes it with her, calls later, and I tell her not to bother bringing it over. It's not much, but it's a little something for her."

"That seems like a lot of ... well, running around to give Mona an extra sticky bun."

Mother shrugged.

"Why doesn't she just grab a couple for herself. I'm sure nobody would mind."

"You don't know Mona Roberts. She wouldn't ask for a handout if it killed her. She's generous … to a fault, perhaps. When she could give, she always did. But these days … well, let's just say it's easier for Mona to take a leftover sticky bun or two than it is for her to ask for a second one in front of everyone."

"How do you know that her finances are so bad?" Mrs. P asked. "Did she tell you?"

Excellent question. One that had been on the tip of my tongue. Well, it would have been. Eventually. When I'd thought of it.

"God, no. She'd never say anything. But I suspected it, and Big Eddie confirmed it."

Mother saw me frown. "I know what you're thinking, Dix. He shouldn't have broken her confidence." She sighed. "Tell you the truth, I'm not so sure Eddie didn't figure it out for himself rather than Mona telling him. He's a pretty smart guy. And I'm Mona's best friend. He discussed this with me because he's worried about her, too. And because he was worried about me."

I gave her the old raised-eyebrow look.

"He wanted to make sure I was all right." She shrugged. "Eddie helps a lot of the widows out with things like that, Dix. He knows a lot about business and investments. Like it or not, years ago women just didn't do any of that sort of thing. Husbands did. They drove the car and mowed the lawn and looked after everything else. Eddie just likes to make sure everyone's looked after … that's all."

"What about Tish? She's staying with Mona, right?"

"She's staying with her, but she's not helping her one damn bit. In fact, if anything, every day Tish McQueen is there, it gets a little harder on Mona. In every way. Let's just say there's only so much to go around. And Tish wants a bit of everyone's share."

I looked over to Big Eddie and Tish still talking in the corner. Big Eddie reached into his pocket and pulled out a golf ball wrapped in a napkin. Well, technically it wasn't *wrapped* in a napkin, so much as Big Eddie was shaking a sticky napkin off his fingers as he pulled the golf ball out. Apparently, the decider himself got first dibs on the sticky buns. That's why his fingers were sticky.

Using his other hand, Big Eddie re-deposited the napkin in his polyester pants pocket. He was holding the ball up for Tish in one hand and with an animated slice to the other, showing her just how far it could be shot. Tish reached for the ball, but with a wink and a mile-wide smile, Big Eddie pocketed it again. And no, Tish's reach didn't follow into Big

Eddie's pocket, but the look she gave him seemed to say someday it might. Then she turned and sashayed away toward the kitchen herself.

"Wonder what's so special about those balls ..." Mrs. P murmured.

A dozen smart-assed remarks leapt to mind, but I resisted giving voice to any of them.

My mother turned to me with one eyebrow delicately arched. Clearly she'd expected me to return that perfect lob.

I shrugged. "Too easy."

Mother turned back to Mrs. P. "I don't know what's up with those *golf* balls, Jane. But I do know that whenever Eddie has Mona out there practicing her swing, she can't shoot worth a damn with the regular white balls, but give her one of those colorful lucky ones and she can drive it half way across the lake."

"Kind of like magic, Katt?" Mrs. P asked, in all seriousness.

"Maybe." Mother's smile was small, but it was real. "Magic's a funny thing, Jane. A pretty great thing when it's used right. Used for good, you know." Inexplicably, her eyes welled up with tears. Be damned if she'd let them fall though; not in front of everyone. And Mrs. P and I both gave her a few silent minutes to put them back in check.

Of course, there had to be a logical explanation for the orange golf ball success. One that had nothing to do with magic. Or even luck, as Eddie maintained. The most likely explanation for their fantastic flight being that Big Eddie had replaced the regulation golf ball with something heavier or otherwise juiced up to make it fly just that much further. Or maybe Big Eddie had so convinced his clients that there was magic in that colored ball, they could shoot it to the moon if they wanted too.

However, I would never say any of this to Mother. And not just because she obviously needed a minute here, and not because she did not always appreciate my cynicism. I wouldn't say anything because there was a fight breaking out in the kitchen.

Nothing was breaking. No fists were being thrown. No one was getting a good old-fashioned beat down. But the yelling that was coming from that little kitchen was enough to clear it.

"Tish McQueen, you're nothing but a no-good, two-bit *flirt*!" Mona accompanied her proclamation with a stamp of her foot. "Everything I have, you want! And I'm damn tired of it!"

"There's nothing two-bit about me," Tish shot back. "And if you're referring to Big Eddie, I wouldn't be so damn sure he's yours after all." She bobbed a hand to her hair, though those blond locks were pretty much frozen in place with styling product. "Eddie Baskin has an eye for the ladies, Mona. Can I help it if he likes the pretty ones better?"

"Oh, since when did you become a lady?"

"Good one, Mona!" Mrs. P called across the room. She never was the queen of subtle.

Tish sent an icy glare in our direction, and if looks could kill, Mrs. P would be toes up. But they can't, so Mrs. Presley just smiled back at Tish. Tish's glare lasered back to Mona.

I kicked Mother under the table. No, not with the *shut-up* assault to the shin she'd given me earlier. More like a *look-at-me* tap, which I followed with the eyebrows raised *what-do-you-think?* look.

She leaned in. "This has been a long time coming," she whispered. "Tish has been after Eddie since the first day she got here. Well, Eddie and everyone else. She was always flirting will all the men. Frankie too." Mother's lips drew thin here. She touched each of her wrists again and looked down as if she'd forgotten that the watch he'd given her was missing.

I trained my gaze back on the confrontation in the kitchen. Tish was staring hard at Mona, and Mona was staring right back. If I thought Tish's stare had been icy, it was nothing compared to the frost in her voice when she spoke.

"Well, then, Mona Roberts," she said, icicles dripping from the words, "suppose I just leave. Suppose I just pack up my bags this very night and head back to Alberta. I've lots to do there. Lots of business to conduct and lots of friends to see. Look after my other interests for a while. Maybe that would be best for all concerned."

In two seconds flat, the look on Mona's face dropped from furious anger to fearful panic.

"Well, I . . . I really don't want you to leave, Tish." Mona mumbled the words.

"Pardon me?" Tish leaned closer.

Bitch. She'd heard Mona perfectly well. I cringed as Mona repeated her statement, loud enough for everyone to hear.

Tish waved a dramatic hand. "Well, it sure doesn't seem that way to me."

"I . . . I'm sorry, Tish."

"Sorry or not, I should go anyway. I'm not sure I like it here anymore."

"Please stay."

Jesus, it killed me to watch Mona so completely chastised and thoroughly defeated.

Everyone was staring at Mona now.

Mother leaned in to whisper — without a prompting kick beneath the table this time — and I had to strain to hear her. "This I just don't understand. I'd have her sorry ass packing in a heartbeat if I were Mona."

"Maybe she's paying her rent?"

"Mona says she's not."

Tish, looking smug and self-satisfied, was about to rain another berating storm down upon Mona. A distraction was needed. Like a titillating Daphne Delicious tale. I was just about to heave a stage sigh and invite them to circle around when another distraction entered the room and I put my porn-primed mind on hold.

The brand new security guard, Dylan Hardy, strode into the room, followed very closely by Big Eddie whose shorter legs scissored to keep up.

Damn, he looked good. Dylan, not Big Eddie. And all over again, thoughts of the night before teased through my mind, causing sensations to tease through other parts.

With put-on awkwardness ("Hello, sir. Pleased to meet you, ma'am."), Dylan was introduced around the room. Apparently, the taker-charger had sneaked out of the room when the kafuffle started to get Dylan, no doubt thinking security might be warranted. Or more likely thinking if anything could break the tension of the Mona/Tish confrontation, the handsome new security guard could.

He was right.

When Dylan's eyes met mine, there was an incredible, unspoken exchange. A barely-there smile packed with knowing, and not letting let on.

Of course, Beth Mary was the first one over to greet him. She gave him a welcoming hug. A long, drawn out (get your hands off his ass, you dirty old woman!) welcoming hug. Tish apparently forgot about Eddie Baskin as she introduced herself to Dylan. And it was with unmistakable, sad relief that Mona introduced herself. Mrs. P was in the kitchen this time, helping herself to a coffee and searching the cupboards for the sugar. And grinning, of course. She stopped long enough on the way back to the table with coffee in hand to ask Dylan, "Are you any good at crosswords, young man?"

"So what do you think, Mother?" I said still staring at Dylan. "Going to go introduce yourself?"

But there was no answer.

While I'd been watching Dylan at this Mona-rescuing meet and greet, Mother had disappeared.

Chapter 8

DYLAN WAS APPROPRIATELY fawned over by the ladies and put-'er-there'd by the men folk of the Wildoh community. With one exception — Harriet Appleton's frown was pulled so tight her forehead looked permanently pleated. She didn't greet the new security guard warmly. She didn't shake his offered hand (and gave Wiggie a scathing look when he did). Harriet pointedly looked the other way.

You'd think Harriet would be delighted to learn that there was more security on the premises. After all, she was the latest victim. She should be thrilled to learn that there was someone besides Big Eddie and the ever-ready Deputy Almond to look after their interests.

Not the case.

Having already been introduced to Dylan earlier by Big Eddie, I didn't rise with the group myself for a second introduction. But that worked well. Very well, in fact. Because from my vantage point (still at the crib table) I could watch everyone gathered in that recreation room and how they interacted with the popular new security guard.

People have no idea how much they communicate through non-verbal cues, and I'm not just talking about tone of voice or gestures. I'm talking about how close or how far they stand from others, their orientation to those in the group, their movements, posture, facial expressions. There's so much to be learned from a lean. Surmised from a slouch. Grasped from a glance. Observed by an ogle.

And speaking of ogles …

Just as I was about to leave the rec room (it's not that I was *worried* worried about my disappearing mother but I did want to know where she'd gone), Lance-a-Lot showed up again, announcing his arrival with that loud, musical truck horn of his.

Dylan was left hanging. Or rather, his hand was left hanging in mid-shake by a blue-haired lady from Complex B who made a mad dash toward the window, damned near taking Dylan out with her walker in her haste. Dylan stood there staring at the horde gathering for the Lance-a-Lot show. He looked a little bit dumbstruck, and maybe even a little bit put out.

What an ill-mannered bunch of biddies to abandon Dylan. If I wasn't so busy elbowing my way past three gray-haired grannies, I'd have said something to them.

Fact-finding missions can be such a bitch.

Lance was at his usual full-mast attention. He gave his customary half turn with a smile. Flexing his butt cheeks for the onlookers, he made his way to the lake and dove in the water. Just like the last time, the ladies relaxed a little once he'd submerged himself, but they didn't abandon their vigil at the window. Patiently they (okay, we) waited as he surfaced and dove, surfaced and dove. Finally, ten or twelve minutes later, Lance started making his way toward shore again, and the ladies came to full, vibrating attention. Lance emerged from the lake, the mesh bag of white golf balls he'd retrieved gleaming in the sun.

As if anyone was looking at those.

Lance drove off, giving his horn one more thrust. People then started to filter out of the recreation room, which was my cue to exit. My cue to go find Mother and see what was up.

"I don't get it. What's that boy got that I ain't got?" Apparently, Big Eddie's joke never got old. At least, not for Eddie.

Mrs. Presley and I passed Dylan on our way out the door. Grinning, she winked at him and he gave her an almost imperceptible little smile back.

"Lance-a-Lot?" He whispered, raising a questioning eyebrow.

I raised sheepish shoulders. "Dives for the balls," I whispered back. That eyebrow did not lower.

"I told you, Dix," Mother said in her *and-I'm-not-going-to-tell-you-again* tone. "I was feeling tired. That's it. I simply left."

"But I didn't see you leave. How could you have just ..."

I was trying her patience. She looked at me with a hand on her hip and a tilt to her head.

I threw my hands up in resignation. "Okay. You just left." But I couldn't resist one long, dramatic sigh. Which of course she chose to ignore.

Katt Dodd was nothing if not mysterious. When Mrs. Presley and I had arrived back from the rec room, Mother was sitting on the sofa, tea in hand, soft music playing. I knew the tune. *Love for this Desperate While*, written by the late, great Peter Dodd himself.

She'd not sat for long after Mrs. P and I arrived. In fact she was up and making lunch in no time flat.

Oh, and yes, very shortly thereafter she was busy selecting my attire for the meeting with Deputy Noel Almond.

"What's wrong with my own clothes?"

Mother looked at me as though I had three heads, and none of them were making any sense. "Come on, Dix. You can't be serious. Wear that stuff on a date?"

"It's not a date!" I protested.

"It's a date." For emphasis, she threw a black sequined halter-top at me.

Hot-potato style, I threw it back.

Okay, for the record, I am *not* opposed to flirty, drop-dead gorgeous clothing. Granted, my 71-year-old mother had a more risqué wardrobe than I had (oh, God, even I know how bad that sounds). But still, I *liked* the stuff I'd brought with me to Florida (t-shirts, shorts, jeans, one blouse and skirt in case I needed to pose as a lady, Capri pants, more t-shirts).

Mrs. Presley was in the kitchen making her spicy pepperoni spaghetti — heavy on the garlic. When we'd been out shopping earlier, I'd made a quick dash in for the basics for Mother. Well, it looked like Mrs. P had dashed herself. She was making enough to feed a small army. Of course, I knew half of it would be heading Mona's way. But like I said ... army style. Yum. I loved Mrs. P's spicy pepperoni spaghetti.

But my serving would have to wait till breakfast the next day. *Not* what I needed to be eating before a ... non-date. Just as well, anyway. As wonderful as Mrs. P's spicy pepperoni spaghetti is, when I eat it late at night, it's been known to throw my sleep disorder into overdrive. Combine that and the stress of the current case, and who knows what Mother and Mrs. P would wake up to find?

Yet, I was glad she was doing the cooking right now. The last thing I needed was her and Mother both ganging up on me over my attire.

Mother held up a hot pink leather mini in her left hand, paired it with a low cut white sweater in her right. She looked at me hopefully.

"Not a chance."

With a huff, she turned again to her over overflowing closet. "You're not making this easy, Dix."

Fine, I'd not packed for a date. But was this really a *date* date I was going on with Deputy Almond? More than likely we were heading to the nearest Starbucks and I'd be paying for my own Caffè Americano.

Was Noel Almond hot? Yes.

Flirtatious? Definitely had been.

Sexy? As hell.

Was he Dylan?

Shit.

Weirdly, strangely, oh God *stupidly*, I was thinking of Dylan Foreman and the other night. How could I *not* be? Not that it had meant anything. Not that it was going anywhere or that it *should* go anywhere.

So why didn't I tell Dylan about this dinner meeting with Deputy Almond? Why hadn't I gotten that message to him? I certainly could have, but I hadn't.

Too damned many questions for one brain.

And let's not forget that Deputy Almond wasn't exactly sweet and kind to my mother. Granted, he'd intimated it was all part of the 'plan' to root out the real culprit, but still ...

I know I complain about her, but she's my mother. And Mother *had* assured me Noel's interrogation wasn't nearly as bad as it looked. But my natural protectiveness toward her had kicked in.

"That security guard has a crush on you." Mother was holding a blue blouse in her left hand now and smoothing her right hand over it.

"Who? Big Eddie? Won't Mona be jealous?"

"Don't be funny, Dix. I'm talking about that new fellow. Dylan."

I pffted my drink onto my chin. "You've got to be kidding." I wiped my chin with the napkin she handed me. "That new guy? Dilbert?"

"Dylan."

Well, now I was *really* glad Mrs. Presley was in the kitchen. She'd have had a field day.

But my interest was piqued.

The thing about my intuition ... I got it from my Mother. So it was interesting that she'd picked up on this 'supposed' crush. Katt Dodd had a sense about these things.

"I saw the way he was looking at you," Mother continued. "Well, you're just as observant about these things as I am, Dix. You must have seen it too."

"I didn't see him look over."

"Of course he didn't gawk. Not in any glaringly obvious way. But he glanced over at you. And these weren't just glances. They held that second longer and went a little deeper. Every chance he got, too. And it wasn't just curiosity. It wasn't a 'where have I seen her before' kind of look. It was one of those rare ones, Dix. That young man had that special gleam in his eyes when he looked your way. I've … I've not seen that look in a long time. But wow, when it hits, it's magic."

I was dumbstruck. Almost into silence. Mother still didn't know Dylan was with me. And yes, all the time, more and more, I was feeling guilty as hell about keeping this secret from her. But it was for her own good. Especially now that Dylan had made his way onto the premises as security. Not that Mother would tell anyone *on purpose*. Not that she'd let the secret slip to Mona or anyone else. Probably. But for now, for her own good, it was better to let Dylan do his work without anyone else being aware of who he really was, including my mother.

Oh crap, I'd tell her as soon as I could.

"Come on, Mother," I fished. "I've got to be … what? Five years older than the new security guy?"

"I'd say more like ten, Dix. Fifteen, maybe."

Grrrrrrrrrrrr.

"But so what?" she said. "What's a few years when it's right? What the heck do the years matter when people fall for each other in this world?"

If she expected an answer … well, she wouldn't be getting one.

Because I didn't have one right then.

"Jumping the gun aren't you a bit?" She had no way of knowing (oh God I hoped she had no way of knowing) how … close Dylan and I had gotten. How close I'd been to jumping a … gun of my own there.

"Life's precious, baby. Life's short. All I'm saying is we have to go for our happiness in the world. Try it. *Trust it.* Grab life by the balls and don't let go."

With that she handed me a red silk scarf.

By the time the doorbell rang, the place smelled to the ceilings of spicy pepperoni, tomato sauce, garlic and onions galore. Yes, it was wonderful. And also by the time the doorbell rang to announce the presence of the good deputy, I was dressed to the nines.

Mother style.

Sorta.

Not in the hot pink and low cuts that mother would have chosen had she had her way. We compromised. I half picked the outfit; she totally picked the shoes. I was wearing a gorgeous silk-screened tank, partly covered by a tiny, cropped Chanel-inspired jacket with a single button closure, and a pretty beige skirt that fell — thank you, Jesus — almost to the knee. Unfortunately, the only shoes I'd brought were low-heeled black ones. Mother, however, had just the answer — strappy, high-heeled Ann Klein sandals. Pale pink (to match the dominant threads in the woven jacket) and barely there.

Without the shoes, I looked kind of hip but polished. With the shoes . . .

Damn, I looked hot.

"I'm overdressed, Mother," I whined behind her as she went to open the door. Mrs. P was already standing there, waiting. Wooden spoon in hand. 'Kiss the kook' apron tied around her twice. "Deputy Almond simply wants to discuss the case," I said to them both. "Nothing more. Just two professionals discussing a case. This is not a date!"

Mother opened the door.

Shit! This was a date.

Deputy Noel Almond stood framed in the open doorway. The uniform was gone. No gun. No handcuffs (fur-lined or otherwise).

But my sharp PI mind did not have to take in these details to conclude that this was a date. No, the real giveaway was the box of chocolates he handed over to Mrs. Presley and the flowers he handed over to my mother. And extra flowers and chocolates, presumably for me.

Damn, that was . . . charming. If I were another woman, I'd probably be swooning. But (as I reminded myself) I was hard-assed Dix Dodd. Men were trouble, and I was immune to their charms.

Yep.

Even the really tall, handsome, muscular ones bearing chocolate.

Though if it was dark chocolate truffles . . . I could see myself slipping.

"Good evening, ladies," he said, walking through the doorway. "Mrs. Presley, you're looking lovely this evening. As are you, Mrs. Dodd." He kissed firstly Mrs. P's hand (she wiped it on her skirt).

Then he kissed my mother's.

"Deputy," Mother said dryly.

If Noel Almond caught the tone of my mother's voice, he didn't let on.

"Yes, you ladies are all looking lovely this evening."

Well, duh, of course we were. But if he expected a titter and giggle or some fool thing like that, well he'd picked the wrong trio.

"Especially you, Dix," he said handing me the flowers and chocolates.

I'm not one to get flustered by compliments. I snorted a half laugh. The flowers were nice — pink and white. Not too showy but not too small. And dammit, still alive even. And the chocolates ... I stole a quick look. Ahhhh, dark chocolate truffles.

Knowing my black thumb, my mother quickly took the flowers from my hands. "I'll just put these in water for you, Dix."

"Say, Deputy," Mrs. P said. "Got a question for you."

Oh shit, this couldn't be good.

Noel smiled. "What can I help you with, Mrs. Presley?"

"Damn crosswords! I'm stuck again. I'm looking for a four-letter word ..."

Nope, definitely wasn't looking good here!

"... useful object used in construction trade."

Noel's forehead knit in concentration. He folded his arms across his chest and laid a manly knuckle to his chin. Then the 'aha' moment. "I think you're looking for a tool, Mrs. P."

She tilted an ear toward him. "A what?"

"*Tool*," he repeated loudly. "I said *tool*."

She nodded in satisfaction.

Noel turned toward me. "Are you ready to go, Dix? I picked out a nice little French restaurant on the boardwalk. I think you'll like it." He held out his arm for me to take.

Oh, come on!

Play along, Dix, I silently reminded myself. The more cozy-cozy Deputy Almond felt with me, the more I could get out of him.

I took his arm. Yep. I took his strong, toned, sexy, all-man arm.

"You two have a nice time," Mother said, politely.

I heard her and Mrs. P talking faintly as Noel walked me to the car. "Truffles, Jane?"

"Dark chocolate ones, Katt. Let's eat them all before Dix gets back."

Noel opened the door to his convertible. Now, I'm not one who's easily impressed by cars. But having to go undercover in various modes of transportation from time to time, I do know a thing or two about them. I can change tires. I can check the oil, and yes, I even know how to connect booster cables without getting a shock.

And what I knew about Deputy Almond's car was this: Number one, it was too freaking low to the ground for my dress-wearing comfort. (I'd be showing more than a little leg crawling into that baby and damned if Noel just didn't keep holding the door open for me. And number two, this was one nice car.

Deputy Almond drove a Corvette convertible. Newer model. Custom painted. Leather seats so soft my ass just kept sinking down in it. And I thought getting *in* had been hard.

"You like the car?" Noel asked as he slid in behind the steering wheel.

"It's very nice."

Not too bad for a Deputy Sheriff's salary.

The top was down and the warm Florida night felt nice on my skin as we drove along. Noel said the restaurant was nearby but I'm sure he took the scenic route to give me full appreciation of the city. And it was beautiful. Relaxing and calm. And the conversation was light and easy. The guy was charming. The guy was interesting.

Okay, I'll admit it. I was kind of having fun. Fun in a professional PI, kick-ass way, you understand?

And after a fine meal and a couple drinks at the Maison Petite Colombe, well I was having even more fun.

"How was the shrimp?" Noel asked.

"Decadent." And oh, and they had been. Broiled shrimp with herbed garlic butter. Sure as hell beat the McMeals I was used to. The burgers-and-fries lifestyle comes with the job. Comes with the late-night stake-outs and traveling quickly from town to town. It comes with the fast pace of the PI lifestyle. It comes with not being able to cook.

"You've got to try the desserts here," Noel said. "They're amazing."

I had no doubt. I'd seen our waiter a few minutes ago at another table with his dessert-laden trolley. Rich éclairs, apricot tarts, chocolate mousse, tiramisu, and a dozen more confections — were displayed. These weren't just desserts, they were works of art. Works, I had no doubt, that ran at least twenty bucks a pop.

"I'd love dessert, Noel. Thank you. But in the meantime," I prompted. "Shall we talk about the case?" I waited a moment. No response. "Noel?" He had to have heard me.

"Just a minute, Dix." Noel's face took on a nostalgic appearance as he looked around the restaurant.

Yes, I'd noticed it ... the last little while, Noel Almond had gotten a little more quiet. A little more subdued. Something was on his mind.

"Been a long time since I've been here." He scratched a hand across his whiskered chin. His eyes took on a faraway look. "This is the place where I met her. This is where I met my Isabella." Noel wasn't crying. His eyes were not tearing up. But those baby blues were certainly misting over.

Isabella?

An old flame?

Was I jealous? God, no.

Miffed? Pfft! Hardly. (Heavy on the 'pfft', thank you very much.)

Curious? Yes of course. Curious as to why the hell men do that! Talk about old girlfriends on a date (there's that D word again) with another woman.

As if reading my mind, Noel smiled and said, "Isabella was a girl I met when I was six years old. I was six, she was eight. I came in here with my grandparents one sunny Sunday. My mother had long ago passed away, and Dad was a military man. Stationed away a good deal of the time. From the time I was six, my grandparents sort of raised me for the most part."

"And you met Isabella when you were that young?"

"She was the first real friend I had. I was a short, dumpy kid. You know the type — big thick glasses, awkward. Tripped over my own two feet. Terrible at sports and geeky as hell. And well, with a name like mine ..."

He left that hanging.

"What?" I asked innocently.

"Noel Almond? First it was Noel Nuts, for about ten seconds. Then it was No Nuts."

"Th-they actually called you that?"

"Dumb, huh?"

"Oh," I said, feeling the heat rush into my face. "Some people can just be so ... immature."

"They were just dumb. Dumb, showing off. Rude. No class. People who don't know any better than to —"

"Okay, I get it!"

Geez, Mr. Chip on the shoulder or what? Just a name, dude! Chill! Then again, I'd sworn my mother to secrecy years ago (pinkie swear over cupcakes and Mountain Dew) as to keeping my real name a secret.

"But with Isabella I didn't feel so alone," Noel continued. He was staring into the candle now as if lost in his drifting thoughts. "She never teased about the way I looked. She just saw what a lonely kid I was and kind of took me under her wing. Isabella's mother owned this place back then, and Isabella and I had free reign after school before it opened for the dinner rush. We did our homework together on a table out back. We danced on the dance floor."

"Sounds like a good friendship."

"It was for years and years. She was the only friend I ever had. The only one I ever needed in this lonely world of mine. Then she died. On her sixteenth birthday, Isabella was killed in a car accident."

"I'm so sorry."

And I was.

Buttttttttttt ... I was sorry in a what-the-fuck, red flag way. My intuition was starting to niggle. I sat up straight. Something was going on here. I didn't have a grasp on it yet, but it was near. The feeling had been fleeting, but it was real. I didn't know what I was yet to clue in to, but holy hell, it was there. I stored that in my memory for later.

Noel did the man-tear wiping thing — the fingers to the bridge of the nose. Something-in-the-eye BS thing. He did the give-me-a-minute snort.

Oh, I'd give him a minute all right.

But if he expected a warm-fuzzy moment, well, to tell you the truth, I just don't have it in me.

And if he was looking for consoling words ... does *suck it up* count?

Yes, of course, I did feel bad about his lost friend. I'm not that hard-hearted. But I just wasn't the right one if he was looking for someone to reach over and grab his hand. If he were looking for words or wisdom to make him feel better ... well that waiter had seemed pretty sensitive. I was just about to excuse myself to the bathroom (I'd wait it out in there) when Noel shook his head.

"Sorry," he said. "I've been talking all night about me. I want to hear more about you."

"Shouldn't we be discussing the case?"

He smiled. "We've got plenty of time. The night is young. And I promise you, we'll discuss the case. I just want to get to know you a little bit better. I've talked on and on about me. Tell me something about yourself."

Damn. He'd hit upon my favorite subject. But still ...

"Come on," he coaxed. "One thing."

"Okay," I said. "I hate crosswords."

"Now there's an intimate detail! Does Mrs. P try to get you to yell phallic euphemisms too?"

I snorted a laugh. "Yep." So the good deputy did know what Mrs. P had been up to.

"Seriously," Noel's voice lowered. "Tell me something about Dix Dodd."

"What do you want to know?"

He shrugged. "Did you always want to be a private investigator?"

"God, yes. I was the kid who looked for every lost puppy. Taped half my parents' conversations. If a friend or a boyfriend told a lie, I could catch them in it quick as a spider traps a fly. I remember when I first heard there was such a thing as a private investigator. I knew that was for me. Growing up when and where I did, that career choice wasn't easy. Things were changing, sure, but it was still rare to see women in some professions. Private investigators were almost exclusively men. Society just wasn't used to seeing women in that role."

My mind drifted a moment to Jones and Associates. I was the first women they hired. I'd been flattered to be offered an apprenticeship there. Flattered and proud as hell. I really had thought I had a future there. Had worked my ass off. But I never got the real cases. Never got the juicy things, no matter how hard I worked. At the end of the day, I was never more than the office girl. As much success as I'd had since the Case of the Flashing Fashion Queen, the way I was treated at Jones and Associates still stung.

Someday, I'd sting back.

The ice clinked in the glass as I raised it to take a drink. A long one.

"But that didn't stop you right? The fact that the field was dominated by men? That didn't stop you from jumping in feet first."

"Truthfully? It did stop me for a while. It'd be nice to say I went after my dreams right away, but life doesn't always work that way. I second-guessed myself. Questioned whether or not I had what it took. Questioned whether it was worth it. Sometimes there's a detour or two along the way in life."

"Did your parents support your decision?"

I was leaning back in the chair at this time. Not leaning back with feet up on the table kind of thing. But leaning back comfortably. Noel crossed his arms and leaned back himself.

"Dad had passed on by this time —"

"I'm sorry."

I waved him off with ... well, a wave. Damned if I wasn't warding off a teary-eyed moment of my own.

"Mother was fully supportive. Hell, half of what I learned ... half of what I *know* ... I probably picked up from her."

"Was she a fingerprint expert?" Noel joked.

"No," I chuckled. "Actually mother had an unusual career path herself." I told Noel about Mother's time on the road, about her being a magician's assistant. Told him everything I'd told Dylan, except I didn't make him think she was a stripper.

Dylan.

Wouldn't have even thought of saying something like that to Noel. Kidding around like that with Noel.

"Your mother must have been a hoot to grow up with."

"All of Peach's and my friends liked her. Our birthday parties were the best. Oh, and when we got Mother in on a game of hide and seek — hell, more like when she got us in on a game — well, she always won. Hands down. Our yard wasn't all that big. Not all that complicated. Peaches and I could never figure it out how she'd always manage to run back to the front step and yell 'home free' before we found her. A master of the disappearing — that was Mom."

I was smiling as I reflected. As zany as she could and did get some-times, it had been fun growing up with Katt Dodd for a mother. Even with Dad so sick, she'd made life fun.

That thought served to propel me back to saving her ass, as I'd come to Florida to do. "So about this case," I began. "I'm thinking that Harriet Appleton has a gigantic stick —"

"From the sounds of it, your mother knows a lot of tricks." The tone of Noel's voice had noticeably changed as he interrupted. "A lot about pulling rabbits out of hats and flowers out of pockets. What about jewels from safes? Rings from jewelry boxes? What about breaking and entering?"

What the fuck? "Wait a minute. What I said was —"

"What you said was most of what you learned you learned from her. PI skills. I'm assuming you meant surveillance of empty properties, getting into and out of places other people couldn't necessarily get into. And of course anyone who knew what to look for on a trail wouldn't be likely to leave one behind now, would they?"

Okay, now I was *pissed*.

"Listen!" I snapped. "What I *said*, you slow-witted prick, was that Katt Dodd had been a great mother. That's it!"

"A great mother with the skills needed to commit numerous thefts at the Wildoh and get away with them. One clever enough to, certainly. And one with the means. Hell, one with the means to commit murder and get away with it too, maybe?"

To add insult to insult (and injury if he didn't watch himself, for I was that close to giving him a thorough ass-kicking right there) he was dialing his cell phone as he talked to me.

The fucker!

He'd used me. He'd lulled me the flowers and the candy and the *aw shucks ma'am* crap, and then he'd used me to set up my own mother.

Shit shit shit! The puppy dog eyes, sad tales of lost friendship. He'd totally played me. When *I* was supposed to be playing *him*!

"Smith!" he barked into the cell. "Deputy Almond here. Go ahead on the Katt Dodd arrest. The daughter confirmed her expertise. Yes, send a couple squad cars over there right now. Marked. I want sirens and lights. Let them know we're coming. Consider her a flight risk. I want that woman in handcuffs. I'll meet you at the station."

He clicked the cell shut and pocketed it neatly. And he stared across the table at me.

"That's all you got, Deputy? The praise of a first-born daughter?"

"How stupid do you think I am, Ms. Dodd?"

"Very."

"That was a rhetorical question."

"Rhetorical? Don't say words you can't —"

"Can't what? Spell?"

"Can't shove up your ass!" For emphasis I slammed my fist on the table.

He stood. "There was another theft this morning. Roger Cassidy had a diamond broach lifted. One he had bought for her granddaughter's christening next month in Miami. He discovered it missing this morning, right after the gathering at the Wildoh."

"Ha! And that makes my mother the prime suspect? Simply because something's gone missing? Wow, great detective work there."

Noel smiled — *damn him*. "One of our officers found your mother's watch at the crime scene. *That* makes her the prime suspect."

Few things in this world shut me up.

That shut me up.

Deputy Almond rose. With a nod and a half wave, he signaled the waiter. From all appearances, he was already on the way to our table, but pushed the dessert cart all the faster when Almond signaled. "Yes, sir?"

"Put everything on my tab, will you, Joey? Oh, and coffee and dessert for the lady, and whatever else she wants. Or maybe she prefers another drink? She looks like she could use one, don't you think, Joey?"

Joey was smart enough not to answer that question. "As you wish, Deputy. Anything the lady wants," he dutifully answered.

Almond slapped him on the back before he turned to me again. "Thank you for the evening, Ms. Dodd. It's been ... well, interesting. And educational."

It took every bit of restraint I had not to get up and kick the shit out of Deputy Noel Almond right then and there. But my tingling toes were pretty determined to kick my own butt as well. He'd played me perfectly. Mirrored my posture as we'd talked. Nudging me more and more to talk about myself. Earning my trust. Chocolates and roses. Flattery (grrrrrrrrrrrr that one stung the most).

But I'd fallen for it.

Yep, we both needed a good boot in the ass.

"There was no Isabella, was there?"

"Of course there was an Isabella. What kind of man do you take me for?"

"Swine variety."

He feigned a hurt look. "I had a goldfish named Isabella when I was nine. Only lived a week though before it died. I flushed it down the toilet. Three times. Damn thing kept swimming back up!" Almond smirked. "Now I must be off."

Oh Christ, people actually said that?

"Business at the station house, you understand."

I glared at the back of Almond's head as he headed toward the door. Despite my best efforts, it still didn't blow up like a balloon and explode.

Damn!

"Can ... can I get you anything, madam?" Joey asked, a little sympathetically and a little bit scared.

I thought for all of one millisecond. "Yes, Joey. Yes you can, as a matter of fact."

He'd already taken a step toward the bar.

"I'll take every dessert you have." I stood. "Every damn one of them."

Joey stopped mid stride and turned back to me. "I don't think the Deputy wanted—"

Fuck what the Deputy wanted.

As quickly as I could, I started handing out desserts. There was a party of ten at a nearby table (wedding party rehearsal dinner — pity the fools). "Compliments of the Sheriff's Department," I said, setting the little plates down. "Here, have two."

"Are you serious?" Bride-to-be asked (two-foot hair — dead give-away), through a forkful of pie.

"Well isn't that nice," a beautiful silver-haired woman said. "Thank him for me, will you, dear?"

Oh I would. Personally.

I was just about to start on another table and hand over the chocolate cheesecake when I realized, 'am I nuts, this is chocolate cheesecake' and I shoved two pieces instead into the over-sized purse I'd brought along (yes, I did think to grab a linen napkin from my table to wrap the cheesecake in thank you very much).

All in all, it took me no more than thirty seconds to unload the trolley completely at this and another couple nearby tables.

Shit! Thirty seconds! I had to get out of there now.

"Five bottles of your finest champagne, Joey, no ten!" I yelled. "Over to the wedding party."

The group shouted a collective "Hurray!"

Okay, the desserts, it looked like I would be getting away with (well, they were already forked into — not much Joey could do about that now) but the champagne?

Joey's face was growing redder by the moment. "Now I know the Deputy wouldn't want —"

"And tip yourself thirty percent!"

Joey stood still for all of one heartbeat before he started for the bar. "Well, the Deputy *did* say anything the lady wanted."

I hightailed it out of the restaurant and spotted Deputy No Nuts (yep, no freakin' nuts in my dull-knife castrating fantasies!) just getting to his car. And in my mind all I could hear was Mrs. Presley's chastising voice: "Give me a four letter word for this situation, Dix."

Fuck!

"Hey, Nutless!" I yelled, not so much to make myself heard over the distance so much as to enlighten everyone in the parking lot. "You're driving me to the station!"

Yes, I would have preferred a cab, but I couldn't waste the precious time.

Smirking, Almond waited and opened the door for me. I yanked it out of his grip, slammed it closed, and opened it again for myself. I got in. Deputy Almond was still smiling as he pulled out of the parking lot.

Why were men such pricks? Why had I let Almond play me like that?

And oh, shit. *What had my mother's watch been doing at the crime scene?*

Chapter 9

As long as I live, I will never forget the look on my mother's face when I walked into the into the prisoner's area of the Pinellas County Jail. She was sitting in a cell with a half dozen hookers, and a small assortment of other poor souls down on their luck. Katt Dodd was sitting in the middle of them, talking to a particularly young-looking dark-haired lady who looked scared to death. With her big round eyes and her trembling bottom lip, the girl looked all of fifteen years old. She wasn't of course. She had to be at least eighteen to be in here (or at least claiming to be eighteen). But right then, she also had to be mothered, and Katt Dodd was doing her damnedest to fit that bill.

Why didn't that surprise me?

But still, when Mother looked up to see me looking at her through the bars of the cell — a smug and satisfied Deputy NO FUCKING NUTS smirking beside me, I know that my mother's tears were not that far away from falling themselves. Despite the stiff upper lip, she looked so helpless. She looked so fragile. Goddamn it, Katt Dodd looked old to me. And I didn't like this one damn bit.

"Well, I bet this is one place you never thought you'd find your mother, huh, Dix?" her voice quavered.

"Certainly isn't one I'll find you in for long. Not if I have any say in the matter."

And oh, fuck, you'd better believe I'd have my say in the matter.

Mother nodded, firmly. One blink of those dark lashes and the tears would be falling. Both hers and mine.

"Well, this is my new friend Bobbie-Sue." Mother said quickly. She squeezed the hand of the girl on the bench beside her. "We're going to keep each other company in here tonight."

"What do you mean 'tonight'?"

Deputy Almond was only too happy to answer that question for me.

There would be no bail hearing until the morning, he informed me. Mother had refused to talk to police tonight, wouldn't until she'd spoken to me and spoken to a lawyer.

Smart woman. And I told her. I made her promise to stick to her guns on that, no matter what. She would.

Of course No Nuts had taken this as an indication of her guilt. He'd so much as told my mother so, but Dodd women don't get intimidated. Nevertheless, it all added up to my mother having to spend the night in jail.

That sent fear up my spine, I'll tell you. I could handle myself with the toughest of crowds. But my 71-year-old mother? I don't know when the shift takes places, but somehow that protective mother-daughter instinct does a complete turnaround in the adult years.

I was half tempted to kick Deputy Almond right in the almonds (they had to be that small) right then and there. Surely a good foot-to-balls kick would earn me a night in jail and I could watch out for my mother. And it would be sooooo rewarding.

"Do it, do it!" urged a little voice.

Mine.

My foot was just itching to fly — heel coming off the floor, toes feeling that special pre-kick tingle that I loved so much …

Then two other officers walked down the darkened hallway. One of them was even clanging/rattling her baton on the bars as she came along. God, I thought they only did that in the movies. They *should* only do that in the movies … it's annoying as hell.

Nevertheless, I was pleased when the two officers stopped in front of Mother's cell.

"You wanted to see us, Deputy?" the officer tagged N. Vega said.

Her partner grunted the same question.

"You two are posted here tonight. Right here. Both of you." He pointed at my mother. "See that one there — the old one? She's under arrest for theft," he said, loud enough so that everyone could hear — me, Mother's cell mates, and especially Mother herself. "And she's a definite person of interest in the disappearance of one Frankie Morrell."

"Frankie?" One of the prostitutes spoke up. She'd been leaning her blue-haired self up against the wall with the greatest disinterest up until this point. "Frankie Morrell? I didn't know he was missing." She was a little older than most working girls. A little bit more makeup around the eyes. She wore a short red skirt, black halter top, and heels that under other circumstances (more pleasant ones I assure you) could be used as lethal weapons.

I made a mental note to get a pair just like them.

Mother turned around and spoke to her. "You ... you know Frankie?"

"Tall guy — like about six-foot-two? Gray haired swept back from his forehead? Glasses that always slipped down on his nose?" Blue Hair answered. "Yeah, I know Frankie."

"When did you see him last?" Noel and I both asked at the same time.

She teetered left, teetered right. "Can't remember. Maybe it isn't even the same guy."

Mother turned back around. She didn't look up at me. It was the same guy I could see it in the blush of Blue Hair's cheeks. I could see it in my mother's eyes

This was one more kick in the ass my mother did not need.

Okay, so now there was a tie for that coveted place on the top of my shit list.

"So you want us here all night, Deputy?" the second officer, J. North asked. "Right here or down the hall?"

"Right in front of the doors, Officer North." He looked at both of them. "This woman is an escape artist. She can't be left alone for a minute. Can't be trusted. Keep an eye on her. And if she gets out of here, I will hold both of you personally responsible. Do I make myself clear?"

He did. To everyone.

Of course, he thought he was pissing me off. Well, I guess that was a given. But I was pleased nonetheless that Mother would be 'watched' all night long. Just in case something went wrong. Guess I wouldn't be kicking Almond in the nuts after all. Which would have ruined the shoes.

And realistically as much as I would have enjoyed a good nut-kicking, I could do mother more good outside of jail than inside. Could and would.

Like get bail money ready.

I was going to post bail if it cost me every last dime I had and every last favor I could call in. I hadn't called Peaches Marie yet. There wasn't a hell of a lot she and her girlfriend could do at the present time while backpacking through Europe. Last email was from somewhere around Glasgow. But if I had to, I'd email Peaches to get money from her.

Goddamn it! I'd do whatever it took.

I'd called Dylan on my cell phone just as I'd arrived at the station, filling him in on what had transpired. He'd listened to everything (and yes, maybe a little bit too silently when I told him I'd been out on a strictly-business meeting with Almond at the fancy French restaurant). I asked Dylan to find a lawyer. The best in criminal law in Pinellas County. Hell, in all of Florida.

As I walked back out to the unmarked police car that would be driving me back to the Wildoh, Dylan called me with a name. I saw the officer shift when I repeated that name. I repeated it twice more, just to be sure, and saw the tightening of the hands on the steering wheel.

Yes, apparently the name Cotton Carson was a familiar one to the police. And not a well-received one. Good.

Dylan elaborated: Cotton Carson was the senior man in Carson, Carver and Associates, attorneys at law. Smart as they come. Tough as nails. Expensive as hell.

I'd pay.

Cotton had thirty-five years criminal law experience. He was known as the Black Suit of Death to local prosecutors. Not only because the man always dressed in black from head to toe, but because he kicked ass in court.

Why, I liked him already!

He'd be at the bail hearing in the morning. Had his secretary shifting things around at this very minute to accommodate it.

"And Dix," Dylan said. "Cotton had one piece of advice he insisted your mother follow."

"That is?"

"Under no circumstances is she to talk to the police unless he's there."

I thanked Dylan. Told him I'd see him later. I clicked the phone shut, and knew Mother would follow the advice I'd given her earlier.

I arrived bearing gifts. Well, not *my* gifts. But I carried them.

I arrived at the door to Dylan's room at the Goosebump Inn bearing the basket of goodies Mrs. Presley had packed with the remnants of her spicy pepperoni spaghetti — still enough to feed an army (and when I considered the great big hulking sons Mrs. P usually cooked for, I didn't wonder why) — and fresh rolls from Mona.

Apparently, Mona had insisted Mrs. P take the rolls when she delivered the spaghetti. Mother and Mrs. P had gone over to Mona's before the big arrest scene, but hadn't stayed long. Tish was there — with her feet up on the coffee table and a drink in her hand while Mona ran around the condo baking and cleaning.

I just didn't get that — Tish was such a bitch, and Mona just seemed to cater to her. But it wasn't just Tish's presence that prompted Mother and Mrs. P to leave. Mona had been busy baking a cake for her upcoming birthday party. Two days from now. Which I thought was kind of sad, that she had to make her own cake.

But it was Big Eddie's cake for the party really, Mrs. P explained. There was going to be a potluck for Mona. ("And it's a surprise, Dix, so don't go blabbing it.") But Mona was making a special dietetic cake. While Mother, Mona and most of the others would be enjoying the finest of ice-cream cakes, a few Wildoh residents (Big Eddie and Harriet included) were diabetic. This was generous of Mona. Well above and beyond what most people would think to do.

A hell of a way above and beyond what I would have done.

I'd told Mrs. P what was going on as soon as I arrived home from the police station. And she gave me her first-hand account of what had happened when the cops had come — in multiple squad cars with sirens blaring. Just as Deputy Almond had wanted, every Wildoh resident had dashed out to witness my mother's arrest. To see her humiliation at being placed in handcuffs.

According to Mrs. Presley, Roger Cassidy had looked angry.

Harriet Appleton had looked smug and satisfied.

Mona had cried. Tish was drunk.

Big Eddie had shaken his head. "But really, I'm not surprised," he'd declared to the crowd in general.

Mrs. P sat on the couch and listened quietly as I filled in the other blanks. I was tempted to leave out the parts where I told Deputy Almond that mother was such a great escape artist, but I didn't. I told Mrs. Presley everything — starting at point A and moving on to Z, hitting all points in between, even when those points weren't so pretty. And I told her about Cotton Carson.

She nodded. "Things'll be fine, Dix. You've got it under control. The lawyer will have your mother out in the morning, and you'll have this case solved in no time flat."

I sighed. I believed her on all accounts, but still this had not been a banner day.

"You say you racked up Almond's bill?" A smile played around Mrs. Presley's face.

"With the desserts and champagne, I'm thinking by at least a grand."

"Wouldn't you like to see the look on his face when he gets that bill, eh?"

I snorted a laugh. "Oh, I'd love to."

Mrs. P got up and went to Mother's room and shut the door. I know she made a call or two in there because I could hear the murmurs through the wall. And then this dear sweet little old lady (ha!) told me with all of her usual warmth, "Get out, please."

Well, okay, not in so many words. (She didn't say please.)

"Go see Dylan tonight, Dix," she said. "You two have to solve this thing before whoever is committing the crimes and planting this evidence plants more on your mother. I packed you a bag: toothbrush and stuff, cozy pajamas and a housecoat."

My initial reaction? I couldn't picture me 'sleeping over'. But the possibly that Dylan and I would be working into the wee hours of the morning was not a remote one. Best to be prepared.

I took the bag from her. "You be all right here alone, Mrs. P?"

In response, she steered me to the kitchen and loaded my free arm down with the basket of food.

"Always."

I followed her into the living room. "You could always come with me to the Goosebump to see Dylan."

She gave me a 'what-are-you-nuts?' look.

Why do I get those so often?

"Don't worry about me, Dix. I'm cozy as can be. You and Dylan just get to the bottom of this." She started flipping through the channels — numbers getting higher and higher. "What was that science-fiction channel you were watching the other night? Maybe they'll play that big monkey-man movie again. King Dong wasn't it, Dix? Wasn't that what you hollered out?"

I locked the doors, checked them, twice, and made a hasty exit.

And now here I was at the Goosebump.

As I stood there waiting for Dylan to answer the door, the smell of spaghetti sauce wafting around me, hungry dogs were starting to show up. They were looking at my basket with … well, puppy-dog eyes. One particularly pushy Labradoodle was sniffing around my purse. Apparently the Goosebump Inn was pet friendly.

"No way, doggie."

Lifting my cheesecake-containing purse up out of reach, I knocked on Dylan's door again, this time a little more desperately. Damn it, he should be around. It was after 9:00 p.m. Surely he wasn't working at the Wildoh at this hour.

Just as I saw a pair of particularly menacing toy poodles tripping their way along the stone walk heading in my direction, Dylan swung the door open to let me in.

He was barefoot. Wearing jeans. No shirt. Just a towel draped around his neck. His hair was tousled and wet, and he racked a hand through it as he stepped back.

"Sorry Dix, just got out of the shower."

"No ... no problem."

His room was a hundred and forty degrees. Okay, maybe not quite that hot, but I was fanning myself nevertheless.

He reached for my goodies. I mean the *basket* of goodies.

But rather than digging in to see what Mrs. P had packed, he set it on the dresser.

I tossed my overnight bag besides it. I doffed my little jacket and flopped myself on the bed. I kicked off my heels one at a time and the *thump thump* of them hitting the floor was somehow satisfying. But it did serve to remind me of my attire. I was still dressed in Mother's finest. Which meant I probably looked as good as I was ever going to. Which seemed appropriate, seeing as Dylan was looking positively edible.

I shook the thought away. "Thanks for organizing the lawyer, Dylan."

"Welcome. From what I hear, he's the best."

He bent his head and gave it a quick once over, then tossed the damp towel onto a chair. And, *dayum*, he made a nice picture. Shirtless, jeans riding low enough to give me a clear glimpse of the iliac furrows that stand out so well on a lean man. Dylan was lean but lightly muscled. And God help me, I badly wanted to trace each of those furrows from hipbone to groin.

With my tongue.

Jesus.

I raised my gaze to the ceiling. *Cotton.* We'd been talking about Cotton Caron.

"How did you manage to get him?" I asked. "I mean, anyone could have gotten his name, but for him to accept my mother's case and rear-range his schedule? To be personally available for the bail hearing in the morning? That must have taken some doing."

"Pulled some strings."

I lifted my head and gave him an arched eyebrow.

Dylan shrugged. "What's the point of having a mother in public office if I don't use that pull once in a while?"

Well, he had me on that one. Dylan's mother, Marjorie Foreman, a prominent lawyer herself back in Ontario, was very politically active in Marport City. It was strongly rumored that she'd be a candidate for Member of Parliament in the next federal election. She was hellishly tough on crime. Pro-women and pro-equality. She was also very pro-environment. She had those who loved her for it, and those who hated her just as passionately for it. Hell, she'd probably made as many enemies in the course of her career as I had. But apparently, Dylan's mother had made a few friends along the way too. Powerful and influential ones.

I sat up on the bed. "And your mom knows Cotton Carson?"

"No, she knows Cotton's political affiliations." He opened a dresser drawer and pulled out a t-shirt. With eyes I knew were way too hungry, I watched him tug it on. "They have mutual friends who have, well . . ."

"More mutual friends?"

"Yeah, something like that."

I rubbed my eyes. From somewhere outside a dog howled. "Oh, Mrs. Presley sent spaghetti for you. I think she fears you're fading away here without a good home-cooked meal."

"Well, she just might be right."

I somehow doubted Dylan was starving to death. The pizza box in the corner attested to it. He had that young-man metabolism. The guy could eat enough for a lumberjack and still wouldn't gain an ounce. Damn him.

Well, kind of damn him. Just a little. I watched him walk across the room.

"You having any, Dix?" Dylan asked, digging out the spaghetti and silverware Mrs. P had packed.

I reached for my purse. "No, it's a cheesecake night."

"Hey, any night where the sun goes down is a cheesecake night."

I saluted him with my own fork (a fork lifted from the restaurant/charge it to the Deputy/thank you very much).

Leave it to Dylan. Five minutes in his presence and I was already feeling better. Why did this guy have that effect on me?

I bit into cheesecake and gave an I'll-have-what-she's-having moan. Oh God, that was good.

"Now where have I heard *that* before?"

Oh boy. I set the cheesecake down on the nightstand. He was, of course, referring to our little rendezvous at mother's condo last night. When he'd kissed me. When I'd kissed him back. When he'd lifted my shirt and touched me with a thousand promises of more.

"Sorry," Dylan said. "I wasn't trying to embarrass you."

"You didn't. It's just that … just that …"

"Just that it's complicated right now. Right?"

He was right of course. About it being complicated. About the timing. But more. I'd checked my heart at the door. Every door. Yes, I felt for Dylan. In every way — physically, emotionally. Holy crap, how could I not care about him? But there was a fine line in life between loving with abandon and being abandoned in love. Between wrapping your arms around someone and having them squeeze the life out of you. Between a tug on the heart and a sharp-bladed knife slowly twisting right through it.

So how could I argue with Dylan's 'complicated' remark?

I couldn't, didn't want to. So, I changed the subject.

"So how is security at the Wildoh these days?"

Dylan answered by stabbing his spaghetti with his fork with a little more punch than normal. "Oh great. Just great. I'm thinking of changing careers."

I shot up a skeptical eyebrow.

"Where else could I spend all day getting smacked on the butt by feisty little old ladies?"

"Beth Mary MacKenzie?"

"She called me Nibs." Dylan shook his head. "Is that some kind of kinky sexual reference I don't know about?"

Why was he asking *me*?

"No, she called *dibs*. Which means technically you're off-limits to the other residents of the Wildoh. She has her eye on you." I feigned sympathy. "Sorry, Dylan."

"All in the line of duty." Forking, twirling, and scarfing down the last of the spaghetti. Dylan set his plate down, walked over to the bed and opened the small night table drawer. Tucked in under the hotel bible, he pulled out a folded square of tissue.

"But this, I did find at the Wildoh," he said. "It pays to vacuum."

So they say.

It looked like the world's smallest golf club. Or maybe the world's smallest hockey stick (yes, I do know the difference! One's for clubbing the bad guys and the other's for smacking them). This looked like something from another dimension. Too small for a child's toy. It might have been a dental pick, but was definitely on the dull side.

"Know what it is?" Dylan asked.

It was the way he asked it. I huffed. "So you don't either."

Dylan sat down on the bed beside me. "But it *feels* like something, doesn't it. You know?" He looked right into my eyes. He wasn't being funny. He wasn't being condescending. Dylan was being dead serious. He trusted my intuition more than anyone. Maybe more than me sometimes. And apparently, he was trusting his own a bit.

And he was right. This *did* feel like something. It was connected with the case. Somehow it had to be.

Enough to call Deputy Nutless and tell him I'd solved the crimes? Or Cotton Carson and tell him not to bother showing up for the bail hearing? Hell no. But enough to trickle some hope.

"Where did you find it?"

"Complex C. In the small lobby off the front doors."

That was mostly the staff complex. And also where Frankie Morrell was renting his bachelor apartment. There were extra storage rooms, utility rooms, and a few bachelor apartments. One of which was Roger Cassidy's.

The police had placed Frankie Morrell's place 'off-limits'. Yellow tagged the door. But I had every confidence Dylan was around other places. Short of break and enter, he would have done some snooping. And he would have done some discreet questioning. Finding physical clues/ potential clues was one thing — but finding out about people — whole 'nother ball game. And Dylan was becoming damn good at it.

"Roger Cassidy is hands-down the cleanest guy I'd ever met," he reported. "I just happened to be in the hall when a courier stopped by to pick up a parcel. Roger was cleaning the peephole in the door. Windex and everything! Later on, he was cleaning the door knob. From what Big Eddie tells me, the police had a hell of a time finding fingerprints there. Like, any fingerprints!"

And so certainly not my mother's!

"But they didn't find incriminating fingerprints at any of the break-ins," I said. "The only incriminating evidence that there even had been a break in were the scratches around the locks."

"Right," Dylan said. "According to Big Eddie, Deputy Almond got lock experts in. Those locks were most definitely picked."

I chewed on all this for a moment.

"Think Roger is OCD?"

"I think maybe. But it's not a 'germ' thing. I mean, he shook your hand. Shook my hand. Plays cards all the time with Mona. Maybe he's just a clean freak."

I'd heard of those — clean freaks. But I'd thought they were just a myth — like Bigfoot and the Abominable Snowman and Size Doesn't Matter. My mind drifted back to my own abode back in Marport City for a minute — socks under the bed, dust on the ceiling fan …

"Eddie, on the other hand," Dylan continued, "is a slob. The biggest slob ever."

That kind of surprised me. Big Eddie was an ex-military man. You'd think he'd be all about order. Precision. "You were in Eddie's apartment?"

"No, I was in his storage room."

"Did you snoop around?"

"Dix! What do you take me for?"

"Oh, good." I was tired. My back was sore. I lay down on the bed while Dylan talked, punching the pillow for emphasis as I did. "What'd you find?"

"Big Eddie keeps a lot of crap in there. Nothing spectacular, though. Few dozen girlie magazines tucked in with the golf mags. Golf balls, of course. And all kinds of paint, including that butt-ugly color they used for the hallway Big Eddie has me painting tomorrow. Brushes, lawn feed, garden hoses, crack fill, sealant, plaster. You know, standard repair stuff."

"Seems Edward Baskin is a regular jack of all trades," I said.

"Yeah, but nothing gets done." Dylan snorted. "He's a slack Jack."

"Find out anything else of interest today?" I said this through a yawn. A powerful one. It had been a late night; I'd been woken up early. And, well, just the running around and tension and mental alertness the day had required.

"Nothing concrete. Nothing absolute …" He pulled a hand over his stubbled chin. He looked down at his hands then back to me again. Whatever it was, Dylan didn't want to tell me. Which meant, of course, it had to be bad news.

"Come on. Out with it."

"You're mother's been selling off the rights to your father's songs. She sold the rights to six in the last four months."

My eyes shot wide. My jaw dropped. It was one thing for mother to get royalties for songs, but to out-and-out sell the rights? This didn't sound like Mother.

I had heard a remake of one of Dad's old songs on an FM station about a month ago. I hadn't liked it. And I hadn't mentioned it to Mother for it was always my understanding that she approved or disapproved who performed his work.

And why hadn't she told me about it? At least it explained the big deposits to her bank account Dylan had discovered.

"Another thing. Everyone thinks your mother is guilty."

"Everyone?"

He shrugged. "Nearly. Not Mona Roberts. But nobody else has a kind thing to say about your mother. No one. Harriet Appleton is especially nasty toward her."

"Fuck." I shook my pillowed head. "What is it with people? Why are they so quick to jump on a bandwagon? To gang up and kick someone when she's down? Well, I'm just going to have to do a little kicking myself. You just —"

"Sshhh! Quiet, Dix." With a roll off the bed and a thump of his feet on the floor, he was standing between the motel room bed and the window. He gave a quick nod to the bedside lamp and I quickly snapped it off, then joined him at the window.

And what to my wondering eyes should appear . . .

But Lance-a-Lot with net in hand, skimming the pool for debris. Only, not the Lance-a-Lot I was expecting. Gone were the happy Speedos. Instead, Lance was wearing loose-fitting cargo pants, a sweatshirt two sizes too big hanging low. He even donned bug-eyed glasses. Oh my God, and Velcro shoes!

Two young women walked by him. I recognized the first — Rosie Sinatra — the gal who'd been at the desk when Dylan checked in the other night. Her friend I didn't recognize, but she wore the same beige shorts and pink short-sleeve blouse as Rosie, so I assumed she too was on staff at the Goosebump Inn. The girls walked by Lance. But they didn't just walk by. They gave him a hella wide berth. Lance didn't so much as glance up at either of them.

"What's going on?" I whispered to Dylan.

"Ah, you recognize him too! I thought you might not, considering the change in his . . ."

"Attire?" I offered.

"Yeah, we'll go with that."

"So, Lance-a-Lot, aka Lance Devinney, has himself another job, huh? Cleaning pools on the side."

"Yeah, Rosie says he does a shitload of pools around. Freelances. She says he's kind of creepy. Never says a word. Never looks at anyone. Just comes in, does his job, and drives away."

The fact that Lance cleaned pools in addition to his diving work didn't strike me as strange, but the rest of it did. "Why would he compose himself so differently?" I asked. "Why act so differently in the two places? Why dress it up for the ladies at the Wildoh and dress down so for the younger crowd?"

Dylan shrugged. He dropped the curtain back into place. I sat down on the bed. "Maybe he's just into older women."

Oh, fuck me!

"Of course, there's nothing wrong with that," Dylan sputtered. "I mean, a younger man and an older woman. Not that you're older as in 'older' older. Just thinking maybe Lance liked the really old ones. Not the ... older ones. Not that you're, like, older ..." He cleared his throat.

Cleared it again (and oh I bit down on the you're-off-the-hook grin that threatened to break).

"So," he said, changing the subject by the best means on earth. "Let's get to work on this." He withdrew the whiteboard from the pile of supplies in the corner. Of all the handy dandy gadgets we'd brought, this — a tool for our minds — was still the one we turned to most.

And so we did again.

Hours later, we had six dozen stick people, lines crossed in and crossed out, diagrams that got downright rude by times (well, Dylan was the one who handed me the marker). We'd drawn up a dozen scenarios. Tens of possibilities. A few possible theories.

It was a start. A damn good start.

"Sleepover, Dix."

Normally, this would have gotten a jolt out of me. But when Dylan muttered the words at around two in the morning, the look in his bleary eyes told me sex was the farthest thing from his mind. And mine, by this point. Plus, I knew I'd wake Mrs. P up if I went back to Mother's. She'd told me to sleep over here. And she did pack my PJs ...

He nodded to a clunky looking chair in the corner. "I'll sleep there if you'd feel more comfortable."

I glanced over to the world's most uncomfortable looking contraption. Dylan wouldn't get a wink of sleep on that, and I sure as hell wouldn't sleep there.

"We can share the bed."

"You sure?"

My heart sped. My mind shifted in a hundred different directions at once. Then braked in safety. "But like you said, Dylan ... it's complicated."

"I said it's complicated *right now*."

Yeah, he had.

I grabbed the PJ bag and headed to the bathroom. You know, Mrs. P is tough as nails. Make no mistake about it. But sometimes she can be kind of, well, nice. Like taking the spaghetti over to Mona. Packing a goodie basket for Dylan. Packing my toothbrush and toothpaste and ...

A see-through teddy! I could picture her now sitting on the couch, laughing up a storm.

I slept in my clothes. Uncomfortably.

Dylan was the perfect gentleman — he kept to edge of the bed, and I took my stretched-out place on the middle. God, we both must have been tired. Dylan was gently snoring before I was asleep, and it wasn't ten minutes until I was in dreamland.

To no surprise, my REM sleep disorder kicked in. And dreamland was wild.

I had that dream I was standing on stage with my high school glee club and I was the only one in my underwear. I dreamed Noel Almond was wearing spaghetti and a pack of Labradoodles was hot on his heels. I dreamed of cheesecake, and sticky buns and golf balls and crib boards. I dreamed of a giant frog and a blue-haired hooker.

I dreamed of Peter Dodd.

When I awoke, every sheet and blanket was off the bed. The lamp and clock radio were placed safely on the floor. Dylan knew I had the sleep disorder, but had never truly seen it firsthand. Until last night, apparently. My assistant was currently hunkered down on the chair in the corner with the bedspread tucked around him.

Under normal circumstances, I might feel half bad about that. But this was no normal circumstance. For I also awoke knowing damn right well who'd set up my mother for the jewel thefts. And I was betting my bottom dollar, this might just lead us also to good old Frankie Morrell.

Chapter 10

WHEREAS THE NIGHT before I looked undisputedly hot, this morning, I looked undisputedly ... well, like I'd slept in my clothes. Rumpled. Crumpled.

But I was too pumped to give it much thought.

When I'd awoken with the knowledge of who the actual thief was, I practically jumped on Dylan to wake him up so I could test my ideas on him. Intently, he was right there with me, following my logic, all the while wearing that thinking-man look of his. He listened to every word. Followed every bit of evidence and supposition I put forth. And when he asked, I had to admit it; yes, my intuition was tingling all over on this one.

He also interjected his own logic. "Going to be hard to prove, Dix."

I gave a Harriet-style hmph.

Dylan was right, of course. But hard never stopped me before.

We had to play it cool. Had to play it carefully and not let anyone know just exactly what we'd deduced until we were ready to spring into that beloved 'aha' moment.

Yes, I admit it. I wanted badly to go straight to Deputy Almond and waggle my know-it-all finger (or fist) in his face and tell him who the real crook was. But I knew I had to wait on this. I didn't want to quietly tell Almond. I wanted to shout it from the roof tops. Hopefully, from the rooftops of the Wildoh. Or at the very least, the rec room. And I wanted to do it with the loudest "Ha! Up yours!" in the world.

Petty of me? Oh, yeah. Big time. But Almond had humiliated my mother in front of the residents of the Wildoh. I wanted to embarrass him and prove him wrong in front of the same.

And personally, I think 'petty' is underrated.

Way underrated.

But there was another reason I'd wait to thump the culprit in front of everyone (I mean besides my penchant for grabbing the spotlight every chance I got). First things first.

And the very first thing to be done this sunny Florida morning was to get my mother out of jail. Despite the crumpled/rumpled way I looked, I headed over to the jail rather than going back to the Wildoh to change. I gave a quick call to Mrs. Presley. She was fine, just having an early breakfast with Mona. Mrs. P said she didn't do a thing last night — just relaxed. Florida was doing her wonders, she said. Big Eddie Baskin had tried to get her to have a go at golf. She'd declined. She had answered a few rude calls from nosy neighbors. Didn't mince words with any of them. Cal called twice — he's lonesome. Craig called once but talked longer — he's more lonesome. Oh, and the young Miss Elizabeth Bee had broken Cal's heart. Apparently, she'd found greener (greener being more moneyed) pastures elsewhere.

Dylan had headed out the door of the Goosebump Inn a good half hour before I did, on the way to his security job at the Wildoh.

"Big Eddie has me doing windows today," he'd said. "Followed by more painting, and caulking around his apartment. Think we can wrap this thing up early?"

I smiled. With any luck, Dylan would be out of that security guard outfit in no time.

I could picture it now.

Damn … could I ever picture it now.

Whoa, Dix. Back it up here.

What I meant to say was, with any luck he'd be out of that security guard outfit, I would introduce him to mother, and we'd have a great time in Florida for the rest of our short stay. Yes, I remembered, Mrs. Presley wanted to go to bingo before we went home. With a fat red marker, she'd been circling the big money ones in the local newspaper.

True to his word, Cotton Carson was at the courthouse when I arrived. I don't know what I expected. Visually, I pictured someone somewhere between Matlock and that cranky guy from Law and Order. I was wrong.

Cotton Carson wheeled himself along the halls of the Criminal Justice Center at a faster clip than the two flustered young articling clerks carrying his briefcase and court papers could keep up with. He growled at the prosecutor, nodded to the clerk, grumbled to the deputy, and smiled sweetly at my mother as she sat down beside him. They'd had the opportunity, of course, of a pre-hearing consultation. And I learned that all this took place in the early hours of the morning. Apparently, Carson had been at the jail before 7 a.m., sent one of his clerks out for coffee and croissants for him and my mother, and spoken to my mother for a solid hour and a half. No, he hadn't needed to be there so early. Nor go over matters with her for such a lengthy time period, but if it got her out of that jail cell, that was good. And if it intimidated the bejesus out of the cops, all the better.

By the time I saw Mother at the bail hearing, she was much more relaxed than I'd left her last evening. Not exactly all smiles; she looked like she hadn't slept a wink. But some of the tension had subsided.

I liked Cotton Carson.

Mother turned in her seat and offered a half-hearted wave to me. She pointed me out to Carson and I could make out the words, 'That's my daughter'.

I wished of course that I could stand right up, jump over the partition and tell Mother the good news. But that fun would be reserved for the Wildoh.

I had put in a voice mail to Deputy No-Nuts before I'd left Dylan's room at the Goosebump Inn. He'd be at the rec room for the early-morning gathering, I had no doubt. If for no other reason, to ask how come I knew so many four-letter words as per the voicemail.

So no, I couldn't jump over the railing and yell my 'aha!' right then and there. But I did relax in my seat a bit, leaning back with a self-satisfied smile. I just damn well knew the day would be ending on a happier note than it began.

I was wrong. Damn wrong.

Oh boy ... wrong.

"Bail is set at one hundred thousand dollars!" Judge Wm. P. Robbins didn't need to bang the gavel. I jumped in my seat without it, thank you very much.

The dick of a crown prosecutor had convinced Judge Robbins that Mother was a definite flight risk with her expertise in stealth, "Expertise to which her daughter attested to in the presence of Deputy Almond."

A hundred thousand freaking dollars!

This was way beyond what I'd expected. Way beyond what I'd

scraped together. Mother would have to spend a few more hours — God if it wasn't for the fact that I'd soon have the fucker in jail, probably a few more days — in jail before I could get this together. Of all the rotten ...

"Ready to go, Dix?" Mother was all smiles.

"There'll be a slight delay, Mother," I sputtered. "That hundred thousand dollars caught me off guard. But with any luck, I'll have you out of here by noon without posting a dime." Of course I didn't know if Noel Almond would move all that fast to get my mother out. And there still was the matter of the missing Frankie Morrell.

One problem at a time, Dix.

Cotton Caron leaned forward and shook my hand. His grip was firm, rough and warm. "Ms. Dodd," he began. "There seems to be a bit of a miscommunication here. Bail has been taken care of. Instructions were left with my assistant last night — no matter what the sum."

Holy shit!

"Holy shit."

My first thought was of Peaches Marie. But on associate professor salaries, both of them, I doubted that either she or her girlfriend would have that kind of cash on hand. And how the hell would she have found out? I know bad news travels fast, but really! That fast across the ocean?

Dylan? The Foremans had money, and they could certainly swing it. But this fast? And Dylan would surely have told me.

Mother looked at me, perplexed. "If not you, Dix ... then who?"

With a snap of his fingers, Cotton summoned forth one of his clerks. She delivered to him a UPS envelope, then backed away practically bowing, to take her seat again.

"This was couriered to my office last evening. It's a blank cheque made out to my trust account. I was instructed to fill in the amount, and get Mrs. Dodd 'the hell out of jail'. It'll take a couple of hours to clear it through the system — less if I hover around the desk sergeant." He smiled at my mother. "I'll do that off the books, Katt. My pleasure."

Despite the assurances she was on her way home shortly, despite Cotton's obvious kindness to my mother, there was worry in her voice when she spoke again. "But who arranged this, Cotton? My friends don't have that kind of money. I sure as hell don't."

I answered for Cotton. "Jane Presley."

The gentleman looked up at me and nodded.

I knew Mrs. Presley was a shrewd businesswoman. I knew she was a thrifty person. And though I'd never given it much thought, it didn't really surprise me that she'd have that much cash at her disposal.

But how did I truly know it was Mrs. P? It was the 'get Mrs. Dodd the hell out of jail'.

"Jane? Jane did this?" Mother's voice was small. "I'm … I'm grateful, but she doesn't even really know me. We just met the other day."

I tried to shrug, but it came out stiff and awkward.

True to his word, Cotton Carson had Mother out of jail in an hour and a bit. I watched him work, or rather, I watched him watching everyone in the Sheriff's office work on Mother's file. He not only watched, Cotton scrutinized. With open hostility. He dogged them with his eyes and chased them with a demanding, unwavering, confident scowl that said 'screw up and I'll have your ass'.

He didn't have to by any means — and he assured us it was off the clock — Cotton Carson drove us home. His articling clerks looked more than relieved as they headed to the bus stop.

"Poor kids," he said glancing at them going. "I ride them hard, but it's a tough business. I'd rather them get used to the grumpy old bastards like me now rather than later when it really counts. Those two will make hellishly good lawyers someday."

"You mean it's all an act?" I asked from the back seat.

"An act?" He smiled at me. He winked in the rear-view mirror. "Hell no. I *am* a grumpy old bastard."

Mother laughed, "Somehow I doubt that, Cotton."

When we arrived back at the Wildoh, it took a minute for the mechanical chair topper to descend the wheelchair from the top of the car. But once it was down, it took no more than ten seconds for Carson to settle himself into it, engage the hand gears and wheel around. He opened the door for mother while I let myself out of the back.

I knew not to dally getting out of the car. I did not linger or stroll or wait for Mother.

Much. Okay, so I'm a nosy daughter. I wanted to know what was going on.

But it didn't take shitloads of intuition to figure out Mother had a little bit of a crush on Cotton, and though he was younger than she, I knew damn well the feeling was mutual. No harps were playing overhead. No birds were chirping delightfully and smiling in that cartoon way (or I'd have to kill them). And if I *ever* see anything even remotely resembling a cupid in the offing, I'd gleefully break every arrow on hand.

Cynical? Who me?

But it was nice to see this flirtation between Mother and Cotton.

I'm not saying Mother was ready to jump his bones. Nor am I implying that it was a case of love at first sight. They weren't holding hands; they weren't smooching away.

But there was something more than a little endearing about Mother's mini crush on Cotton. Namely: he wasn't Frankie Morrell.

Yep, I don't miss much.

Cotton and Mother said their good-bye on the small front step. A long, extended goodbye. Oh yes, all the nosy neighbors were hiding behind their curtains, peeking out the window watching them. I know, for I was hiding behind the curtain on one of the living room windows watching them watching. At the smaller window. Mrs. P had kicked me out of the better view. Mother wasn't on many people's happy list right now. And the rumor mill at the Wildoh was already running on tales of her.

So of course Mother knew as she stood out front with Carson, she was being watched. She knew it as she said goodbye. As she took his hand, and he smiled at her very fondly. And Katt Dodd knew it too, when she bent to kiss the gentleman on the cheek and aimed her ass at the lot of them.

The first thing Mother did when she got inside her condo was to hug Mrs. P.

"It's not such a big deal," Mrs. P said, and her shrug came easily. Or as easily as a shrug can come through the bear-hug grip of Katt Dodd. "You got troubles . . . we all got troubles. And I'll get it back just as soon as Dix cracks this case wide open." She snapped her fingers for emphasis.

I had to smile at that one. I was closer than even Mrs. P thought.

Mother was exhausted. She'd been up all night, mostly consoling Bobbie Sue. Turns out the young lady (aged sixteen) had been out on the mean streets all of two days before being picked up by the cops. She'd run away from her home in Delaware. From what Mother related to me (though she'd never break Bobbie Sue's confidence and give the specific details, even to me) she didn't blame Bobbie Sue one iota for leaving home. Things had been bad there. Very bad. But Mother convinced Bobbie Sue there had to be a better life out there than one of selling herself on the streets. By the end of the night, Mother had convinced her to take a bus to North Dakota where she had an aunt she was fond of. Phone calls were made. Tears shed. Truths told and promises given. Authorities notified.

Bus fare paid (compliments of the blue-haired, Frankie-knowing hooker).

One hundred and seventeen bucks shoved in her pocket (thanks to Officer North who took up a collection around the station overnight).

Drive to bus stop given (compliments of Officer Vega who reportedly waited at the bus stop until Bobbie Sue was safely boarded and the bus was heading down the road).

Hugs and hope given (by everyone there).

A prayer or two said.

And strict instructions from Mother to call collect when she settled in.

That was women for you.

Chapter 11

MOTHER WAS STILL upset over the missing watch. More so than ever after it was discovered at the scene of the latest crime. But where it showed up didn't seem to bother her near as much as who had found it. Roger Cassidy. But why would that bother my mother? I was pretty sure there was nothing going on between the two of them.

"I just don't understand how it could end up at Roger's," Mother said, worriedly. "I've never even been in his place."

Well, I understood how that watch could end up at Roger's. I just had to prove it.

Mother was very anxious to have the watch back, but of course, the cops were not about to return it. It had been bagged and tagged as evidence.

"Worst-case scenario," I told her, "I'll buy you a new watch."

She shook her head. Not in a 'no, no, don't spend your money on me' kind of way, but more in a 'you just don't understand' kind of way. And she wasn't about to elaborate.

Maybe I didn't understand. God knows I'm no Dear Abby. Maybe such a gift from Frankie really meant something to my mother. Even if Frankie didn't seem to anymore. And what about that hooker back at the jailhouse who claimed to know Frankie? What about my mother's flirtation with Cotton Carson?

Whatever the case, soon enough the real thief would be exposed and Mother would be cleared of suspicion for those crimes.

Then it would be a heck of a lot easier to concentrate on the disappearance of Frankie Morrell, with mother no longer a suspect in the thefts. At the very least, it would deflect suspicion away from my mother, which in turn would make those who'd been suspicious of her in the first place feel guilty as hell. Good. I hoped they'd lose a month of sleeps. I hope they'd hang their heads in shame.

Like I said before, pettiness is underrated.

"Pinch-Me Pink? Or something more subdued? Like …" I looked at the label of my own tube as I pulled it from my front pants pocket — "… Chapstick."

I held up the choices for mother. She grabbed her Pinch-Me Pink while I smeared on the Chapstick. But she hesitated in her reach. And damn it if I didn't almost hear her sigh.

Katt Dodd was wearing down. I didn't like to see this.

Power naps taken (yes, even by me), we were geared up for the afternoon at the rec room. Everyone freshened up. It was Wednesday. Three days since Dylan, Mrs. P and I had arrived in Florida and two days until Mona's birthday party. Something about the Florida weather — all that sun and fresh air, I slept like a log, thoroughly and deeply. Though an hour hadn't been near enough to fully rejuvenate Mother after the night she'd had in jail, it did help. She was ready to face her accusers again. And she was ready to face her only friend at the Wildoh, Mona Roberts.

I hadn't told Mother yet that I'd solved the crime. Why? Well, I knew she'd argue with me when I told who committed the crimes and was trying to frame her. This was going to hurt Mother.

Also because I'm a great big freakin' show-off. I wanted to do this — have the whole it-was-the-butler-with-the-candlestick-in-the-library moment — in front of my mom. A person just never outgrows that. Whether it's jumping in the pool, riding a bike with no hands, marching down the aisle at graduation or kicking a jewel thief in the crotch — really, a person just never outgrows those 'look, mom!' moments.

Mother stiffened noticeably when we walked into the rec room. Well, noticeably to me, and no doubt to Mrs. P, who flanked her on the other side. But Mother's obvious tension was probably not that noticeable to anyone else. Katt Dodd's million-dollar smile beamed across her face.

The rec room was packed. A smiling Mona sat at the crib table, but flanked by an angry Roger Cassidy and an even angrier Vanessa Trueman. Annamarie Tildman didn't so much as turn her head mother's way. She just stared down into her crib hand, boring a hole into the cards with her eyes. Beth Mary was nearby in the kitchen, and her glance at mother, Mrs. P and me was brief and to the point. She was obviously firmly now on the "I-Hate-Katt" bandwagon. With her hands behind her back and one foot hiked up onto the wall, a short-skirted, tight-sweatered Tish leaned up against the wainscoting. Big Eddie looked frankly chastising as he surveyed the three of us. I didn't see Wiggie for a minute. Not because he was completely hidden behind Harriet standing in front of him there by the windows (he was only half hidden), but because he looked just that despairing as he stood there. Harriet herself was in her typical hmph-mode. She stood heel to heel, toes out and arms crossed so tightly in front of her, it looked like she was going to slice her skinny self in half at the middle. (One could only hope).

And then there was Dylan Hardy (yes, heavy on the 'har') standing close to one wall. White paint flecked his muscled forearms. Under my gaze, he crossed his arms across his chest, which did lovely things for his biceps. He really did look every inch the security guard/handy man. Poor guy. With any luck, he'd be putting that paintbrush down very shortly.

And guess who else was there?

"Well, hello Katt, Mrs. Presley, Dix! So good to see you all again. As always, ladies, you're looking lovely. Did you enjoy the chocolates and flowers?"

Noel Almond.

Of course the asshole had shown up. The voice mail I'd left for him had been pretty explicit. When. Where. What would be happening. The only thing I left out was 'who'.

But I was surprised that he hadn't shown at mother's door before this little meeting. I know cops, and they don't like surprises. They don't like having their thunder stolen. They don't like when smart women come in and show them up by doing their jobs for them.

So yeah, I was surprised. And a little suspicious. Did Deputy Almond know something I didn't? Something I should?

Mrs. P was so kind as to answer Almond's question. "We certainly did enjoy the presents. I love chocolate. Can't go wrong with flowers. But I wonder, Noel, did you enjoy your bill from the restaurant where you and Dix dined last night?"

Apparently, Deputy Almond had yet to receive that bill, for he looked truly taken off guard by Mrs. Presley's comment. But he wasn't the only one.

When I shot a look at Dylan, his face was carefully, tellingly blank. He'd known that I'd met with the deputy; I'd told him as much. I think I even told him it was over dinner. I just hadn't mentioned it had involved chocolates and flowers. Shit.

Almond recovered quickly, pushing any uneasiness he might have felt from Mrs. P's jibe aside, and smiled again. "The main thing is that our Ms. Dodd had a wonderful time last night. Fine French restaurant, a little laughter, coziness, small talk … Did I mention how helpful the talking part was?"

Grrrrrrrrrr.

Okay, firstly the 'our Ms. Dodd' sounds like something out of a Jane Austen novel, and I'm the last candidate for a character in one of those. Secondly, did he have to blab to the whole world I was so foolishly manipulated?

"Why Deputy," Tish purred. "A French restaurant? You'd think you'd have taken a real lady."

"Maybe someday I will, Tish." He smiled at her and winked.

Oh God, he *winked!*

I cleared my throat. Twice. This one was for my mother.

I nodded to Mother and Mrs. P, who each took a seat on the small sofa at the room's far end. Sensing something was up, Mona left the crib table and joined them.

With a quick look to Dylan (who was still unsmiling), I began. "I am sure the fact that my mother, Katt Dodd, has spent the night in jail hasn't escaped the notice of anyone here."

Beth Mary faked a hand-to-chest, I-had-no-idea gasp, but dropped it when she looked around the room and realized she was the only one pretending.

"It would be pretty hard to miss such a thing," I said, "since Deputy Almond was kind enough to send a full police escort to pick up my mother. Apparently, the Sheriff's Department feels they need full backup to escort a compliant, upstanding, innocent (if I said little old lady, Mother would kill me) woman to jail." I looked to Almond. "Did I mention innocent?"

His expression had not changed — the smirk had not dropped, the eyes didn't betray anything but that annoying amusement I loathed. "Katt Dodd, innocent?" he said. "That's not where the evidence leads."

I laughed. "Oh, that's exactly where the evidence leads. I know who the real thief is."

Yes, I can't help it. My own personal theme song was playing through my mind.

Harriet grunted. "I hardly think we need be wasting our time listening to this." She turned to Deputy Almond. "Is this how you conduct your investigations, Deputy? By letting some ... some porn star," (and she said it like it was a bad thing!) "make accusations? Refute evidence?"

I glared at Harriet Appleton. And though Wiggie (looking paler by the moment) seemed to deflate behind her, she didn't budge under my best evil glare.

"My first thought — hell, my first prayer — Harriet, was that you were responsible for the thefts."

"Don't be ridiculous!" she said.

"Like I said. That was my first thought. But unfortunately, wishes don't always come true. You're a loud-mouthed, obnoxious, mean-spirited old coot, but you're not a thief."

"Is this what we have to expect from this little show of yours, Dix?" Tish poured her words into the room. "One by one, you go around insulting us? This your hard evidence? Name calling?"

"Not quite Tish. And may I ask where you were on the night the broach was being stolen from Roger's condo?" My eyes narrowed.

"That's easy," Tish said. "That's idiotic also. I was down at the Roxie's Bar. Ask Buckie, the bartender with the mermaid tats on his forearms. He'll tell you."

"I will."

I wouldn't. I had nothing on Tish. Just wanted to see if I could get her to answer me. God, I loved the power. Okay, now with that out of the way ...

I addressed the crowd again. "Any one of you could be responsible for the thefts. You all know each other. You know where each other lives. Hell, if my guess is right, you know the details of each other's lives very well — right down to the rings on and off fingers, the birthdays, weddings and funerals. I've seen this community. Everyone knows everyone else's business."

"It's called caring, Dix," Mona said. "And that's not a bad thing."

She was right of course. And she squeezed my mother's hand as she said it.

Oh I wanted her to remember those words.

"I know it is, Mona. And for the most part, it's a great little community you have here. But there is a thief in the henhouse. A rooster in the tool shed. A goat in the foyer. An umbrella in the ..."

Jesus, I really do suck at metaphors.

I quit while I was ahead. (Okay, so maybe I wasn't ahead, but I quit anyway.)

"Get to the point, Dix."

Okay, if anyone but Noel Almond had said that, I would have gotten to the point. Because I was damn good and ready to. I would have gotten to the point right then and there. But because Noel said it, my first inclination was to drag it out as long as I could

No chip on my shoulder. Much.

"My point is," I said. "The real thief here at the Wildoh is not Katt Dodd as you've all been so willing to believe. My mother has been set up. Set up by the *only* one who could possibly do such a thing. By the only one who had the technology. The capability to enter locked doors so very well."

Harriet hmphed. "Your mother's the escape artist. The one with the expertise."

"Ah," I said. "Big Eddie Baskin is the one with the keys. Big Eddie, aka the Taker-Charger, is the one with the access to every accommodation on site, day and night, without suspicion. The one who could sneak into my mother's place, take her watch and plant it for evidence at Roger Cassidy's"

"That's preposterous!" Mona leapt up. Judging from the brilliant flush on her face, I'd say her blood pressure had just shot up to *way-too-big-a-number* over *holy-shit*. She looked ready to rip me apart in defense of her boyfriend. "Eddie is as honest as the day is long. I've known him for years! We ... we all have." She looked to Mom. "I'm sorry, Katt. I want your name cleared as soon as possible. I know you're not one bit guilty. But we were together the night the watch went missing. All night, Dix. I stayed over at his place."

There was a collective mumble of agreement around the room. Mom looked at me with a half sympathetic "You sure, honey?" look.

Okay, usually when I reveal the culprit, it's to a little more fanfare than this. A little more '*Dix, you're so wonderful. So great. Fantastic. Smartest PI ever.*'

And the absence of fanfare would have been fine. Except for one thing. While everyone else was hotly denying Big Eddie Baskin's guilt, Big Eddie wasn't. He wasn't saying a word. Silently smiling.

I didn't like when the person I had just accused stood silently smiling. Not at all.

The hush went in a wave around the room and crested in the middle where Big Eddie stood. Big Eddie walked over to me with an unsettling confidence. All eyes were upon him now. Well almost all eyes were on him. Dylan was watching me. So was Deputy Noel Almond, damn it.

"Interesting theory you have there, Dodd." Deputy Almond. said. "But it's full of holes. Completely full of holes. Keys were not used in the break-ins. All locks were picked."

"Exactly!" I said. It didn't take a genius or crack PI to figure that one out.

But the tides had turned. I was on the defensive now. Right about this time, Big Eddie was supposed to be defending his position, justifying his every move. Damn it! He should be flustered. Panicking and giving me more rope to hang him with. But that wasn't happening.

I continued. "Eddie couldn't use his keys on the break-ins. The cops would be smart enough to be able to tell if a lock had been picked or key had been used. No, Big Eddie had to be sure that he wouldn't be suspected. He had to make it look like the locks were picked, thus he picked the locks."

No reaction. Geez! No reaction.

"I found this." I held out the tiny golf club-ish/hockey stick-y thing. "I was snooping around yesterday when I found this on the floor."

"That's ... that's Eddie," Mona said. "It's just one of his charms."

"One of my many charms, Mona," he said, winking at her.

Dear God, why wasn't he turning pale? Why wasn't he blustering and running from the room? At the very least sitting down. Big Eddie was looking far from the criminal I was trying to peg him to be. Far from a man with something to hide.

And then there was the polyester pants thing ...

"Search me." Big Eddie spread his arms wide, palms open in an offering gesture.

"Ew —"

"No, I'm serious," he said. "I get my groceries brought in. I sold my car a month ago. I've not been off the grounds for weeks. Haven't had to. And I've been so damn busy with repairs around here. Harriet's ring went missing just two days ago; Roger's broach was stolen last night. If I was the one who took the jewels, then I'd have to still have them. Check me." Again he spread his arms, oh and yuk, his stance. He turned to Noel Almond. "Deputy, get your colleagues in. Get the feds. Hell, call in the Marines if that's what it'll take to shut this girl up."

Oh, I was getting mad. And a little worried. I looked at Dylan. His brow was lined too. He was still in character — still Dylan Hardy, the thick as bricks security guy, but where no one else could, I could read the concern on his face.

Deputy Almond took the floor. "Whereas Big Eddie brought it up ..." he punched him in the arm in some stupid male bonding ritual. As if he'd shot him with HGH, Eddie Baskin stood a little taller. "I'm going to bring my officers in to search the place. The whole place — all the grounds and everyone's condo. I don't have search warrants. But I don't need them if there are no objections. You're all gathered here. This seems to be pretty much everyone. Does anyone object to a search of their premises?

The fucker! How could anyone object?

Harriet glanced at Wiggie, and he actually kept eye contact for a change. Tish only smiled, but it wasn't her place but Mona's that was going to be searched, so why should she mind? Mona's face shot red again.

"And remember," Almond added for selling emphasis. "We still have a missing person on our hands in the suspicious disappearance of Frankie Morrell. If everyone is agreeable, and we can bypass the warrants, we'll possibly be one step closer in solving that murder."

"Who said anything about a murder?" I said. "All you have is a missing person's case."

He looked over at me that dismissive, 'oh-are-you-still-here?' look I was too damn used to from my years working at Jones and Associates. Then he smiled broadly, as if I was supposed to melt or something. "Right, Dixie. Until we actually find out where your mother ... um, I mean, where the body is stashed, *then* we get to call it a murder."

Within the hour, fifteen officers were pulling into the Wildoh.

I recognized Officer North from the other night. Almost imperceptibly, certainly apologetically, she waved at my mom. One by one, while the residents waited in the rec room, the condos were checked.

Big Eddie insisted that the officers start at his place — his shop, his apartment. He helped all he could. Thought of places to check that the officers perhaps would not (air ducts, vacuum cleaner bags). He unlocked every door for them, pointed out every wall safe, and stood by while each was opened. All the while Dylan tagging along in good, old thick-as-a-brick fashion in case any heavy lifting was required.

Oh, and guess what they found?

Not a damn thing.

Not one single shred of evidence to point to Big Eddie, or anyone else.

Chapter 12

So what did I learn from the search?

I now knew that Roger Cassidy had the largest collection of big boob magazines on the planet — dating back to when the big boobs of yesteryear had yet to be dwarfed by their silicone sisters. Harriet and Wiggie had separate bedrooms (surprise, surprise). He slept on a twin bed while she reserved the queen-sized bed for her own pencil-like form. Beth Mary had the second biggest big boob magazine collection on the planet — though hers wasn't as neatly stacked as Roger's.

Vanessa Trueman's place was neat at a pin, while Quinn Foster hadn't done the dishes in a week (which is two days longer than my record, thank you very much). Big Eddie had piles of underwear — literally. Boxers. And about two weeks' worth of laundry undone. He wasn't the least bit embarrassed by his slob state. Laughed it off. Happy as a clam the whole time Deputy Almond and the others searched his place.

Many of the residents seemed to swear by Bengay. There were too many litter boxes around for a residence that was supposed to be pet free. Six out of ten people really do not make their beds up before leaving the house in the mornings (I would have guessed higher), and hotel-stolen ashtrays are the norm rather than the exception.

Yes, through Dylan, I learned all the above and more (in many cases TMI) about the Wildoh residents.

Oh, and I also found out that Mona Roberts slept on the floor in a sleeping bag in an empty room. No furniture. Nothing in the closets. Just a few meager belongings spilling out of one old suitcase on the floor.

And of everything Dylan told me, this latter fact surprised me the most. While Tish McQueen enjoyed the big double bed in Mona's master bedroom, Mona slept on a sleeping bag on the floor in the one unfurnished spare room. Mona's cupboards were all but empty, her cookie-jar money stash (all old folks have one — it's the law or something) consisted of three bucks in Canadian change.

But despite all these interesting discoveries, there was no sign of any of the jewels gone missing. Nothing. Nada. I'd figured that the items stolen earlier would be long gone by now, but I'd have thought Roger Cassidy's recently stolen broach would turn up. It hadn't even been 24 hours! According to the notes taken by Officer North, with all the commotion, no one had been off the complex in that time frame. No one except for ... FUCK!

Katt Dodd, of course.

Me, Mrs. Jane Presley and Katt Dodd.

This trip just kept getting lovelier by the minute.

Actually Mrs. P just laughed off Deputy Almond's suggestion that she was in cahoots with my mother. We're talking knee-slapping laughter. She laughed all the harder when he later tried to turn on the charm. Mrs. Presley was driving Almond nuts (no pun intended). But I have yet to see something or someone that Mrs. P is afraid of. Or someone who could sweet talk her. Not after all those years of running a no-tell motel like the Underhill.

And though I wasn't worried about Almond's accusations about me (and the prick wouldn't dare try to sweet talk me after the other night), well, I was getting more pissed off by the minute.

"Happy now, Dix Dodd?" the king of polyester pants asked me when the search of the premises had been completed.

I didn't answer Big Eddie. If he was looking for an apologetic mumble, a sheepish hanging of the head, he was barking up the wrong goddamn tree.

Fact was, I was not happy. But nor was I convinced of Eddie's innocence. In fact, more and more my intuition tingled. I just knew somehow Big Eddie Baskin was connected to all this. But how? If he'd not left the complex in weeks (and why the hell not?), and the jewels truly weren't to be found on the premises, then where were they?

"Maybe you should stick to writing those dirty books and let the men-folk handle the investigations?" Noel Almond suggested helpfully.

The suggestion stung all the more because Deputy No Nuts knew I was no writer of books, dirty or otherwise. I was a PI, dammit, and at least as good at my job as the 'men-folk'. But to protest would be to blow my cover, and I wasn't ready to do that yet. So I bit my tongue and said nothing. And bit it. And bit it some more. God, the man infuriated me!

I was also genuinely worried that no evidence had turned up in connection with the missing jewelry. But too, on this Wildoh search, I thought some sign of Frankie Morrell might show up.

A snapshot.

A piece of clothing.

Another blue-haired hooker, lounging on a sofa.

A lily pad with identifying evidence.

Of course, Mom had her little green heart-shaped evidence still in the freezer. Yes, she was still sure that had been Frankie's way of trying to win her back.

But as far as hard (okay, remotely believable) evidence as to the whereabouts of Frankie Morell … that would come later.

Oh boy, did it ever.

That afternoon, Mrs. Presley thought she'd get some Florida sunshine. There was no golf this afternoon (guess Big Eddie exhausted his balls the day before and it wasn't Lance-a-Lot's day), so she pretty much had her pick of the lounge chairs outside the rec center, and that was where she was headed. No, Mrs. P wasn't the most welcome guest at the Wildoh. Everyone associated her with Katt Dodd. Hell, half of the Wildoh residents thought she was the head of some Ontario granny jewelry-fencing ring, and the other half thought she was the mistress of a mafia kingpin, ready to make one call and they'd all have horse heads in their beds by morning if they pissed her off any more. Mrs. P really shouldn't have told them that.

So in her oversized Hawaiian top, below the knee shorts and sombrero that shaded every square inch of her small body, Mrs. P set off. Despite all the goings on, I think she was having a good time in Florida. She'd never complain, of course. And I was damned determined to get her to at least one of those monster bingo games she so wanted to attend. She certainly knew the severity of the situation. But it didn't worry her. "Ah, you'll get it figured out Dix," she said as she headed for the door.

"I don't get it," I told her. "It feels like it should be Big Eddie. My intuition … Mrs. P, it's jumping all over Big Eddie."

"Maybe it's hormones," she suggested. "Maybe they're causing you to not see straight. Woman your age … wouldn't be the first time hormones sent things out of whack."

Anyone else I would have whacked.

I thanked her from my seated position on the couch. Tossed out a two-thumbs-up.

But truthfully, I was getting worried about this case. And as she set out the door, I tucked my arms around myself and let my smile fade. I was missing something. But what? Big Eddie was too damned cocky to *not* be guilty. Too damned smug about the whole thing. But without evidence...

"Cupcake, Dix?"

I only realized how very deep in thought I was when Mom's words jolted me back to the present. I scooted my feet off the couch and she sat down beside me, sighing as she did. Mother had been in the kitchen baking, and before me now sat a tray of chocolate cupcakes, with inch-high frosting.

Well, they wouldn't be sitting there for long.

Oh God, they were good. Rich. Sweet. Decadent.

But in the time it took me to scarf down two of the chocolate delights, she'd barely picked the paper off hers. (This is a reflection on her mood and lack of appetite rather than my gluttony and love of all things chocolate. Yeah, we'll go with that.)

"I got an email from Peaches Marie," Mother said.

"Is she having a good time?"

"Yes," she said, brightening a bit. "She and Rosemary were just heading up to the Shetland Islands. I like Rosemary. She's good for Peaches Marie. Gets her to lighten up a bit, you know."

Lighten up? My barefoot, vegan, sister with a penchant for yoga positions that make my bones creak just thinking about them, needed to lighten up? If Peaches Marie got any lighter, she'd float away.

And if Mom thought my sister was tightly wound, I'd hate to think what she thought of me.

"Did you tell her about everything going on here?" Though I tried to make it sound casual, I had to ask.

"No." Mother sighed. "Why worry her yet? Let her enjoy the trip. Let her have a good time while she still can. Before ..." It wasn't quite a sob that ended her sentence, but as close to sob as I'd heard from my mother in a long, long time.

I did not like that all-hope-abandoned resignation in my mother's voice. She was giving up. Mother reached over beside her on the couch, and pulled a rose-colored, knitted afghan over her knees.

She wrapped it around her legs and ran her hand over the rough pattern. "I wonder if I could make one of these," she mused. "I wonder ... I wonder if they let a person knit in jail. You know ... they might not with the long-pointy needles and all."

I set my cupcake down. "Mom," I said. "There is no way in hell —"

"I'm an old fool, Dix," she said. "Noel Almond is out to get me. And I know that he will."

"But you're innocent."

She huffed. "I know this. You know this. Jane Presley ... Mona Roberts. That's a tally of four in my corner."

"Pretty good number."

She tried to smile. "Dix, I didn't steal any jewels. No matter how bad things got, I'd never steal from anyone, let alone my friends. Times have been hard lately and I've had to sell off the rights to some of Peter's old songs." She looked at me sheepishly.

"You did?" Of course, I already knew this, courtesy of Dylan's digging, but I feigned surprise. "Mother, why didn't you tell me?"

"I didn't tell your sister either, if that's what you're wondering."

"It wasn't."

Of course it was.

"Dix, I didn't tell you because I didn't want to worry you. You've enough on your mind with your growing business. I didn't want to be a bother."

"You're my mother, you're never a bother. We're —"

"We're family," she finished for me. "And I've done my best by both you girls. But I never wanted to burden you with any of it. Not when your father was sick. And certainly not now."

It was true. She'd been the one. It was only when I was grown up that I realized the sacrifices she must have made. The tears she'd hidden. The times when there was barely anything to hold on to — Katt Dodd had held on. For us. For my father. For herself.

She didn't deserve this shit now. She didn't deserve to be framed for these crimes. And she didn't deserve a daughter complaining about her wildness. About her going out and whooping it up in her latter years after all she'd done for us. Now some asshole was quite willing to let my mother spend her golden years behind bars for crimes she hadn't committed.

Damn that Eddie Baskin. I'd find the truth of this matter if it was the last thing I did.

"I'll figure this out, Mom," I said.

I got up and marched off to the kitchen.

"There's more cupcakes on the counter, Dix."

God, did the woman know me or what?

But I wasn't after more cupcakes. I got two tall glasses and ice from the freezer. And lastly I grabbed two cans of Mountain Dew from beneath the cupboard.

Mother's eyes widened then misted when she saw me carrying them back.

I sat down on the sofa again — beside her, yes, but closer somehow.

"I'm ... I'm scared, Dix."

"I know." The pop cans clicked as I pulled back the tabs and fizzed the contents into the tall glasses. "Remember when you promised me you'd never tell anyone what my real name was?"

She nodded emphatically. "And I never did."

"I never doubted. Because you promised me you wouldn't."

She smiled. "If I recall correctly, it was more than a promise. It was a pinkie swear."

"It was a pinkie swear over *Mountain Dew and cupcakes*," I said. "That makes it ironclad."

We linked our pinkie fingers together.

"Mom, I promise you, I'll get to the bottom of this."

She blinked rapidly. "Thank you, Dix. I have faith in you."

I spent the rest of that day like a woman possessed. It was one of those hot-as-hell, muggy Florida days. Sweat rolled off me, refusing to evaporate in the hideous humidity, and I kept the water bottle filled. I talked to all the Wildoh residents who would talk to me. None of them yet knew that I was a private investigator. They still thought I was the not-too-bright, erotica-writing daughter of Katt Dodd. So although they talked to me with hostility, it wasn't guarded hostility.

Except Big Eddie. He wasn't the least bit hostile. The fucker was still just a-grinning. I knew he was the culprit. He didn't seem to care. Smug son of a bitch.

I snooped around every complex, watched the comings and goings of everyone that I could. One of those people coming and going was Dylan, going about his security/maintenance duties. He nodded at me politely each time we passed, me on my overt fact-finding mission and he on his covert one.

I charted. I plotted. I drew little stick figures and great big question marks, as I tried to tie each and every individual into Big Eddie Baskin.

I thought about motive.

I considered money.

I pondered access.

And I had no doubt Dylan was doing the same.

And why was I looking for connections to Big Eddie? Because he had to have had an accomplice, that's why. Someone had to be working with him to get the jewels off the property.

And I didn't like how these lines of thought looped and led.

That evening Mother was almost her old self again. Apparently the pinkie swear promise was all she needed to buoy her spirits. She insisted we all 'doll up' and head out for a night on the town.

I did the DD (designated driver, not Dix Dodd) while out with Mom and Mrs. P But I enjoyed a nice, cold glass of wine when I got home. And only as I relaxed and sipped, did I realize how tired I was. Pooped. Beat.

And I slept like the dead. I didn't stir until the next day, when I awakened to my mother screaming and pointing a shaking finger to the empty wall safe.

Chapter 13

I COULDN'T BELIEVE it.
   Yet there it was ...
   That safe was not twenty feet from where I'd slept all night! How could someone have broken in and gotten by me? It just wasn't possible. And it was also highly risky. Whoever broke in here had to be pretty damn sure I'd not wake up. But how?
   Then I stood up from the sofa bed and reeled sideways. What the hell? I sat down again. The dizziness passed quickly, but when it did, I realized my brain was shrouded in a fog that was just beginning to dissipate. And not a sleep fog. I blinked.
   Jesus, someone had slipped me something! But who? When? Oh, where should the ass-kicking begin?
   My own, perhaps. Instantly the answer came to me.
   I'd been careless yesterday. The damn heat, I'd carried a water bottle around with me all day. Of course, I'd set it down everywhere I'd gone. To take notes, to run to the bathroom at Mona's. I'd set the water down to shake hands with Roger (whose other hand was covered with chocolate ... geez, I hope it was chocolate).
   Damn damn damn! Anyone could have slipped something into my water. I'm never that sloppy. But if I had in fact been slipped a mickey, why the delayed reaction? Why hadn't it hit me until hours later? How could it not hit me until ...
   Oh, shit, until I'd had that drink of wine after dinner. It must have been something fairly innocuous until it was intensified by alcohol. That *perfectly* predictable glass of wine.
   Or, shit, shit, shit, maybe someone slipped something into the wine itself? Slipped *into* Mother's condo in order to slip it into the wine. Not that I could prove it. I'd polished off the last of it, a partial bottle of Shiraz. The same one Dylan and I had drunk from the other night. There'd been

just enough left for a single glass.

Whatever the method of delivery, in the water or in the wine, it had worked. It had been lights-out drowsiness when my head hit the pillow, which I attributed to stress. I'd crashed early, thinking my subconscious might solve the mystery my conscious mind seemed unable to crack.

Mother was crying. Even the nerves-of-steel Mrs. P looked a little shaken.

Shaking the last of the cobwebs away, I headed to the sliding door. Damn it! Not only was it unlocked, it had been left mockingly ajar! One white panel of the sheers rippled out into the wind. There were no telltale wet footprints. No muddy hand prints on the wall. And no water on floor this time, no little piece of greenery — heart-shaped or otherwise. I checked the lock. Of course, it wasn't broken.

"How could it be?" Mother asked me, bewildered.

How could I answer her?

I made two calls. The first one, I made easily, to Dylan. He was at the Goosebump. I know I woke him up — that was evident by the groggy "'Lo". But his alertness was instantaneous upon hearing my voice and the panic I tried to keep from it. Dylan Foreman was pretty good with his own bullshit buster. I told him what had happened. He'd be right over. He'd throw on his Dylan Hardy security uniform and be there as quickly as he could. He didn't bother to tell me not to worry. That would just be too damn condescending in the circumstances.

"Thanks, Dylan."

"And Dix," Dylan said, before he hung up. "One of my contacts came through with that information on Frankie Morrell. Appears he does have a thing for hookers — blue-haired, sharp-clawed, whip-brandishing ... you name it. He's been picked up twice in the last year soliciting undercover female cops. And apparently, he has some pretty kinky tastes when it comes to the services he pays for."

"How kinky?"

"You don't want to know."

That was all I needed to know.

That was going to break my mother's heart.

But if Frankie was into assorted games with hookers, I wanted him nowhere near my mother. Not that I wanted him missing or dead. Just no-damned-where near my mother.

The second call I made reluctantly. Yes, I had to call Deputy Noel Almond. That was a hard pill to swallow. I didn't mind waking him up. Hell, I was silently pleading *please be asleep* into the phone even as I dialed his cell. But I just didn't want to ask for help from the bastard. But there was no way around it. He had to know about this crime. And while I had him on the phone, I filled him in on the new info on Frankie Morrell.

On the missing ring news, Noel seemed a little surprised. Heavy on the little. I know the guy is trained to hide emotion, but I'm trained to catch the flickers of it.

When I told Almond about Frankie's fetish for floozies, all he said was, "Well, that's interesting." But he said it with absolutely no interest in his voice. Not a bit.

He'd known. Nutless bastard! "Perhaps your investigation of Morell's disappearance should have been geared in that direction, rather than my mother's?"

I heard the chuckle before the phone clicked dead.

When I told Dylan I thought I'd been drugged, he looked stricken, sick for a moment. Then just plain angry. I was fine I assured him, and though he didn't go into some macho-male going-to-kick-me-some-ass mode I find so tiresome, clearly he would love to get his hands on whoever slipped me the sleeping aid.

Perhaps he would.

I'm not stupid. Well, not *that* stupid. Dylan's concern and anger went beyond the typical employee/employer thing. Beyond 'friends'. I knew it.

He made a quick trip into my mother's before reporting to Big Eddie for work. He'd been painting, sorting tools, vacuuming like a madman under Big Eddie's instruction. Clearly, Eddie Baskin was taking advantage of the perceived slow wit of Dylan Hardy and getting him to do a month's worth of grunt work.

We had to admit it then, to Mother, that Dylan was one of the good guys, on our side trying to solve this case. Sheepishly, I had to admit it.

"Don't hang that head too low, Dix," Mother said. "I've known all along."

Of course she had. This was my mother.

"I've seen the way you two look at each other," she said.

"Ah, you should see them when they think they're alone!" Mrs. P added.

Lovely.

There was another knock at the door.

Big Eddie was taken aback a moment when he walked into mother's and saw Dylan there. Whereas I myself was taken aback to see Big Eddie. No one had called him. He had to know he wasn't the least bit welcome. But as he walked in through the door, he was followed by Deputy Almond.

"What are you doing here, kid?" Big Eddie asked Dylan.

Instantly Dylan Foreman donned the Dylan Hardy face.

"Saw the door open here, Big Eddie," he said.

"And you walked right in?"

"This nice lady," (he pointed to me) "invited me in."

Big Eddie grinned at me. "You look tired today, Dix," he said. "Didn't you sleep well?" He was baiting me. Clearly, clearly, he was doing everything he could to yank my chain. He was that confident. Had *he* slipped me the drug? My bets were on it.

"Slept like a baby, Eddie. But not nearly as well as I'll sleep tonight." I smiled at him. Yes, I was fishing for a reaction. And yep, I got it.

And I saw it — the slightest waver to his grin. His eyes slid over to Almond before they slid back to me. What did I have? Not much — suppositions. But I'd gotten what I wanted — I wanted to throw Eddie off the slightest little bit. But I felt it too. The niggling was there. Hormones, my butt!

While I was watching Big Eddie, Almond was watching us both. Carefully.

"Say, Deputy," Mrs. P said. "Give me a —"

"What, Mrs. Presley?" He rolled his eyes and turned to her. "A seven-letter word for castrated?"

Mrs. P gasped. "Do all you sheriff's deputies talk such filth to little old ladies? What I was going to ask for was a boost up."

He did a double take. "Excuse me?"

"I'm too short. And there's something at the back of this safe."

We all were there in an instant, elbowing for room.

With a pointy right (hers) to the ribs (mine), Mrs. P won.

There was indeed something at the back of the safe.

"Dust?" I asked. Well, that was the first thing that came to mind.

"Come on, Dix," Mrs. Presley said. "This isn't your apartment. Dust doesn't grow that thick here."

She had me there.

"Maybe it's bird poop," Dylan said.

We all did a double take on that one.

"What?" he said. "Birds poop."

"Yeah," Big Eddie said. "Yeah ... they do poop, Dylan. Now just shut the hell up."

Almond reached in to touch it, his fingers coming away with grains of fine sand.

"Know what that is, Eddie?" Deputy Almond asked.

Big Eddie wet his lips before he answered. Apparently, the strain from staying on his tiptoes was getting to Big Eddie. His bald head was gleaming with sweat.

"Not sure, Deputy. Could be anything really."

"Looks like sand."

"Lots of sand in Florida."

Eddie clumped down to flat footed again.

Almond nodded. He turned to Mother. "So, Mrs. Dodd. How very unfortunate that suddenly you're a victim of crime too."

Already, I did not like where this was going.

"Why, just yesterday your daughter hiring a pricey lawyer to get you out of jail, you're the prime suspect in all these crimes — and let's not forget the disappearance of Frankie Morrell — and suddenly, surprise, surprise, you too end up being the victim of a robbery. What are the chances?"

My jaw dropped. I could not believe what I was hearing.

"Yeah," Eddie said enthusiastically. "Seems pretty coincidental to me too."

Fucker!

"Easy, Dix ..." I only realized my hands were fisted when Mother put her hand on my arm. She turned to Almond. Oh, how she turned to Almond.

Katt Dodd was back. My pinkie-swearing, lipstick-wearing, kick-ass mother was back.

Almond stood there smirking in that condescending way some men have. He stood there waiting, no doubt, for my mother to cry. Fall down and fall apart. Dissolve into whimpering. Lose it in hysteria.

The guy just did not know women.

And he sure as hell didn't know my mother.

See you can only push a Dodd woman so far, and losing the ring that my father had given her was the final push that Katt Dodd needed before she started pushing back.

"Deputy Almond," she said. "Since these thefts began I have been nothing but cooperative with you. Since the disappearance of Frankie Morrell, the same. I've told you everything I know in every instance."

I knew the tone. Oh, God, I knew this tone. Peaches Marie and I had received the same the morning after we'd sobered up from our first high school ... ah, sleepover. This was the I've-put-up-with-all-I'm-going-to tone. This was Katt Dodd's I'm-smiling-but-I'm-going-to eat-you-alive tone.

"Now what I see happening here, Deputy Almond," my mother continued, "would seem to constitute police brutality. Harassment at the very least. You've been accusing me for weeks, yet your evidence is flimsy to non-existent. Anyone could have gotten my watch and you damn well know it. Well, Deputy, I am sick and tired of it. I've tried to be polite, cooperative and friendly. But no more. Now, you're going to write up a report on my missing family jewels. And you're going to give this matter all the attention that you'd give to each and every other crime in this complex."

He tried to stare her down. "Since when do I take my orders from you, Mrs. Dodd?"

Katt Dodd reached into her pocket. She pulled out her Pinch-Me Pink without hesitation, smeared it on thick and smacked her lips together before she smiled at him. "I'm just asking you to do your job, Deputy. That ring was very special to me. And if you don't apply the same diligence in solving this crime as you did the others, I will hold you personally responsible. And I will bring a lawsuit against not only yourself, but the entire Sheriff's Department."

"You think that scares me?"

"I don't know if that scares you or not. But maybe this will: this is Florida, Deputy Almond. There are a great many ladies and gentlemen of my age here. And I assure you, when I am cleared of these crimes — *and I will be* — it is my intention to campaign tirelessly to get your elected Sheriff kicked out of his job. Every gray-haired granny will be after his ass by the time I'm through, and I'll make sure he knows it's because of *your* actions, Deputy. Because of *your* harassment of an innocent senior. I have friends well beyond these Wildoh walls, and some in very high places. And I assure you, I am far from shy in front of the cameras. Would that be enough to unseat a Sheriff? Maybe not. But I'm betting he'd be prepared to cut your ass loose to take the heat off himself."

Noel stared at her, but silently. Hell, she'd shut us all up.

"You think my magic is all in my head," Mother said. "Just an old woman's foolishness. Well, just watch how quickly I can make your job disappear. Your reputation."

(And if I was judging things correctly, I bet his gonads, too, right about now.)

"Go ahead, try me," Mother said. "You'll find Cotton Carson is the least of your worries." She went right up to him and got in his face. "Piss me off one more time, Deputy, and I swear to you the moment I'm cleared of these ridiculous charges, I will not only sue you for harassment, dereliction of duty and anything else I can think of, I will *fucking mobilize* a gray wave."

Deputy Almond tried to stare my mother down. Failed. Though not miserably. The stare down lasted way past when my eyes began watering. But he failed nonetheless.

Muttering under his breath, he punched a few numbers into the cell.

"North? Deputy Almond here. Get forensics down to the Wildoh again. We've had another theft."

Call completed, Deputy Almond sat on the sofa. "Can I bother you for a coffee, Mrs. Presley?" he asked, sweetly.

"Certainly. Cream, sugar, or spit?"

Well, he didn't think that one over for very long. "Never mind."

He opened up his handy-dandy notepad. Clicked open his pen. "Now, let me ask you a few questions, Mrs. Dodd," he said to my mother.

Big Eddie sat down, his charm-filled necklace giving a *tink* with the motion. God that thing must weigh a pound. About six mid-life crises rolled into one.

"Time for you to go, Eddie," I said.

He looked at Almond. Almond nodded. "Yeah, Eddie. This time . . . I'll handle it myself."

"Don't you need someone to safeguard the scene until forensics arrives? To make sure it doesn't get, you know, contaminated?" he asked. "I can do that."

"I'll look after it myself this time."

"You sure, Noel?"

"Quite sure."

Eddie left, growling at a head-hanging Dylan as he went.

Mother sat on the sofa. She smiled at Almond as though he were the sufficiently chastised child and the time-out was over.

I learned a lot from this exchange. Relearned some too.

First, Mother's strength. That was a refresher course. Katt Dodd had gone through some hard times in her life, especially when our father was dying and she had to be strong for Peaches and me. And now that the Dodd diamond was on the line, her real strength showed through again. The diamond meant the world to Mother, but she was the real rock here. She was the real family jewel.

Secondly, I learned never to accept coffee from Mrs. P when she's ticked at you.

Thirdly and more importantly, I learned that Deputy Noel Almond didn't believe my mother was guilty either.

Chapter 14

I HUNG AROUND while the forensic guys did their job, watched as they took fingerprints and samples. Closely. Noel Almond did too.

When they were gone, and a coffee-seeking, caffeine-deprived Noel Almond himself was out the door later that morning, I set out in search of Dylan. I didn't have to look far. Big Eddie had him doing a shitload of work again today. As far as I could see, the only 'security' Dylan was providing for Eddie Baskin was securing that he'd get lots of rest and relaxation. Poor Dylan had been vacuuming, cleaning, painting, mowing lawns, trimming hedges — you name it — while Eddie enjoyed the free time.

And sure enough, as I headed toward Complex C in hopes of finding Dylan, I watched Eddie heading toward the lake's driving range.

Yes, his he-vage rode down too low and his pants rode up too high. And yes, he was smiling as he headed out to play golf. But I saw it ... that fixed grin was just a little bit strained as he made his way to the driving range.

And apparently, Big Eddie was feeling a little off his game this fine morning for within the ball-filled mesh bag that he carried in his left hand, a glowing orange ball stuck out like a ... well, like a glowing orange ball among a whole bunch of white ones.

Big Eddie needing some of his own magic spin on that ball, perhaps? Not so very confident in his own drives and slices? Little shaky these days?

Good.

Fan-freaking-tastic!

I wanted him rattled. Rattled men make mistakes. (Not to be confused with that other well-known maxim, men are rattlesnakes.)

I found myself checking things over as I approached Complex C where Dylan was working again today. You know, a pat to the hair, a tug to the shirt, stomach in chest out kind of thing. But no, I *wasn't* primping. Well, not a lot. And certainly not for Roger Cassidy, who with a scowl and muttering a slew of four-letter words, met me in the doorway on his way out. Well, kind of met me in the doorway. More like on the step as he slammed the door closed behind him when he saw me aiming to enter.

I watched him storm off in a huff.

Dylan knew I was coming, but he wasn't hanging around the entry-way waiting for me, nor did I expect him to be. We were still undercover. For a while yet, I was Dix Dodd, erotica queen of the north, (that in itself was telling — Almond knew my real persona, Almond was keeping it mum) and he was Dylan 'heavy-on-the-har' Hardy.

I met a few other grumpy people in the hallway. Grumpier, of course, when they saw me. Grumpier still when they saw my fuck-you smile. But that was fine. Nothing out of the ordinary in my line of work. I sloughed it off.

I knew I'd find Dylan in the supply room in the basement. I'd like to say that was a brilliant deduction on my part, but we'd prearranged the meeting spot.

Dylan was mixing paint when I arrived. Well he was kind of mixing paint. The can was definitely open. There was a wooden stir stick in it. There was a roller brush in the unspotted tray.

He dropped the ah-shucks, thick-as-bricks persona the moment he saw it was me rounding the corner. "You look different, Dix."

Those first four words threw me back a bit. What had he noticed? A glow to my skin from the Florida sunshine? More lightness in my blond hair from the same? A lightness to my step? Roses in my cheeks? A sparkle in my eyes? A —

"Oh, it's your shirt," he said, nodding. "Your mother ironed for you."

What can I say? The guy knew me.

There were two stools in the work room behind the long lami-nate-topped counter. I took a seat on one of them. Dylan sat down beside me. He half leaned, half pivoted as he reached for the two coffees on the shelf below.

Yes, he *did* know me. I'd jacked up on caffeine before I'd left Mother's, of course, but this was a welcome bonus. I grabbed my cup from Dylan, and our knees touched as he swiveled a bit to touch his Styrofoam cup to mine in a salute.

And yes, this small knee-to-knee contact did send a little thrill shooting through me.

Okay, more than a little thrill. Compared to Almond ... well, there was no comparison. And yeah, I swallowed down the wee bit of guilt I felt over the other night's date/non-date thing.

What was it with Dylan Foreman? What was it with *me*?

Dylan didn't move his knee away. I waited to see if he would, half wondering if I should edge away myself. But I didn't and he didn't, and the moment passed when either of us could have done so without awkwardness.

My mind drifted to the other night when Dylan and I had gotten more physical. Closer than just touching knees ...

Did I say *drifted*? My mind *shot* back to that memory like it had been launched from a rocket.

Dylan taking the glass from my hand, hauling me down on the bed. His body so solid and exciting against mine. His mouth on my mouth, his hands on my body. Oh, God, his mouth on my ...

"Still, thinking about Big Eddie, Dix?"

My sexually-charged, rocket-launching mind pulled a 180 and came crashing right down to earth.

"Er, yeah. Big Eddie. That's right. He's the one responsible for the thefts, Dylan. I know it."

I did know it. All signs pointed to Eddie Baskin. More importantly, my intuition was screaming and pointing the bony finger of blame at him. But the way he acted when I accused him, how easily he accepted the search of the premises ... Now, that baffled me. How could he be that cocksure that the jewels wouldn't be found?

He couldn't be. Unless they were no longer on the premises.

But Eddie said he'd not been off the grounds for weeks. Had no need to. No extra money to be spending these days. And it happened that no-one had left since Roger's broach was stolen. But the small tool/charm Dylan found in the hallway, the opportunity, my clamoring intuition ...

"So, who is his accomplice?"

Clearly Dylan had gone over this same ground in his own mind and reached the same conclusion I had.

"It has to be someone on the inside," I said.

"Right."

"Someone close to him, obviously. And someone who wouldn't raise the suspicions of the residents."

He nodded. "For sure."

"Someone he trusts."

"Someone he'd take off to Cuba with, you think?"

Huh? Where had that come from? "Maybe," I said. "But really, Dylan, what does that have to do with ..."

From his back pants pocket, Dylan hauled out a piece of paper. A photocopy. I quickly unfolded and read the document. "Holy shit."

"Yeah," Dylan agreed. "Kind of puts a rush on the situation, huh?"

Rush wasn't the word for it. We were way past rush — rush was yesterday. The page Dylan handed to me was a copy of a travel agency itinerary from Ridley Travel. Apparently, Eddie Baskin *was* heading to Cuba, via Cancun. Tomorrow evening. Flying first class.

"Where'd you get this?"

He smiled. "I found it when I was dusting Eddie's apartment."

"Dusting?"

"Yeah," he said "My favorite. I got the pleasure of dusting Big Eddie's place — I'm sure the first time in years. Anyway, Eddie left me alone there while he did some errands. And well, he had a ticket for Cuba that just needed a good dusting."

"He left this out in plain sight."

"Hell, no, but dust gathers on the inside of locked drawers. In envelopes marked 'confidential'. Even the ones that need to be carefully steamed open."

I smiled at my apprentice. I'd never been so proud.

"And while there is only one ticket here. The credit card receipt that I also, ah dusted off. Is for double the total on the ticket. Exactly. Big Eddie is flying first class. And he's not flying alone."

"Leaving with his accomplice?"

Dylan nodded. "That would be my guess."

"Tomorrow ..." I looked at the itinerary again. "That doesn't leave us much time."

"It'll be enough."

God, I hoped so. But there was still so much work to be done yet. We had to figure out who Eddie was working with, and fast. "So Big Eddie has a ticket," I mused aloud, perusing the itinerary closer. "One way, first class." I raised an eyebrow as I read further. "He must have been stealing these jewels for a while. I mean, apart from the Dodd diamond, if he fenced everything, it wouldn't fetch more than a few thousand dollars. Enough for a first class ticket, sure. But enough to skip town on?"

"I know. Makes you scratch your head, doesn't it?"

I looked the pages over again. "This is good investigative work, Dylan. Fine work. Brilliant, in fact."

"Just *brilliant*?" He cocked his head and smiled. "Come on, Dix, give me a six-letter word for it. I know you want to. Starts with G."

"Pfft." Dylan and I were far too competitive for me to dub him the genius of our duo.

"Come on, Dix. You gotta admit it was sheer genius the way I came in here posing as Dylan Hardy. The way I snuck around, did all this damned grunt work just so I could get closer to the unsuspecting suspect."

"Work?" I snorted a contemptuous laugh. "Why, look at this place. It's a mess." I ran a finger over the counter and held it up for inspection. "You call this clean? You call this dusted? Why I've seen cleaner counters in my —"

Dylan saw it the same time that I did — the little grains shiny on my fingertips.

"I call it sand," he said.

While I'm no sand expert, this was just too coincidental. Fine sand at mother's condo; fine white sand right here. And when I looked closer, there wasn't just a dusting of it on the counter, there was a trail of it. Leading all the way to the cabinet in the corner.

Dylan and I stared at each other. Then did a double take back to the cabinet. It was padlocked.

"Got the combination?" I asked, not even trying to keep the *please please please* out of my voice.

Dylan frowned. Obviously the answer was no. Then that I'm-so-smart look crossed his handsome face. He grabbed a screwdriver and started working on the cabinet's hinges.

"I would have thought of that," I said.

I wouldn't have thought of that. If I'd picked up a screwdriver, it would have been for leverage to pry the damned door off. Or a chisel and hammer to beat the lock off it. But leaving the cabinet and lock intact made so much more sense.

"Were you present when Almond's team searched in here?" I asked him.

"I was in the room, but not over here. Had my ears open. No one noticed anything out of the ordinary. It's just sand, after all."

Sixty seconds later, the left side of the cabinet door was off. Among the expected stuff — the pile of girlie mags, the florescent paint (presumably for the magic golf balls), duct tape, more duct tape, six rolls of quarters and two rolls of dimes — there was something else. Filled half way with fine sand, was a child's plastic beach bucket.

"Didn't the bucket of sand strike anyone as off when they searched in here?"

"Apparently not. Of course, lots of places use sand in their outdoor ashtrays. Probably no one would have given it a second look."

Not even Noel Almond?

Dylan stuck his hands in and began sifting through the sand.

"What the hell?" Dylan mused. We both felt it . . . the anticipation . . . like when you're a kid and plowing through the Styrofoam popcorn to find the Christmas gift hidden inside the big box. "Nothing."

"I don't get it," I said. "Why keep sand under lock and key."

I didn't have the answer.

But I knew this was the question.

Oh, and then there was another question in the room. "What the hell are you two doing?" Big Eddie Baskin asked.

"Boss!" Dylan said, reverting to his security guy persona. He pulled his hands from the sand as if he'd been caught with them in the proverbial cookie jar and wiped them on his pants.

How much had Big Eddie Baskin heard?

"I didn't expect you back so early, Boss," Dylan said. "How'd you make out playing golf at the lake? Get a hole in one?"

Golf balls pinged and bounced on the floor like angry white punctuation marks as Big Eddie threw the bag down.

"What the fuck's going on here?" He growled.

Dylan spoke quickly. "Miss Dodd here," he gestured to me as if Eddie needed direction as to which Miss Dodd he was talking about, "bet me I couldn't get into the cabinet." He smiled widely. "Guess I showed her, huh?" He turned to me again. "Pay up, lady!"

I didn't have my purse with me, but pulled a folded twenty from my pants pocket and put it in his hand. "Guess you were right, Dylan." I looked to Big Eddie, smiling to piss him off all the more.

He was thinking things over. Wondering how much I knew . . . just what I'd figured out so far by my access to the cabinet. His eyes shifted from Dylan to me, and back to Dylan again. But he wasn't jumping down Dylan's throat, so apparently he believed him.

Dylan was still grinning like a fool. "Twenty bucks!" He turned to Big Eddie. "It was only supposed to be ten, but when she found out I didn't know the combination, she doubled it! Guess I showed her," he repeated, pocketing the money, still grinning.

The guy deserved an Oscar.

If I was reading Eddie's glare correctly, it was me he wanted to tear to shreds.

He said. "You'll find no jewels in there. Don't you think you'd be better off hunting to see where your mother stashed the ring?"

"What's the sand for, Eddie?" I asked.

"Building castles."

"That ring meant the world to my mother."

"Then she shouldn't have lost it, Dodd."

"I know you took it."

"Prove it."

"Oh, I will."

He chewed on that a moment. Then he kicked me out — out of the maintenance room, out of Complex C. And I could hear the reaming out he was giving his poor, simple "security guard" even as I walked away from the building. But I wasn't worried about Dylan. He could handle Big Eddie.

The sand. I clutched tightly the handful I had in my pocket. Sand is sand? Well, I'd seen enough CSI shows to know things aren't always as they appeared.

I didn't yet know who Eddie's accomplice was, but I was getting closer to fingering him. I didn't yet know what the sand was for.

But soon enough I would.

Chapter 15

THE REST OF the day was uneventful. (Note here I say the rest of the DAY. The evening was significantly eventful, thank you very much.)

After Big Eddie kicked me out of the complex, I resumed snooping and talking to the Wildoh residents. Or rather, trying to talk to them. I was, after all, on the proverbial shit list, so it was not an easy task. When I walked into the common rec room, a wave of people cleared out around me. And, yes I carefully guarded my water bottle at all times. Just as carefully guarded my reactions and interactions.

But more than anything, it was a figuring day. I was close. Very close. But how did the sand fit in? How did Big Eddie stash the jewels so very confidently? So very thoroughly without worrying about a thing? Who the hell was his accomplice?

And the frustrating-as-hell part was that I knew the answers to these questions were all right in front of me somehow. Sticking right out there for me to grab a hold of. Red flag waving!

What the hell was I missing?

I have faith in my skills. And given enough time, I knew I could answer all these questions, figure this all out. But that was the problem. Time was the problem.

Too damn many questions.

And here's another question.

Why did everyone at the Wildoh still believe I was Dix Dodd, erotica writer? Almond could have given me up on that, but clearly he hadn't, as I soon ascertained from those I tried to converse with. No one at the Wildoh was any the wiser about my PI status.

Not saying that anyone was overly friendly to me. The only time I didn't have to wring words out of people was when I asked about Lance-a-Lot and his pool cleaning. Beth Mary piped up with "He'll be here tomorrow!", but quieted when she realized she was supposed to be ostracizing me.

Group mentality. I'd seen it before. Confronted it before. Everyone (with the notable exception of Mona Roberts) was on the 'Dodd sucks' bandwagon. T-shirts, bumper stickers, banners. Okay, no one had gone that far yet, but how far off could bumper stickers be?

Give me time. Oh, Lord, give me time.

"So have you got things figured out yet, Dix?"

Mother wasn't quizzing me. Certainly she wasn't fretting (much). She was simply asking. She didn't seem terribly worried. Why? Mountain Dew and cupcakes will do that to you I guess. It was as if Mother had relinquished worry over to me.

Kind of cool.

Yes, she'd be glad when these things were resolved. Yes, she'd be glad when the jewels were returned to their rightful owners. (Especially her diamond to herself). And yes, she'd even be glad to know where Frankie Morrell was. Though, as more and more time passed, I believed the latter was the least of her concerns.

She and Mrs. P were dressing up for a night on the town. Cotton Carson, though he couldn't attend with the two ladies himself this evening, had gotten tickets for Mother and Mrs. P to dinner theater, live band, five-course meal — the works.

That male attention was helping Mom become her old self again. Not that she *needed* the male attention, but, well, it was kind of nice. Kind of fun.

I was staying in this evening. Dinner was microwaved macaroni and cheese. No live band unless I broke out the musical spoons. As for male attention ... well, Dylan was on his way over. But we'd be white-boarding it all the way.

I had on hand enough dry-erase markers to make even the most industrious kindergarten teacher green with envy. We'd be working our asses off this night.

He'd have to sneak past Big Eddie, who would wonder what his security guard was doing there after hours. But at least I didn't have to sneak him in past my mother.

I was glad she knew. And in a dumb, giddy way I wouldn't admit to under threat of death, I kind of wanted Dylan to get there tonight before

Mother and Mrs. P left for their evening out.

Mother had confronted me with my interest in Dylan/his interest in me.

"I know things, Dix," she'd said.

I'd responded appropriately with another chin-spraying 'pfffft' (quickly becoming my trademarked move), but Katt Dodd smiled anyway.

And smiled all the more when Dylan did show up at the door before she and Mrs. Presley left.

It wasn't the coffee he bore (though that set my own heart just a-jumping). It wasn't the stack of notes he had tucked under his arm. Nor was it even the circle-a-word book he dropped off to Mrs. P just to be ... well, just to be Dylan. It was the way he looked at me. That's what put a smile on my mother's face. Okay, maybe it was also the way her tough-as-shoe-leather daughter looked at Dylan. Maybe that made her smile a bit, too.

Well, it was good to see him.

"Hello, Dylan," Mother said.

Dylan shook her offered hand.

"I never did get to thank you for Cotton Carson's attendance at court the other day. Dix tells me you arranged it. And I'm very, very grateful for that."

"My pleasure, Mrs. Dodd."

"Katt. Call me Katt. Dix has told me so much about you, I feel as if I know you already."

For the record, I'd not told my mother 'so much' about Dylan already. She was one to tease.

"Did Dix tell you how good looking he was, Katt?" Mrs. P asked.

"Why, she did, Jane. And she was right."

"Did she mention tall? Handsome?"

"Oh, yes."

Dylan wasn't blushing. But he was grinning ear to ear.

Me? Well, I didn't blush but ...

"How come your cheeks are turning red, Dix?" Mrs. P asked.

"Just hot in here, Mrs. Presley," I answered.

"Hormones," she said. "Gotta watch out for those hormones."

Did I mention I couldn't wait for Mother and Mrs. P to get out the door?

Dylan and I did get down to work as soon as they left. Well, once I had coffee in hand and cupcakes (Mother made more, bless her heart) passed out. Now, with caffeine and sugar sufficiently perking our systems, we were ready.

We had to crack this thing wide open before the family jewels ended up in a pawn shop somewhere. Yes, the police were surveying those dens of iniquity carefully, not just for mom's ring but for the other missing items. Still, the longer that diamond was missing, the slimmer the chances of getting it back.

I swallowed down a bite of cupcake remembering my promise. Mom had such faith in me. I'd find that ring if it took forever.

So Dylan and I brainstormed. We charted. We looked at this from every angle until my head pounded. But be damned if I could figure out just how Big Eddie was dumping the stuff. Damned if we could figure out who his accomplice was.

Around ten, Dylan and I took a break. Not a wine break. And we sure as hell didn't need another coffee break. The cupcakes were gone. But we just had to break to clear our heads a bit.

While we'd been working, Dylan had started the evening sitting across from me. Then he'd moved beside me on the pulled out sofa bed, and then well … closer beside me.

Planned? Hell no. We'd just been that into what we were doing.

But as we took our much-needed break, it was then that I realized how close I actually was to Dylan Foreman. And damned if I didn't see it in his eyes, he was realizing it, too.

"Dix, about the other night …"

He didn't have to explain which night. It was there in those gorgeous liquid brown eyes of his. As we sat there on the very same sofa bed, close, alone, it was all coming back to the both of us.

It happens sometimes when the stakes are high, and you're with someone you've been completely open with. Scarily open.

Briefly I wondered if he was trying to hedge his way out of the situation. Make excuses why it shouldn't have happened, and why it would never happen again. This wasn't just me letting him off the hook. This was me jumping the hell off it. If Dylan was looking for a way out, then a way out I would give him.

"Really Dylan, you don't have to say anything."

So he didn't.

He didn't say one word as he pulled me into his arms.

Wordlessly — oh, Lord, *breathlessly* — I went.

Just like that, we were prone again, body to body in the sagging center of my mother's sofa bed.

His kiss was exquisite. Slow and unhurried, lush and luxuriously sensual, like that time months ago when he'd kissed me for the first time. He kissed me like only a man who truly enjoys kissing can kiss a woman. He kissed me like every woman dreams about being kissed, slow and thorough and sweetly arousing. And I tried to be easy and unhurried, too. To enjoy the slow build. I really did. For all of about fifteen seconds. Because, God help me, I was sooooo far beyond needing a slow build. My poor, sex-deprived hormones were clamoring to get on to the main event.

Unable to do anything else, I answered his sensual invitation with ferocious sexual urgency. To my undying gratitude — which I expressed with an approving moan — he came back at me with a rough and ragged passion that matched my own. His mouth was suddenly hard on mine, demanding that I accept the invasion of his tongue. And oh, God, *did I!* I accepted the thrust of his tongue as avidly as my body was aching to accept another invasion. Meanwhile — *yes!* — his hands swept over my body with unmistakable carnal purpose. Like he *owned* it. Like it was his to control.

With no warning, he rolled me under him (*God, yes!*), and I almost came. And this despite the fact that neither of us had shed a single article of clothing. The feel of his weight pressing me into the mattress, the heavy pounding of his heart against mine …

Then he raised himself on his arms, causing his lower body to press into mine, at the juncture of my parted thighs. And no way was that a flashlight I was feeling. I moaned and arched against him.

Dylan groaned. "It's the uniform, isn't it, Dix?" His words were teasing, but his voice was satisfyingly hoarse, the gaze that roamed my face gratifyingly intense. "Go on, admit it. The security guard getup makes you hot, doesn't it?"

Giddy, I laughed. "Oh, yeah, baby, that's it. The uniform. As far as I'm concerned, you can be Dylan 'heavy on the har' Hardy forever."

He surged against me in a thrust that all but had my eyes rolling up into my head. Inside, my hormones broke into a praise-Jesus-Dix-is-gonna-get-laid-RIGHT-NOW hallelujah chorus.

"Make that heavy on the *'hard'*," he said.

At his words, something broke loose in my brain, started rolling and tumbling in there.

Nooooooo! my hormones screamed. *Stay with it. Stay right damned here! Get us laid, damn it!*

My brain wouldn't listen.

Heavy on the hard. Heavy on the hard. Dylan's words kept echoing in my head. I strained to catch the significance. *Heavy on the hard . . .*

He bent to press his mouth to my neck, skimmed up my throat to my chin, my temple, my forehead, but I was all but oblivious. The tumblers in my head kept rolling, rolling . . . Then stopped as everything clicked home.

My arms tightened around Dylan reflexively, and I cried out. "Omigod, omigod, omigod, omigod, omigod!"

Dylan froze for a second, then groaned and lifted his head to look at me. "What are the chances I just discovered a new G-spot, and that string of *omigods* was not about the case?"

"I know what happened! I know who did it! I know who the accomplice is. And oh, shit, I know where Mother's diamond is!"

He rested his forehead on mine and exhaled. "Of course you do."

His frustration was palpable. Poor guy. He might have reached for me first, but I was the one who'd fired the starter pistol. I was the one who shot us from zero to sixty in ten seconds, and here I was calling a screeching halt to our lovemaking. "Oh, Dylan, I'm sorry . . ."

"Nothing to be sorry about." His breath fanned my forehead. "Just give me a second."

True to his word, he collected himself quickly. With a sigh, he rolled off me.

I leapt out of bed. "It was the damned hormones!"

"I have no idea what you mean by that, but I presume you're going to explain." Dylan said, adjusting himself in his jeans. "So, what did I miss?"

"Oh, it's not what you missed. It's what *I* missed. It's been out there all along. And I . . . I just couldn't see it." I looked at him sheepishly. "Hormones."

His brow furrowed. "If this is one of those female things that I really don't want to know about . . ."

I smiled. This would take some explaining to Dylan. And explain I would. Leisurely. We had time now. Not all the time in the world, but more than enough.

I knew what to do.

And oh, the pleasure I would have doing it!

Chapter 16

DYLAN WAS JUST leaving when Mother and Mrs. P rolled in at two in the morning. Not intoxicated, but both ladies had had a wonderful time. So Dylan turned himself around and sat back down for a little bit while we explained to Mother and Mrs. P all we had surmised. Mother was disappointed as I told her what I'd deduced. She conceded that it made strange but perfect sense, but I caught the look of deep, deep disappointment in her eyes.

"You going to be okay?" I asked.

Of course she would. She was a woman, after all.

Dylan and I talked it over and agreed we should keep the Dylan Hardy persona a few more hours, if for no other reason than to keep Big Eddie feeling comfortable.

Big Eddie? Well, Big Eddie was going down (and not in the good way). The conclusions I'd reached last night only solidified his guilt.

We decided to break the case at Mona's party. I know, I know, not nice to disrupt her birthday celebration. But it was when everyone in all three complexes would be gathered together. Hell, even Deputy Almond had promised a spitting Beth Mary that he would show up for a piece of cake. But I think Noel was showing up for a different reason. No, not for any interest in me. But I think the guy knew I was getting closer. What other explanation could there be for his not blowing my cover?

We were the last to arrive, but it was not a fashion statement kind of thing. And not just because I liked to show off. (Though I dearly love to show off.) It was strategic. By the time we arrived, everyone else was already there. The whole gang. Yes, including Almond and a few of his fellow deputies. Which raised some eyebrows, mine included. Why had he brought his posse? What did Almond know? Almond's presence didn't surprise me. He was, after all, a familiar figure at the Wildoh. But not with backup.

When Mother, Mrs. P and I walked into the rec room, we got a cool reception, to no one's surprise.

Well, strictly speaking, we walked *through* the rec room to assemble on the outdoor patio. Apparently there had been some sort of kitchen accident. Burned buns of some kind. Doors stood open airing the place out while the smell of charred food hung heavy like a blanket in the air. We did the hand waving through the air as we walked through the smoky room.

Once again the only exception to the concerted shunning of Mother and company was Mona. But even she seemed off today. We weren't greeted with her usual arm-waving enthusiasm, and her habitually happy expression was nowhere to be seen.

How much did Mona know already?

We arrived before the cake was cut. Before either cake was cut. Mona being Mona had made a diabetic cake for Big Eddie. These cakes, various drinks and a couple of fruit trays sat on a table surrounded by every single Wildoh resident. Even Dylan was sitting when I arrived. He quickly jumped up, gave his chair to Mrs. P and in fifteen seconds had secured another one for my mother from inside.

I'd stand. He'd stand.

Mona soon enlightened us as to why the doom and gloom at her own birthday celebration. She cleared her throat. In retrospect, I think that was more to get hold of her emotions than to herald the beginning of her speech. Her eyes welled with tears held back. I hated knowing they'd probably soon be falling, thanks to what we'd be disclosing.

"You've all been such good friends to me," Mona said. She looked at my mother. "You more than anyone, Katt. My years here at the Wildoh have been some of the best in my life. After my husband died, and my daughter moved away to start a family of her own . . . I . . . I never thought I'd find a place for me again. Not one where I could truly belong. But I did. I found it here at the Wildoh with all of you. Beth Mary, Roger, even you Wiggie. Harriet. Of course with you too, Big Eddie. And that is why it pains — desperately pains me — to tell you all that I'm leaving."

Okay, I had not seen this coming. Not at all. Apparently, I wasn't alone in the shock as the collective gasp of dismay reverberated around the room. Well, almost 'collective'. While some clutched hands to their

Family Jewels

157

chests and others held fingers to their mouths, one resident seemed singularly unsurprised. Tish McQueen sat in her lawn chair sipping her drink, dangling one finely shod leg over the other.

Mona continued, "I've decided to sell out. Tish has decided to buy in. Thank God for Tish. I'm very glad of that. The market's down, as everyone knows, but Tish … Tish has agreed to take my condo off my hands."

I just bet Tish had agreed to take it off Mona's hands. No doubt for a song. In addition to being a stripper of extraordinary reputation, Tish was a shrewd business woman. There was no question in my mind that she had beaten poor Mona down in price over the past weeks, whilst convincing the poor woman that she was her savior. And all the while depleting Mona's resources by sponging off her while she 'made up her mind', putting Mona in an even more desperate bind.

"Oh Mona," Mother said, genuine tears filling her eyes. "Where will you go?"

"Well, I'm not really sure on that …," Mona answered.

"Maybe you could stay with Tish?" Dylan suggested. I could tell this was eating at him too.

Tish didn't miss a beat. "Oh, no. I haven't got the room."

Mona slapped on a smile that wouldn't fake out a toddler. "I'm sure everything will be all right. Tish's lawyer is drawing up the papers today, and I'll be signing the condo over to Tish tomorrow. By the end of the month, I'll be gone."

"Are you going too, Big Eddie?" I asked innocently.

Eddie turned beet red. "No. Of course not."

"Really?" Dylan scratched his head. He knotted his forehead. "When I was dusting around your place the other day, I saw all those suitcases out, half packed and stuff. So I thought you must be moving too."

"No, kid," Big Eddie said. "You're mistaken. Now why don't you just shut up and —"

"Oh, then you must be just taking a trip, eh, Big Eddie? I saw your passport out on the dinette table."

"Just … doing some spring cleaning. Now shut the hell up, kid."

As if on cue, Lance-a-Lot truck's rumbled into the yard. The musical horn trumpeted his arrival. And despite the action going on right before the crowd at the Wildoh, more than a few people turned his way. Including me.

Speedos? *Check.*

Mesh ball-gathering bag dangling down? *Yep.*

Grin? *Check.*

Swagger? *Oh yeah.*

Oh, yes, the boy arched his back, and strutted his stuff before he dived into the lake to do his ball gathering work. Even Noel Almond sat up a little bit straighter as Lance dove under the water's surface.

Right on cue, Big Eddie said, "Now, what's that boy got that I haven't got?"

"Nothing, Big Eddie," I said. "At least, not yet."

That sent a few eyebrows soaring. Everyone looked to me to see what I'd say next.

"Let them have it, Dix," my mother said.

She smiled at me, and I had to smile back. "Damn right, Mother."

Just like the other day, all eyes were on me. But unlike the other day, this time I had it *all* figured out. I hoped.

"Well, Big Eddie," I said. "I'm surprised to hear that you're not taking a trip."

"Why's that?" he asked cautiously.

I huffed. "A man who works as hard as you do — day in and day out. Taking charge. Making sure all runs smoothly. Why, even those golf lessons of yours must be exhausting. I just thought you'd probably be ready for a vacation. Some downtime."

"I'm good, Dodd. Thanks for your concern."

I threw my head back and laughed. Not because it was that funny but because I wanted to sound bitchy. "Concern? My only concern as of late, Eddie, is you getting away before I could prove my mother's innocence and your guilt. Before I could figure out who your accomplice was. But I don't have that concern anymore. I'm good."

There were murmurs of "Oh shit", "Here we go again", and even a "What's that girl smoking?" from the crowd. I really couldn't hold it against them. After all, we'd been here before with the big — and unfortunately anticlimactic — reveal. Who could blame them? But this time, it would be different.

My eyes raked the crowd. "Most of you believe me to be Dix Dodd, erotica writer, but I'm not. That's just my cover. I asked Mother to tell you that so I could join you unawares."

"Our under-wares?" Beth Mary asked, looking bewildered.

"No, she said *unawares,*" someone said.

"I wear boxers," Roger volunteered.

Veronica touched his arm. "As long as the waistband holds, I think you're okay."

"No," I said. "*Unawares.* As in you didn't know my real occupation. In reality . . ." I paused dramatically, "I'm Dix Dodd, private detective." *Da-da-da-daaaaaaaahhhhhhh!*

Okay, no one exclaimed shock or surprise, but they had to have *felt* some.

Tough audience.

I cleared my throat. "I got a fax from Deputy Almond a few days ago advising that my mother was in trouble. Advising that she was a suspect in these thefts, as well as in the disappearance of Frankie Morell. In order to keep everyone off their guard while I investigated, I posed as an erotica writer."

"*Poorly.*" Tish sniffed. "I knew all along you couldn't write that stuff."

Okay, I should have let that go.

Of course, I couldn't.

"Really?" I smiled sweetly at Tish while my mind raced. I had to make this good. "I guess I didn't tell you the right story. Maybe I should have told the one about the woman who has been lusting after the handsome young handyman . . . I mean gardener, who is tall and dark and has the most amazing hands. And then one night, the gardener lets himself into her house when she's there all alone, and the two of them pretend he's a complete stranger who has invaded her house and she's totally at his mercy and has to do everything he wants. *Everything.* No matter how depraved. Except everything he wants is everything she's been fantasizing about. And then he pushes her up against a wall and makes her watch in the mirror as he —"

Dylan coughed. "Um, Dix . . ."

I blinked, coming back to reality. Tish stood there, her mouth hanging open. Actually, everyone's mouth was pretty much hanging open. Roger adjusted his boxers.

"Sorry. Got a little off track there for a moment, didn't I?" I began pacing as I talked so the crowd would have to visually follow me. "Anyway, getting back to the mystery, I was going to say that it took me awhile to figure things out. Much longer than it should have. And do you know why it took me so long?"

"You're stupid?" Tish suggested.

"You're drunk!" Beth Mary clapped her hands as she answered.

"No, that's not it," Mrs. P answered. "It was the hormones. That's what got in the way wasn't it, Dix? Just like I said all along."

"You were right, Mrs. Presley." I smiled at her. "Yeah, it *was* the hormones getting in the way, fogging my good judgment."

Ever so pleased, Mrs. P leaned back further on her chair.

Everyone looked lost at this point, except for Mother, Dylan and Mrs. P. But some looked less lost than others. Noel Almond was listening a little more intently.

"I turn you on that much, Dix?" Big Eddie laughed, but it was nervous laughter. "Got you all flustered into thinking I was the crook? Well, wouldn't be the first time I'd turned a lady's head. Ha, ha."

"Nothing turned on here, Eddie," I assured him. I thought of saying my stomach was turning, but that would be just plain mean. "Except for my stomach turning a little." Sometimes, I'm just plain mean. "But my point is I'm still absolutely certain you're the thief. More so now than ever. The powder on your hands the one day, the sticky stuff on them the next. The little charm that could so easily be used as a lock pick. That was brilliant, by the way, picking the locks. Anyone investigating would ask, 'Why would anyone pick a lock if they have the keys?' That would effectively dismiss you as a suspect. Oh, and then there is the matter of my mother's stolen watch."

"I . . . I told you, Dix," Mona ventured. "Eddie was with me the night Katt's watch went missing."

"I know you did, Mona. You provided him with the perfect alibi. But it wasn't Eddie who took the watch. It was —"

Eddie sighed loudly. "Look Dodd, we've been over all that." He sat back a little easier. "I thought you had something new to tell us. Same old same old. You want Deputy Almond and his boys to search the place again? Is that what you want?" He looked at Almond, looking for the Deputy to return his rolled-eyed look. Almond didn't. Big Eddie shifted his attention back to me. "You didn't find anything before, but go ahead and look again if you want. You won't find anything here. Not on me. I can guarantee you that."

"Not even a pocket full of sand, Eddie?"

"Sand?" he asked.

"Sand?" Almond said. He was all ears now. "What about the sand, Dix?"

I saw that I was somewhat losing the crowd, not the least reason being that Lance-a-Lot was strutting his stuff out of the water, swaying those hips, slicking his hair back. Sun glinted off the bag of white balls he carried and glinted off his sun-kissed chest. Did I mention today's

Speedos were yellow? Sun was glinting down there too.

"Sand is used to make mortar, Eddie," I said. "A sealing agent. Sand, lime, water makes mortar. The powder on your hands, that was lime. I saw you applying it to the garden on the day you hired Dylan. Sand — there was a bucket of it in the supply room locker, as well as grains of it in Mother's safe. Water? Easy enough to come by."

"That makes no sense, Dix," Eddie sputtered. "If I wanted a sealant, I would have just bought a sealant."

"Yeah," I said. "But you know if you had bought a sealant, then we'd be looking for a sealant. Just like if you'd used keys for the break-ins we'd be looking for someone with keys. You're not that bright Eddie; but you're not that stupid. You covered your tracks pretty damn well."

"So, what are you saying, Dix?" he asked. "You think I've been stealing the jewels and sealing them into the walls or something. Hiding them in the brickwork?"

"My officers are thorough," Almond said. "If there had been freshly sealed or modified areas, they'd have found them. They looked." His demeanor had changed. I wasn't the only one to notice. Big Eddie noticeably squirmed under Almond's steely gaze.

"Ah, but they weren't looking in the right place, were they?"

And it was here Big Eddie's eyes shifted. Right to where I knew they would. For Lance-a-Lot was just about to get into his truck.

"Hey, Lance!" I cried, racing the short distance from the patio to the parking lot.

He turned at my voice, broad show-time smile still plastered on his face. The smile dropped, however, when he saw me bearing down on him as fast as my Sketchers would carry me. And though he didn't scream out loud, I knew a shriek was building as I skidded to a stop, pulled out the waistband of his Speedos, dove my hand in and grabbed his crotch.

And pulled his penis off.

His *fake* penis.

Shrieking, Lance fell to the ground. But I was so delighted to have gotten the prize, I waved it around triumphantly.

"Oh, Dear God," Wiggie shouted. "Not him, too! Not again!"

Beth Mary screamed through the chorus of exclamations:

"What have you done?"

"Holy shit!"

"Oh, sweet Jesus!"

Holding the hollow phallus aloft, I walked back toward the group on the patio. I noticed Deputy Almond had taken up position very close to Big Eddie, and one of his boys was edging toward Lance-a-Lot's vehicle.

"Keep back!" Roger shouted at my approach. "For the love of God, keep away from me!"

I stopped my dick-waving advance.

"What?" I shouted. "It's a fake!" Belatedly, I realized I might have instilled post-traumatic stress disorder in several, if not all, of the men present. "A *fake*," I repeated. "A trick dick! "

"No magic there," Mother interjected.

"But it's more than cosmetic," I added. "It's how Big Eddie has been smuggling the jewels out of the Wildoh. With Lance the pool boy — the pool boy who left a little piece of water plant on the floor when he broke into my mother's apartment to take her watch."

"You said we'd not get caught, Uncle Eddie! You said we'd —"

"Shut up, kid," Big Eddie said, sitting down. "Just shut up now."

Lance shut up now. Sat down. Crossed his legs so easily.

I turned the phallus upside down and two bright orange golf balls rolled out into the palm of my hand. "Dylan? Want to do the honors?"

"Got it, Dix." Handyman Dylan produced a drill from the tool box he'd brought along. A moment later, the first golf ball was opened.

"My granddaughter's broach!" Roger exclaimed.

The second golf ball, of course, contained Mother's diamond.

"I believe this belongs to you, Mother," I said, handing over the Dodd family diamond.

"I knew you'd solve this crime, Dix," Mother said, happily. Proudly. "Really I did."

"Once those hormones got out of the way." Mrs. P winked.

"Yeah, so did I." Deputy Almond had already slapped the cuffs on Big Eddie and one of his deputies was doing the same to a very shriveled up (in every way imaginable) Lance.

I did a double take as Almond's words registered. "*You* were sure *I'd* solve it? All of five minutes ago, maybe."

"No, right from the start. From the time I faxed you." Almond slanted me a look. "Your reputation precedes you, Miss Dodd. My cousin in Marport City spoke of you."

The hackles on the back of my neck rose. "And who would that be?"

"Detective Head of the Marport City PD."

Oh dear God. Richard Head (aka Dickhead)! Detective Head and I were far from good buddies. Arch enemies is more like it. I could only imagine what he'd told Almond. "Whatever he said about me, Deputy, I'd take it with a grain of salt. A very big one."

"He said you were a severe pain in the ass."

"Okay, maybe it wasn't *all* lies."

"And that you were one hell of a good PI. He said if anyone could crack this open, it would be you, especially if your mother's freedom was on the line. Oh, and he said he'd kill me if I told you he said you were a good PI."

In my mind, I was already composing the email. *Dear Dickhead, I didn't know you cared. Your recommendation means so much to me. NOT. Curl up and die. Hugs and kisses, Your friend, Dix.*

Then it struck me — *that's* why Almond had arrested my mother! That's why he was bent on painting her as the guilty party despite the flimsiness of the evidence. That's why he'd been antagonizing me. To give me the incentive he figured I needed to crack the case. The bastard! I felt my blood pressure rising. To think I'd been feeling kind of bad about that restaurant bill!

"I've known for weeks that Eddie Baskin was committing the thefts. I just couldn't figure out where the goods were going," Almond said. "I needed someone on the inside. Someone so on the inside she didn't even know I'd put her there. Someone with the smarts, and more importantly, the motivation, to figure this out."

"And you knew if you rode my mother hard enough, I'd be damned motivated. Not to mention the way you baited me along the way, pissing me off. All to spur me into action."

"Guilty as charged." He turned away at the sound of the approaching sirens and was smiling when he turned back around. "Sorry about all that, Dixieland," he said, using one of Dickhead's few G-rated ... um, nicknames ... for me. He turned to Eddie Baskin, who wasn't looking so very big, and Lance a ... Little. "You have the right to remain silent. Anything you say ..."

The arms that wrapped around me were my mother's. "I knew you'd save me, Dix."

Mona came to stand beside us as we watched Big Eddie and Lance being placed in the police car.

Big Eddie looked back at Mona. "I've always loved you, Mona!" he shouted. "Ever since the day we met. Will you wait for me, sweetheart?"

Her eyes were full of tears. She put a hand to her chest, and tried her best to swallow down the lump in her throat. And Mona Roberts gave

Big Eddie the only answer a woman like Mona could give. "God, no!"

"What about you, Katt? Were you waiting for me?"

The voice came from within the rec room, just inside the door. Deep. Gravelly. Croaky as if the owner of it were parched. And everyone went inside to see the wet, muddy, worse-for-wear Frankie Morrell dripping water on the carpet.

Everyone but Mother, that is. She was hightailing it across the grounds of the Wildoh, making a disappearing act of her very own.

Chapter 17

THE GALS OF the Goosebump Inn all gathered around when the police came to check on Lance's rental. It was all there. All of it, even Harriet's missing ring. And more.

Apparently, Big Eddie had been working and waiting for years, spying on his fellow Wildoh residents, gathering information on who owned what. Building confidences. Planning who to steal from, and who to set up. Frankie's disappearance was just a convenience to him. When he had the plan ready, he called his nephew, Lance (oh poor boy; not aptly named) and put the plan into place. And it would have worked, had it not been for . . . me. A fact I told everyone who'd listen, and even some who wouldn't. (Harriet Appleton held her hands over her ears in a very childish way.)

Later in the day, Mother had a talk with Frankie. It wasn't that she'd run away from him back at the rec room. She'd run away from the moment. "Too much, Dix," she explained. "Too much, too soon." Well, it wasn't much of a talk in that the communication was pretty much one way. Mother's way. All the way.

"We're through, Frankie Morrell."

Frankie pleaded his case. He'd been lost. Disoriented. Wandering around in the swamp for days. Oh my word, he could hardly remember a thing! Frog amnesia, mother assured him. Frankie swore that had to be the case.

Deputy Almond, however, was putting his money on a different excuse for Frankie's amnesia. Apparently an over-zealous dominatrix (aptly titled the Dark Intruder) had taken a session a little too far with a few select clientele. One of her leather-clad clients had gotten away and called the police. Whereupon the old dom had figured it was game over and released the remaining gentlemen before the police raid.

That case was still open, with numerous charges pending against the Dark Intruder (and surprisingly no more men coming to the fore to testify against her). Almond was anxious to talk to Frankie. Anxious to get him downtown to ask a few questions and get a few answers. Though I didn't know how anxious Frankie would be to talk about these alleged dungeon days.

Deputy Almond told me this discreetly. Not within range of the prying ears of the Wildoh. He saved Mother that humiliation at least.

But I hated to have to tell these things about Frankie to Mother.

Turns out I didn't have to. She was through with Frankie. Completely. Eternally. No, it wasn't Cotton Carson. Nor really even Frankie's disappearance (which was, after all, her frog-related doing). In fact this breakup had been a long time coming. That's what they'd been fighting about before Frankie had even disappeared. That's what the watch had been about. Not only did Frankie give her that expensive piece of jewelry to try to win her back, he'd had it engraved. That's why mother had been so desperate to get it back. Not because of the expense of the gift, or soft sentiment toward the giver, but because of what Frankie had had engraved:

Katt Dodd, marry me?

It was a personal thing. A privacy thing. And now, a done thing.

"Are you going to call Cotton, Mom?" I asked her.

She smiled. "Maybe. Probably. He's nice enough."

"I think he'll be your knight in shining armor," Mrs. Presley suggested.

Katt Dodd smiled at her. Smiled at Dylan and me standing there in her living room. "Oh, I don't need a knight in shining armor, Jane. I've got daughters."

"I told you before, Katt," Mona said. "I do not take charity."

"Oh for Pete sake, Mona. How can it be charity? It's your birthday. With everything going on, I didn't get a chance to go out and buy you a present. The least you can do is let me take you out for a night on the town."

Mrs. P was finally getting her wish. We — me, Dylan, Mom, Mrs. Presley — were all bingo bound. It was our last night in Florida. Our flights were booked for tomorrow — one way to Marport City. The BMW would stay with Mom. Least I could do. No, not quite. The least I could do was insist — finally insist — that my mother sell me the condo. I'd been there too long free of charge. She needed the funds. With business the way it was, I could easily now get the mortgage. Sure it would mean giving up some things — such as the new fancy-schmancy office in favor of going back to the old office (I heard the plastic aloe vera still rested in peace on the window sill), but that was fine.

Dylan had rented a Lexus to drive us around in style. I'd made reservations at the Maison Petite Colombe. And after dinner, we'd be playing at the biggest bingo hall in Florida. High-dollar bingo around the clock, satellite hookups to link the biggest games across the state, big screen TVs to display the numbers on, the whole shebang.

It didn't take a hell of a lot of arm twisting to convince Mona to join us. Tish was having some decorators over and Mona didn't really want to be there for that. (The papers weren't even signed yet, and Tish was going in for the kill.) Plus despite Mona's stiff upper lip, finding out about Big Eddie's betrayal had to hurt. Mother had offered her a place to stay as long as she needed, but with a despair that frightened me, Mona refused.

But she would come out with us this night.

Mother was worried, too. I could tell. But it was an edged worry as we got ready. One that I could not place. She was more thoughtful than usual. Not lost in thought so much as working within thought. We dressed — dolled ourselves up for the evening. Mother wore the new watch I gave her. And lastly she put on the family jewel. The diamond ring Peter Dodd had given her.

"I'm worried about Mona, Mother," I said. "Where will she go?" Dylan had done some checking, or rather some *more* checking on Mona Roberts. The granddaughter was well again. Cancer in remission. Getting stronger every day, thanks to Mona covering the hospital bills, which had depleted her own savings. But financially, Mona's daughter was barely scraping by. There was not enough for the two of them, and Mona didn't want to add to their burden.

Of course, Mom looked like a million bucks. Young. Full of life.

Mona came over around six, and despite the situation in her life, looked almost as wonderful as Mom did. She smiled best she could.

The doorbell rang shortly after her arrival.

"That'll be Dylan," Mrs. P said.

I knew it was. I caught myself then. The little tummy sucking anticipation, the smile that threatened to play. I knew it wasn't a date. Even as I walked to the door, and swung it wide, I knew it wasn't a date.

Oh shit.

It was a *date*.

Dylan looked like a million bucks, too, in his faded jeans, print shirt and navy Hugo Boss jacket. Casual but damned elegant. His hair was freshly washed and tamed, and his skin glowed. I'd bet the Manolo Blahnik mules (Mother's) on my feet that he'd been to a barber for an old-fashioned straight-razor shave. He looked, and smelled, good enough to eat.

Oh, and he was carrying flowers. Lots of them. And it was with school-boy charm that he pinned a corsage on Mona, Mrs. P and my mother. The ladies all giggled as they walked out to the car. The big bouquet of red roses could only be for me.

I smiled as Dylan handed them over.

"Thank you, Dylan." I tipped onto my toes to kiss his cheek.

He smiled down at me. "What happened here … between us …" He glanced to the fold out couch where so recently we'd teased and tantalized each other. Where we'd gotten so close.

My heart lurched. Sent up that big red flag again. Because Dix Dodd didn't do close. End of story. But somehow my mantra wasn't doing for me what it was supposed to do.

"Don't worry, Dylan," I said. "What happens in Florida stays in Florida."

Dylan sighed, "I wasn't worried, Dix. But we can't just ignore what happened."

"Oh my, look at the time," I said, ignoring him.

I expected at least a huff of frustration. But instead Dylan grinned. Just a bit a first, then widely.

"This isn't over, Dix Dodd," he said, pulling me into his arms. "Not by a long shot."

He kissed me again. Long. Hard. Masterfully. Just like the handyman … er, gardener … in my fantasy would have done.

I felt myself slipping. *Oh shit!* … Dix Dodd was kinda, sorta, almost doing … closer.

And, oh, Lord, it still scared the hell out of me. Enough to pull away with a shaky laugh. "Come on, let's go. They gals are waiting for us."

We had the same waiter at the restaurant. Actually, we had the same table. And whoa, big surprise — Deputy Noel Almond was sitting at it. He rose when we marched in.

"Hey, Deputy," Mrs. P called. "Give me a seven-letter word for —"

"Apology," he offered, cutting her off.

Mom looked at him. "That'll almost do."

Almond smiled. "Tell you what. I'll make that apology … and I'll also pick up the tab for the meal."

"You haven't seen how much Dix can eat," Mrs. Presley offered, helpfully. "Like a horse. She just never stops."

Gee, thanks, Mrs. P.

"Oh, I think I can manage," Almond said. He looked directly at me. "We found everything, Dix. Thanks to you. All the items that were reported missing — and a few that hadn't — were found in Lance's room at the Goosebump. And you were right about the banking angle, too. It'll take a few weeks to straighten everything out, but thanks to you, Eddie Baskin won't be bilking anyone out of their life savings."

"How'd you figure that out, Dix?" Mona asked.

I shrugged, the picture of modesty.

Okay, I preened.

"From what Mom told me, I knew he helped a lot of people with their banking and financial affairs. Which got me thinking … why stop at stealing jewelry from residents when he could probably talk them into granting him signing authority on their accounts and totally clean them out? People trusted him enough. Then I figured it out — the jewelry thefts were just a ruse, a way to make everyone suspicious of everyone else at the Wildoh. That way, he looked like a hero when he rode in to help 'protect' their assets."

Almond hung his head. "I shoulda figured that myself."

I could have told Almond to take it easy on himself. He wasn't privy to the same information I'd had, specifically, the fruits of Dylan's less-than-legal search. He didn't know Eddie Baskin was the anxious owner of a first-class ticket to a country that would welcome and shelter an embezzling weasel. His thought processes weren't guided by the knowledge that there necessarily had to be some higher stakes hijinks going on than mere jewelry theft.

Yes, I could have let him off the hook. But I didn't. He'd been a prick to manipulate me.

As it happened, he let himself off the hook.

"Yeah, I shoulda seen it coming, maybe," he said. "But give Big Eddie credit. He's smarter than he looks. By infecting everyone with paranoia, he pretty much guaranteed folks wouldn't talk to one another about money matters. Of course, we'll also do a forensic audit of the Wildoh's books. It seems the owners trusted him nearly as much as the residents did."

His warm gaze found mine and I relented. I think the guy really was sorry. And well, he *was* paying the bill ...

"Have a seat, Deputy," Mother said.

Almond and Dylan's hands both shot to pull out the chair for me. If it had been yanked out any further it would have been placed at the next table. The men looked at each other, eyes locking. And it was Noel's hand that came off the chair. Dylan waited as I sat (and then I had to do that scooting thumping into the table thing that drives me nuts) while Almond attended to the older ladies.

"So you're picking up the tab, eh, Deputy?" Mrs. P affirmed as she looked for the priciest item on the menu.

"Of course, Mrs. Presley. Everything's good here, and fairly reasonable."

"Did you get your bill yet from when you took Dix out?" Mother asked.

Since Noel's head didn't shoot off his shoulders, it was a pretty safe bet he hadn't. He just sat there looking a little confused.

"Oh, I'm sorry," Mother said, when she realized Noel hadn't yet gotten my pumped-up dinner bill. "How rude of me." And in the very next breath she said. "I'll have the lobster. Oh, and it's such a special night, we must have champagne. Maybe a nice blanc de noir? Ah, here's a good one ..."

Noel said nothing. Just kept smiling. And smiling. We could run this night into a small fortune for him. I knew that was what he was thinking.

Okay, the guy had been a jerk. And I am honestly and truly the last female on earth to forgive jerks. These chips-on-shoulder things? Yes, they too are underrated. But he was really trying now. Really trying to be the good guy. The nice guy. He'd been an ass. But didn't everyone deserve a second chance? He'd offered to pay for this little dinner by way of apology. Did we really need to hike the bill up as high as we possibly could?

"I'll have the lobster too," I told the waiter. "And oh, I'm so thirsty. Better make that two bottles of champagne for the table. And it's Mona's birthday," I pointed to the menu-scouring woman across the table from me. "Can you have your chef improvise a birthday cake? Some of that excellent cheesecake I sampled the other night would do nicely."

Mona popped her head up from the menu. "I don't know what to order. It all looks so good."

"Try the lobster," I suggested, grinning at Noel Almond, who was just then ordering soup.

It was a lovely meal. And the cheesecake was the single most decadent thing I've ever had in my mouth (I know what you're thinking — we
won't go there. And I said 'single'.)

Yes, it was a very pleasant meal indeed. But then Dylan stood.

Mrs. P and I looked at each other for a panicked moment.

Surely he wouldn't.

Dylan cleared his throat. He *tinked* the side of his wine glass with
his fork, drawing all attention to himself. (Okay, the six-foot-four frame
combined with the handsome-as-hell looks did not hurt. Let's just say
he drew *more* attention to himself.)

He turned to Mona.

Oh no oh no oh no oh no

"Say, Dylan," Mrs. P said into the moment. "What do you say we
wrap this night up and head out to bingo? If you'll just go warm up the
car — "

It was a try, bless her heart, but Dylan was not to be dissuaded.

"Mona," he said. "I don't have a gift for you. The least I can do for
you on this special night is sing Happy Birthday to you."

I closed my eyes and braced myself. Not with my hands on the
table, not my feet on the floor, but kind of with my head cocked to the
side while every muscle in my body tensed. Every hair stood on end.

Oh Jesus it was bad. Every frigging 'yo-ooo' was a like a pin sticking
into my ears. Every off key syllable he belted out made me cringe all
the harder.

And God help him, Dylan had no idea.

None whatsoever.

I opened my eyes on the last *yo-ooo*, only to witness half the staff,
customers and two seeing-eye dogs beneath the corner table (they'd
not been beneath it when he'd started singing) cringing just as I had.

Mother's eyes were wide and shocked. Noel Almond looked as
if he were considering whether an arrest was in order. Mona's mouth
dropped open in what could only be described as ... well, horror. A
waiter dropped a silver serving tray on to the floor — and just left it there.
Somewhere I heard the click of a cell phone closing (damn, I hoped it
wasn't a camera phone).

And nobody moved.

Not a muscle.

Dylan leaned in toward me. "Look, Dix," he said. "They're speechless."

"They are that," I said with a shaky voice.

Slowly, normal restaurant sounds returned as people got over their shock *(how could a man who looks so damned* good *sound so damned* bad?*)* and resumed eating their meals.

"Does he have a clue?" It was Noel Almond whispering in my ear. "Does that young fellow have any idea how bad he is?"

Young fellow?

It was the way Noel said it. Not in a derogatory way, necessarily, but pointed. And whilst he was settling his hand on my knee under the table.

Yeah, that surprised me. Not Noel's question; hell, anyone who's ever heard Dylan sing wonders the same thing. And certainly not the hand on my knee. No, the surprise was how little I felt as Noel Almond squeezed.

Also a surprise was the strong inclination I felt to pull towards Dylan. I shifted away from Noel's hand.

"Ready to go everyone?" Mrs. P was getting anxious. Bingo was a calling.

"Would you like this bill added to the previous night's?" It was our waiter.

Oh shit. I'd assumed they'd already processed a credit card payment for last night's meal. If the waiter added this night's hefty, soup-sucking tab to last night's and handed Noel the bill . . .

"Yes, Mrs. P," I said. "Let's go. Don't want to keep those balls waiting!"

"What balls do you mean this time, Dix?"

Jesus, Dylan, wipe that grin off your face.

Mona laughed. "Got to be the bingo balls, Dylan."

Just as the waiter was making a beeline for the table, we were waving goodbye and making a beeline for the door.

"There . . . there must be some mistake," I heard Noel say as he looked at the bill. As the door swung slowly closed.

"Yeah, there was a mistake," I mumbled as I walked to the waiting Lexus. "You pissed off Dix Dodd."

But that wasn't the only mistake made that evening. The second I can claim as my own. All my own. Yep. When I decided that surely I could play as many bingo cards as Mrs. P. After all, she was just a little old lady, right? So when I stood in line behind her, watched her buy her sheets of cards, handful of specials, breakopens, bonanzas and tickets for the various draws (including wild card, fifty-fifty, door prizes and a chance to spin the great big wheel), I said "I'll have the same."

No wonder Mrs. P had giggled.

By the time she'd set up her row of troll dolls and dabbers, I suspected I was dealing with a professional here. By the time the first game was in play, I knew it. I could barely keep up.

Thankfully by the time the big game — the one that everyone had come for — where ten bingo halls were linked via satellite with a grand prize of two hundred and fifty thousand for a full card in 45 numbers, I was ready. (Ready in that I knew enough to buy only one card for the special game when the floor seller came around.)

Mrs. P had her usual six in front of her. Dylan dared two. Mother and Mona (apparently old bingo pros themselves) each had six cards in front of them. Mrs. P had already bagged five hundred dollars on a sputnik game, Mom had won the chance to spin the big wheel (she'd won a free night of bingo, taken a deep bow and high-fived most everyone along the aisle on her way back to the seat). But, okay, these are long bingo nights.

Mona stifled a yawn.

I leaned over to mom just before the big game was to start. "Poor Mona. Of all the people who should win, she deserves it."

"Night's not over yet, Dix."

"Close enough."

Mother didn't answer. The caller had begun with B4 and heads were down and dabbers were dabbing. This was it — the last game. And truthfully, I was glad the night was ending. It did kind of hit me how tired I was as I sat there dabbing. Number after number. B after I after N ... you get the picture. Yep, dabbing away. Then ... holy shit!

I looked up at the board and gave a gentle kick to Dylan under the table.

"Ouch!"

Okay, my gentle sucks.

I gave a don't-look-now, tipped-eyed look to my cards. I was set.

Freakin' set for a quarter of a million dollars!

I 18 was all I needed.

Dylan's eyes grew round. His mouth dropped down.

We were at the 40th number. I had five numbers to get that I 18. The big screens not only displayed the number up and the one after it, but if a person looked really, really closely, you could see the next color up.

"I 17," the caller called.

Oh boy. Oh boy! OHFREAKINBOY! There were three I's in a row coming up after that one. Three freakin' I numbers. One of them had to be mine. My heart was pounding. Dylan was completely ignoring his own cards now and staring into mine.

"You're going to win, Dix," he murmured. We didn't want to break the luck and let everyone know.

"As long as no one else calls in the meantime I —"

"BINGO!"

On I 17.

Everyone in the hall jumped amid the chorus of 'oh shit'. Jumped up to see who'd won. Looked around in disbelief to see who was looking down at her cards in disbelief.

And that was Mona Roberts.

Mona held her breath as the floor worker called the card in to the caller.

The place erupted in applause as the caller announced. "That's a good bingo. Pay that lucky lady one quarter of a million dollars."

Mona was crying. Mother was crying. Mrs. Presley was clapping and laughing out loud. Hell, I might have had a tear in my eyes too.

"I won't have to move now, Katt," Mona said. "I won't have to sell out to Tish. Oh, my God, I can tell her to pack up her ugly ass and get out of my condo! I . . . I'm going to be all right. I really am!"

I grabbed my mother's arm as we headed out of the bingo hall. Not that she needed the help, but because, well, I wanted to. And no, I'm not going soft. I'm still a million miles away from being a touchy-feely person. But it was somehow okay to do right then. I stopped her by the exit, and looked out at Mona in the parking lot, clutching her huge check in her hands, hugging strangers, smiling for all she was worth, and even laughing out loud in her joy as Dylan opened the door of the rented Lexus for her.

"Pretty lucky, huh, Mom?"

Mother smiled at me through her Pinch-Me Pink lipstick. "You know better than that, Dix Dodd. Luck had nothing to do with it." She took my arm again and we started walking around the car. "That was pure and simple *magic*. Now do you finally believe?"

Dylan opened the car door firstly for mother, and then for me. But he paused as his hand held on my door. He waited for me to look into his eyes. When I did, his gaze was warm, happy. A little hungry.

"What happened in Florida . . ." He pulled me close for a quick kiss that should not have stolen my breath so completely. ". . . was meant to happen in Florida."

Oh, *bingo*.

He stepped back and opened the door for me.

Did I believe in magic? Did I dare?

I slid into the back seat beside my mother, who winked at me and grabbed my hand. Maybe, just maybe, I could.

Epilogue

I WAS KIND of sad to leave my Florida nights. I caught myself sighing as I packed my suitcase (included in which were my newly purchased granny panties, turtleneck sweater, and that Florida Gators bobblehead collection that I just couldn't resist). Yes, I would miss my mother, and Mona, but I knew they both were okay now.

Mona did kick Tish's ass to the curb (literally!) and Mom did call Cotton Carson. They had a date for next Thursday. Frankie went a-wooing elsewhere. Big Eddie and Lance were guests of the Pinellas County Jail awaiting trial. Noel called my cell a dozen times. I let it ring.

And I'm delighted to report that Mrs. P thoroughly enjoyed her trip. The bingo was the highlight for her, of course. Not just winning the five hundred bucks, but seeing Mona's life come back together the way it should be. Oh, she was anxious to get back to her boys (who by this time were calling twice a day to ask, snuffling, when she was coming home), but the vacation had done her good.

We were flying home, of course. Late-night flight but direct to Marport City. Which was fine with me. More than fine. I was anxious to get home and back to business. I'd called my old landlord. Yep, my old suite was still available (no surprise there), and I'd be back in it the first of next month. Thank God I'd gone month-to-month on the new place and would only lose a month's rent. Ah, but I'd miss those plush carpets in those chair tipping moments.

"Hey, Dix! Got a question for you."

I sighed. Mrs. P had been doing this for a good half hour now. We were barely in the air and it was a hell of a long way yet to go. We'd done about twenty crossword clues so far. And my patience was wearing thin.

Yes, Dylan and I were competing again, and he was winning. *Again.*
Twenty to zip, or thereabouts. So far, Mrs. Presley was keeping the
clues clean (maybe that's why I was so far behind Dylan?), and yeah, the
competitive side of me was getting a wee bit ... pissed.

Anxious even.

Irritated.

I really, really wanted to get one.

"Here's one you might be able to get, Dix. I'll say it real slow to give
you a chance."

"Gee, thanks Mrs. P," I grated.

"What's a five-letter word for cock —"

"Penis!" I shouted. "Wohoo! I got one! I got one!"

Oh God. I more than shouted. Jumped up, and banged my head
on the overhead compartment as I turned with a *woot!* to Mrs. P sitting behind me. To a smiling Mrs. P and a planeload of jaw-dropped,
shocked passengers.

I sat down quickly. Three nuns in the row beside me crossed themselves at once. An irate mother covered her teenage son's ears (while said
grinning teen gave me the thumbs up; apparently, he had one too). A
group of college-aged kids at the back of the plane broke into applause.

"Er ... Dix," Mrs. P said. "I was going to say *cockpit dweller.*"

"Would that be a *pilot*, Mrs. P?" Dylan offered helpfully.

"Yeah, it fits right in. Thank you, Dylan." Then in sterner tones for
me: "Geez, Dix. Where'd you learn to talk like that?"

I couldn't sink down far enough in the seat. Fortunately the flight
attendant came by just then distributing blankets. I grabbed one from
her and quickly disappeared beneath it. Better.

Better still, Dylan declined a blanket of his own and crawled underneath mine with me. Which I thought was very brave of him, considering
I'd just informed my fellow passengers that I had a penis.

Eventually (like within ten minutes) the laughter died down. The
nuns stopped praying. And soon thereafter, people actually started doz-
ing off. Mrs. P herself began her gentle snoring behind us. The lights were
dimmed except for a very few overhead reading lights. Dylan reached
up and turned off both the lights above us.

Under the security of the blanket, I felt Dylan's hands begin to move.
Nothing that would get us arrested. Subtly. Discreetly. Sweetly, even.

But wow. Just ... *wow.* I felt like a teenager — horny and anxious
and dare I say ... smitten?

Oh shit! Dare I?

After long, breathless moments, he found my hand, lifted it and grazed the back of my knuckles with his lips.

My pounding heart skipped a beat.

Then he leaned back in his seat, offering me his shoulder for a pillow.

I settled my head against him, placing my hand on his chest beneath the blanket. Under my palm, I felt the strong thudding of his heart gradually slowing.

Oh boy.

Thank you for investing the most valuable commod-
ity you have — your time — in reading our book.
We hope we managed to make you laugh!

Word of mouth is the most powerful promotion any book can receive.
If you enjoyed this book, please consider spreading the word. You
can do this by recommending it to your friends, posting a review
wherever you bought it, or reviewing it at Goodreads or other such
places where readers gather, and mentioning it in social media.

Again, thank you!

N.L. Wilson
(aka Norah Wilson and Heather Doherty)

Read on for an excerpt from *Death by Cuddle Club*,
the next Dix Dodd Mystery.

Other Dix Dodd Mysteries
The Case of the Flashing Fashion Queen (Book 1)
Death by Cuddle Club (Book 3)
Covering Her Assets (Book 4) — coming late 2013

Other books by the writing team of Wilson/Doherty
Young Adult/New Adult
The Summoning (Book 1 in the Gatekeepers Series)
Ashlyn's Radio
Comes the Night (Casters Series, Book 1)
Enter the Night (Casters Series, Book 2) — coming February 2013
Embrace the Night (Casters Series, Book 3) — coming Summer 2013
Forever the Night (Casters Series, Book 4) — coming Fall 2013
Read about the Casters series at http://castersthebooks.com

Available from Norah Wilson:
Romantic Suspense
Every Breath She Takes
Guarding Suzannah, *Book 1 in the Serve and Protect Series*
Saving Grace, *Book 2 in the Serve and Protect Series*
Protecting Paige, *Book 3 in the Serve and Protect Series*
Needing Nita, *a free novella in the Serve and Protect Series*
Paranormal Romance
The Merzetti Effect — A Vampire Romance (Book 1)
Nightfall — A Vampire Romance (Book 2)

About the Authors

NORAH WILSON is a Kindle best-selling author of romantic suspense and paranormal romance. She lives in Fredericton, New Brunswick, Canada, with her husband, two adult children, beloved Rotti-Lab mix Chloe, and kitty-come-lately Ruckus Virtute. (Yes, she has two names.)

HEATHER DOHERTY fell completely in love with writing while taking creative writing courses with Athabasca University. Motivated by her university success, and a life-long dream of becoming a novelist, she later enrolled in the Humber School for Writers. Her first literary novel was published in 2006. While still writing dark literary (as well as not-so-dark children's lit), she is beyond thrilled to be writing the Dix Dodd cozy mysteries and paranormal/horror with Norah. Heather lives in Fredericton, New Brunswick with her family.

Connect with Norah Online:
Twitter: http://twitter.com/norah_wilson
Facebook: http://www.facebook.com/NorahWilsonWrites
Goodreads: http://www.goodreads.com/
author/show/1361508.Norah_Wilson
Norah's Website: http://www.norahwilsonwrites.com
Email: norahwilsonwrites@gmail.com

Connect with Heather Online:
Facebook: http://www.facebook.com/heather.doherty.5
Email: heatherjaned@hotmail.com

Ðeath by Cuddle Club

A Dix Dodd mystery

Copyright © 2011 N.L. Wilson (Norah Wilson and Heather Doherty)

Description

Vindication is Dix's when her nemesis Detective Richard Head (aka Dickhead) shows up at her door, asking for her help on a delicate matter. Delicate because he can't turn to his own PD without admitting he's a member of a newly opened Cuddle Club. There have been a couple of deaths of Club members, ostensibly of natural causes, but Detective Head wants to take a closer look.

The task for Dix? Infiltrate the Cuddle Club, ferret out the truth, and report back to Dickhead. Simple. Well, except for the fact that Dix is about as cuddly as a porcupine. Good thing for her that her assistant, the handsome, much younger and infinitely more cuddle-friendly Dylan Foreman, is eager to go under the covers ... er ... under cover with her.

Head was right, all is not as it seems at the club. As Dix has always maintained, cuddling can be dangerous to your health. In fact, it can be downright deadly.

Excerpt

A S A THANK you gift, my mother sent me pastries. Isn't that sweet? Oh, wait, did I say *pastries*? No. Not pastries. That's what a normal 70-year-old woman might do. Yep, a normal mother would send her culinarily challenged PI daughter yummy treats as a thank you for getting her out of trouble in Florida. For saving the diamond my father gave her (AKA, the family jewels). And — let us not forget — keeping her 70-year-old butt out of jail on a trumped-up murder rap. But Katt Dodd will never be accused of being normal. What she sent me were *pasties*. Yep, stick-'em-on, twirl-'em-round pasties. (Well, I couldn't get my twirl on, but I could get a pretty good sway thing going.) Bless her skinny-dipping little … heart.

Yes, so, post-Florida, I was now the not-so-proud owner of be-tasseled hot pink pasties. Ah, a wardrobe fit for a queen. A *drag* queen. Not quite so appropriate for a professional, 40-ish, amazing-yet-modest private detective. Possibly the most amazing private detective in all of Marport City, Ontario.

Okay, so I'm not so modest.

And yeah, maybe not everyone saw it that way, especially not the guys back at Jones and Associates — the good ol' boys club where I used to work. But, hey, they'd bet — openly — that I'd never make it on my own. That I would be out of business within a very few months, and would come back crying on their doorstep when I landed on my ass. Well, I've shed a few tears in these past months, but none over them, and sure as hell none on their cruddy doorstep. I guess they don't know how well-padded that ass of mine is!

Wait, that didn't come out right.

I did mention I'm 40, right? I've got my fair share of padding there.

But what the hell — isn't 40 the new … 40? I wouldn't exactly call me a cougar, though some would. Actually, some do. How I love them all the more for it!

This would probably be a good time to mention Dylan Foreman, PI in training. Smart, sexy as sin — and OMG, so handsome! Tall and lean, but plenty wide at the shoulders and narrow at the hips, just like I like them. (Or high, wide and handsome, as my mother would say.) Thick, dark brown hair, chocolate brown eyes. And all of 28 years old. He'd been my apprentice since shortly after I hung up my shingle in the dilapidated rental office building on the outskirts of town. My friend since day one. And lately, dangerously close to a friend with benefits.

Yes, Dylan had joined me back when I was in that tiny, grungy suite, which was all my budget would stretch to. You know the kind of office building I'm talking about. Worst part of the city, motley characters hanging around the alleys out back. And inside, that faint, what-the-heck-is-that? odor in the stairwell (though you really don't want to know). And the tiny, dusty office itself with the dead aloe vera plant on the window ledge . . .

And here we were, home again.

Yes, we'd moved back. Go figure. The very same office we'd left behind when the success of the Case of the Flashing Fashion Queen allowed us to move into better digs.

Why were we shuffling back into the old place? Economics, of course.

I'd bought Mother's condo from her. Now that she was living full time in Florida, I couldn't continue to live there rent-free under the pretext of looking after the place. No more use of the BMW, either, since we'd returned it to her in Florida. All of which meant I was no longer able to afford the cushy office with the thick-piled carpet that seemed to bury your feet up to your ankles when you walked through it. (I have calf muscles of steel now.) I even had to return that tweeting, all-in-one copier/printer/fax machine I so loved (I just nipped in under the grace period to rescind the contract). And the voice-changer? It went back, too. I kept the high-tech coffee pot, however. I mean, c'mon — it ground the coffee beans and delivered frothed milk.

The move back to our old digs couldn't have been better timed, though. Business had been dropping off as of late, no doubt due to the dismal economy. Amazing how blind an eye people could turn to philandering spouses during hard times. Divorce was costly for everyone, and not just emotionally. So we didn't mind the decrease in rent that went with the lower class of accommodation. Maybe in this part of town, people who could afford a divorce might be more comfortable consulting a PI whose offices were a little further removed from their usual spheres. One could only hope.

So yes, Dix Dodd, PI, and Dylan Foreman, PI apprentice, were busy unpacking on this fine, quiet Saturday in October. Unpacking boxes, arranging furniture, blowing up Blow-Up Betty and tucking her into the corner. Amazingly — or perhaps not so amazingly — no other tenant had occupied the office since we'd moved out. I uprighted the aloe vera plant and discovered it was plastic. Huh. It still looked half dead. Now that was realism for you.

We had a couple of mini-bottles of sparkling wine chilling in the mini-fridge (hey, I'm all about class). That had been Dylan's contribution (the fridge, not the wine). I'd bought the bubbly, intending it as a reward for us when we finished the unpacking. Dylan's dark eyes had seemed to grow just a tad darker when he'd seen those little bottles. Probably for the same reason my whole body had flushed hot standing in the liquor store four hours ago when I'd bought them. We'd been dancing around each other since Florida. My logical brain still thought it was a bad idea, but my libido disagreed. So far, Dylan had seemed to be content to let the two Dix's duke it out, but he wasn't above stacking the deck in favor of Lust-Crazed Dix. And he damned well knew which Dix had bought the sparkling wine.

So, as we unpacked that fine Saturday, all was quiet. Even with the sharpened edge of awareness between us, it was fun. All seemed good and right, just as it should be.

When will I ever learn?

Quiet didn't last out the afternoon. Fun escaped out the window (and probably got beat up; I tell you, it's a tough neighborhood). And good and right? Ah, that didn't last out the afternoon either.

Because there came a knock at the door. One that made my intuition tinkle like those little bells they put on the end of pasties tassels — Whoops, sorry. TMI. Let's just say the hair on the back of my neck stood up against my collar.

And then the door opened.

Damn.

I regarded the tall, slightly rumpled man standing in my doorway with astonishment. I rubbed my eyes and looked again. Still there. "Oh, crap."

He strode into my office, letting the door fall closed behind him. "Nice to see you, too, Dixieland."

You guessed it. It was my nemesis, the very last man I expected to see at my door. Well, minus an arrest warrant and handcuffs. Yep, it was none other than Detective Richard Head, of the Marport City PD, known by the unkind, uncouth, and just plain immature as Dickhead.

"*Dickhead?*" I said. "What are *you* doing here?"

He mumbled something unintelligible as he walked through to my office.

Dylan and I followed him into the room. I shot a glance at my desk. Five minutes ago, I'd dumped a box of my personals on my blotter, ready to fire them into the various drawers. I gave a quick scan of the items. No, no tampons. No neatly wrapped maxi pads. What a shame. Dickhead tended to go green around the gills around that kind of stuff.

I turned back to him. "Sorry, I didn't catch what you mumbled. Could you repeat that?"

His jaw worked a minute. Finally, he said, "I need your help." The words were grating, reluctant, and he turned toward my desk, no doubt so he wouldn't have to see the glee in my eyes at his admission.

A quick look at Dylan revealed he was just as astonished as I was. Understandable, considering that it wasn't that long ago that the good detective had been hot and horny to land me in jail for the murder of one of Marport City's rich and famous. I had ultimately solved that case (naturally), saving my ass in the process and causing Detective Head much gnashing of teeth.

Dylan came to stand by me. Was it my imagination, or did he stand a little closer than normal? And was he trying to make himself even taller than his 6' 4"?

"Detective," Dylan said.

"Foreman," Dickhead acknowledged, but he gave Dylan just the briefest of glances before turning his attention away again.

The masculine pissing contest barely registered. I was too busy savoring Dickhead's earlier words. *I need your help.*

"What are you grinning for, Dixieshit?"

I let my smile widen. "Ah, the memories."

With a barely suppressed growl, Detective Head sat. Well, sort of sat. We hadn't gotten around yet to bringing the chairs up from the moving van, so he half leaned/half sat on the edge of my desk. He looked down at the assortment of pens, pencils, odds and ends of makeup ...

"Wow. Why do you have so many pairs of tweezers?" He turned to me with a close and scrutinizing look.

"PI stuff," I answered hastily, fighting the urge to raise a hand to my upper lip. "Every good PI has at least a couple sets."

"A couple? Looks like you have a half dozen."

"Yeah ... well, I'm a damn good PI"

Dylan, I noticed, was looking a little confused, too. Oh God.

"So what brings you here, Dickhead?" There. That should change the subject.

Except it barely got a rise out of him. That snide smile he habitually wore (well, at least in his interactions with me) was gone. And — unless I was badly mistaken — so was a good bit of the confidence he usually carried. "Like I said before, I need your help, Dix."

Dix? He wasn't taking the opportunity to make fun of my name. This had to be serious.

Still, I was suspicious. "*My* help?"

Okay, I've had a couple high-profile cases, but my specialty is trailing cheating spouses. In fact, that's how Dickhead and I had met. I'd been trailing him on his ex-wife's dime. Were they back together, and *he* was suspicious of *her* now? No, that hardly seemed likely. She'd taken him to the cleaners. No way were those two living under the same roof again. In fact, Dickhead had been forced back under his mother's roof out of economic necessity, last time I checked. (Did I mention divorce was expensive?) Was he seeing someone else and wondering about her fidelity? Or — oh, wait, hold the phone! — maybe it was his mother! Was the old girl seeing someone? Some old gent who seemed a little too smooth and who needed checking out? (Hey, if you knew *my* mother, you'd know I'm not even kidding.)

Dickhead rasped a hand over his chin. I couldn't help but notice that it was a strong, attractively stubbled chin. (And no, it didn't do anything for me. But just because I despised the man doesn't mean I'm blind. Objectively speaking, he's not a bad looking guy, if you like 'em muscle-bound and lantern-jawed.)

"It's complicated." He cleared his throat and inserted a finger beneath his collar to loosen his already loose tie. Man, he looked uneasy. Stressed. Which made me feel uneasy and stressed ... because it was just *killing* me not to mock him.

"You want me to tail some —"

"No!" The clipped word cut me off, and yet he was still unwilling to elaborate. What was eating at him so?

Dylan cut in, "You're involved with a gang and you —"

"That ain't it either, Foreman."

Dylan and I glanced at each other. Oh, yeah. It was *on*. And it was my turn.

"You lost your badge to a hooker and you need us to track her down!"

Dickhead snorted. "Get real."

I shrugged. Seemed like a pretty real possibility to me.

Dylan's turn: "You … you found out you have an illegitimate son, and you want us to find him!"

Damn, that was a good one.

"Jesus, Foreman."

I was up again. "You … you were looking out the window while recovering from a broken leg. And … and you saw your neighbor across the courtyard acting suspiciously. And now his wife is missing and there's a little dog digging up the flowers and —"

It was Dylan who snorted this time. "That's *Rear Window*, Dix."

Whoops. Hitchcock's best. No wonder it seemed so brilliant.

Dickhead glowered as Dylan and I continued to throw out increasingly ridiculous scenarios at his expense. He clearly wasn't enjoying this as much as we were. In fact, I think it was safe to say he was annoyed. Then again, he wasn't exactly jumping in to enlighten us as to the real reason for his presence, was he now?

And that's when I got it. That's when it really sank in. The guy was *here*, at *my* office. He didn't like me any better than I liked him. This was serious. This was —

"Murder," he said suddenly. "I think someone's been murdered."

I blinked. "You suspect a *murder*?"

His brow furrowed fiercely. "That's what I said, isn't it?"

Testy.

"Why don't you go to the police, then?" Dylan asked, beating me to the punch. "You *are* a cop, after all."

Dickhead cut Dylan a hard look before turning back to me. "It's complicated," he said again. And judging by that look of consternation on his face, I had no doubt of it. "I don't *know* there has been a murder. I only suspect there's been one. I have no proof. No evidence. No motive. And no one willing to come forward."

"Not even you?" I didn't have to work hard to inject the words with incredulity. "You suspect a murder may have taken place, but you're not willing to come forward?"

He glared at me. And if looks could kill … well, I'd not have made it past the third grade, but that's not important right now.

Then something remarkable happened. The light of battle went out in his eyes as he reined himself in. At that, I felt a frisson of unease crawl up my back like a spider. What the hell was going on here?

"No, not even me, Dix." Dickhead heaved an in-for-a-penny sigh. "It's a club. An exclusive and private club that I belong to. Members are dying."

"How many?" Dylan asked.

"Two in the last month. The M.E. called it natural causes, but it's just … fishy to me. Feels wrong."

"Did you know the deceased?" I asked.

"Not well. Only by first name and … well, not well. But they seemed healthy enough. Not at all sickly."

"Old?"

"Yeah, *old*. About your age, Dix."

Mentally, I punched his shoulder. Hard. Oh, and physically, I did the same. Dickhead had been expecting it. Hadn't even flinched in that *totally worth it* kind of way.

"The point is," he continued, "in both cases, each of these folks was at the club one night, dead the next day. No sign of foul play. But I don't like it."

"Yeah, but without any proof—" Dylan started to say.

"But you feel it in your gut," I interrupted.

It was with serious eyes that Detective Head considered me now. "You know it, Dix. In my gut. I know you do."

He was right. I'd had my share of those niggles and nudges of intuition, and I wasn't foolish enough to imagine I was the only one. Hell, cops were famous for it. Gut instinct, jokes aside.

This was it. This was real. This was a case I'd be taking. And I told Dickhead so.

"You'll need to infiltrate the club," he said.

Here's where I got nervous. "Want to elaborate on what kind of club this is?" I was having visions of needing to wear a neoprene cat suit and leather boots with five-inch heels.

"It's a club. An exclusive … club."

Somehow, I didn't think I'd be at a quilting bee. "Right. A club. So you said."

Dickhead scrubbed a hand down his face. "It's a cuddle club."

"I'm sorry, you had your hand over your mouth. It's a *what* club?"

"I said cuddle club. It's a cuddle club!"

"Ha!" I snorted. "Good one."

He wasn't laughing.

"I've heard of those," Dylan said.

"Yeah, well, I've heard of the Great Wall of China and that doesn't mean it's real."

Sa-lam!

Oh, wait, did I say *Great Wall of China*? Er, not so much of a slam, then. How did I screw these things up? I should have said *the Tooth Fairy* or *honor among thieves* or *monogamous men*, but no —

I realized then that both men were just looking at me, obviously waiting for me to say something (preferably something comprehensible this time). I looked at Dickhead then turned back to Dylan. "He's not kidding, is he?"

He wasn't.

Oh boy.

I cringed. Man, did I cringe.

The phone rang in the outer office and Dylan excused himself to go answer it.

I asked Dickhead a few more questions: When did they meet next? Where? What did I need to wear to fit in? I almost choked on his answers, but I took the case anyway.

And I named it Death by Cuddle Club.

Made in United States
Cleveland, OH
06 December 2024

11409635R00114